ASSASSIN BY ACCIDENT

CARNIVAL OF MYSTERIES

Welcome

Traveler

E.J. RUSSELL

Cover Art by Dianne Thies, https://LyricalLines.net

Editor: Meg DesCamp

ISBN: 978-1-947033-57-3

First edition: August 2023

Contact information: ejr@ejrussell.com

ASSASSIN BY ACCIDENT

CARNIVAL OF MYSTERIES

Welcome

Traveler

E.J. RUSSELL

ABOUT ASSASSIN BY ACCIDENT

If a megalomaniacal earth mage kidnaps your little sister, do you:

A) Kill him

B) Kill him

C) Kill him

D) Magically indenture yourself to him to ensure her safe return

Welsh water horse Nevan Quirke would have happily opted for A, B, or C, but had no idea where his sister was hidden—so, option D it is. He's not a fool, though. He made sure to limit his obligation to a single task.

Unfortunately, he neglected to nail down a few *tiny* details before the geas brand was seared into his skin, and now:

A) He can't shift

B) He can't swim

C) He can't drink

D) If he fails, he'll be bound to the mage for eternity

Oh, and that task? Assist in an assassination.

If only he weren't so *thirsty*.

And if only his partner for the heinous job weren't the most appealing man Nevan has seen in his entire two-thousand-year life.

Assassin by Accident takes place in E.J. Russell's Mythmatched universe and is part of the multi-author Carnival of Mysteries Series. Each book stands alone, but each one includes at least one visit to Errante Ame's Carnival of Mysteries, a magical, multiverse traveling show full of unusual acts, games, and rides. The Carnival changes to suit the world it's on, so each visit is unique and special. This book features grumpy/sunshiny, hurt/comfort, mistaken identity, opposites attract, unexpected derring-do, and of course an HEA—no matter how little the men in question think they deserve it.

CHAPTER 1

*I*f the thrice-damned earth mage hadn't informed Nevan Quirke that he was bound for Oregon when he'd ejected Nevan from that ridiculous secret stronghold, Nevan would have known anyway.

Because *rain.*

It darkened the shoulders of his black leather duster. Matted his overlong hair to his head. Dripped under his shirt collar and between his shoulder blades to dampen the linen shirt under his suede vest.

In other words, it was *glorious.*

He lifted his chin to let the drops patter against his face, taking a deep breath. And nearly choked. Because what *wasn't* glorious was the stench emanating from the dumpster inside the tiny brick-walled courtyard where Yvo had plunked him. Gagging, Nevan spotted a break in the wall and sprinted for open air.

Once clear of the garbage stink, he was assailed by the scent of frying meat. He glanced at the building looming beside him. *Burgerville USA.* That explained the aroma of grilled beef with the hint of caramelized onions.

He turned in a slow circle, assessing his surroundings. The

restaurant sat in the middle of a strip mall parking lot at the intersection of two busy streets. The corners to the south each held strip malls as well. To the east lay a small regional airport.

I know this place. Or at least this area. Before the Faerie Convergence, Unseelie fae had maintained a portal in a nearby wetlands. Nevan had heard rumors that the portal had been reactivated afterward, open to both Seelie and Unseelie, but since he rarely ventured out of Faerie, he'd never bothered to check.

He sighed. The wetlands were out of his reach now, portal or no portal. In fact, there was no wild water anywhere in sight other than the rain.

Goddess, he was so *thirsty*. He lifted his head and opened his mouth, trying to catch the rain on his parched tongue, but only succeeded in torturing himself with a few stray drops. He eyed the lowering clouds. Gray, but not ominously dark, which meant this drizzle was probably the most he could hope for. What he needed was a fecking monsoon. Or better yet, to break this damn geas—and preferably the mage's neck along with it—and return to his lake under the waterfall.

To go home.

But he refused to return to Faerie without his little sister. And fecking Yvo Offerman, earth mage, entitled narcissist, and pain in Nevan's arse, had spirited Lulu away, hidden her some-where even Nevan couldn't find. He would do anything, *anything*, to rescue her from Yvo's clutches, which was why he'd struck this demon's bargain with Yvo in the first place.

He wasn't a complete fool. He'd made sure the deal was for a single, *specific* task. Although Nevan wasn't technically a demon, he'd learned from demon experience: Never enter a bargain with a mage without a well-defined, *near-term* exit strategy or you could become bound to their will forever. Nevan valued his freedom too much for that. Besides, if he were enslaved to a mage's will indefinitely, who would look after Lulu?

The task he'd agreed to had seemed simple enough: Accept

an object from Yvo's contact in the Outer World and convey it back to the stronghold.

"My contact will do all the work," Yvo had said. "You're simply the"—he'd tittered—"pack mule."

"Ceffylau dŵr are *not* mules," Nevan had growled. Monsters, yes. Mules, no.

Yvo had waved a hand. "Pack water horse, then, if you insist. The function remains the same."

Nevan clenched his left fist over the geas brand, the mark of his servitude. The burn as it was seared into his palm after he'd agreed to Yvo's terms had never entirely faded.

Soon, though. All he had to do was follow Yvo's instructions, the geas would be fulfilled, and he and Lulu would be free.

The Burgerville door swung open and a couple of human teenagers emerged, each of them holding a monster-sized drink cup, which they slurped from in between spates of giggling. If Nevan had any moisture to spare, his mouth would have watered. As it was, he swallowed, his dry throat clicking.

I really should have checked the fine print on that geas vow. But he hadn't demanded particulars. Just plowed ahead and agreed to do Yvo's bidding in exchange for his sister. After the bargain was struck, however, Yvo had informed him with ill-concealed glee that until he'd completed the job—although the pretentious arsehole had insisted on calling it a *quest*—not only was Nevan barred from shifting, and from immersing himself in life-sustaining wild water, but from taking into his hand any drink that contained even a drop of water. And since all beverages other than pure ethanol—which was poisonous to him anyway —contained at least a tiny percentage of water, Nevan was destined to be dehydrated until he finished this *quest*. Any attempt to sidestep the terms would result in A) pain, B) more pain, and C) possibly forfeiting and putting not only Lulu, but himself in Yvo's power for good.

So perhaps he was a complete fool after all, especially since he hadn't asked what exactly he'd be *accepting* and *conveying*. No, those details had emerged after the brand was already seared into Nevan's flesh, and Yvo had taken far too much relish in informing him what he'd agreed to, all the while taunting Nevan by swishing a bottle of pure spring water in his hand.

"You're to go to Starbucks," he'd said, a self-satisfied smirk on his face as he brandished the water. "But no venti macchiato for you."

"Which Starbucks?" Nevan growled in response. "There are about a million of them. Do I have to check each one?"

Yvo scowled. "Of course not. This is a *time-sensitive* quest. I know where the target is *now*, but tomorrow? The next day?" His lower lip stuck out in a pout. "For some reason, my spells can't predict when they'll move on, or where." He shook the water again. "That's why I've imposed these extra... incentives on our little arrangement. So you won't be tempted to dawdle."

"I'd have never done so regardless. I want Lulu back as soon as possible." He narrowed his eyes as he glared at the mage. "Far away from you."

"Tut tut. I'm not such a bad fellow. Who knows? Luljeta might decide she prefers to stay with me in the end, after all. Her sort has the potential for dark or light."

"Since you've stooped to kidnapping a child, you're definitely dark."

"Light. Dark. Dark. Light. *Pfft.*" Yvo tossed the bottle from hand to hand. "So *subjective*, don't you think? One person's sunlight is another person's anathema. Consider vampires. If you—"

"I don't want to consider vampires. I don't want to consider anything except this task."

"Quest," Yvo said testily. "It's my *quest*."

"It might be your quest, but it's just a task for me. One I must complete to get my sister back. So I go to a Starbucks, which I'll identify how?"

"No fear. I'll drop you within sight of it, although not *too* close." He tittered again, making Nevan grind his molars at the irritating sound. "Large, imposing men appearing spontaneously out of thin air tend to draw too much unwanted attention from humans. You'll arrive in a secluded spot."

"Thoughtful of you."

"Yes, isn't it?"

Nevan refrained from rolling his eyes at Yvo's self-congratulatory tone. Clearly, the arsehole's sarcasm detector was just as deficient as his sense of humor. However, Nevan supposed he ought to be grateful. Mages weren't quite as scrupulous about remaining unobtrusive as others in the supernatural community, probably because while they wielded magic, they weren't themselves magical. Not like Nevan or Lulu or any other supe.

The supe council, though, was *extremely* particular about violations of the Secrecy Pact. If any supe exposed the existence of the community to humans, they might as well kiss their freedom—and possibly their lives—goodbye. However, Nevan doubted Yvo's plans were formulated out of concern for Nevan's well-being, or for anything other than his bloody *quest*.

"Proceed to the Starbucks, where you'll meet your contact."

"And they'll turn over the item? That's the job, right?"

Yvo's expression tightened at the word *job*, but he recovered his smug self-satisfaction soon enough. "While the contact is the *means* of retrieving the item, you'll need to accompany them as surety while they complete their part." Annoyance flickered across his face. "Guild contracts are so *restrictive*. There's no *trust* in the worlds anymore."

Alarm bells clanged in Nevan's brain. "Guild? What guild?" So few guilds still operated in the modern world. None of them were good news, but one was worse than the others.

"The Assassin's Guild, of course."

And *there* was the other shoe. Because if the Assassin's Guild was involved, it meant somebody, somewhere, was going to die. "I didn't sign up to be an accessory to murder."

"Ah-ah-ah." Yvo waggled a finger at him. "You said *anything*. Anything for Luljeta, provided it was a single task." He shrugged.

"You didn't specify that the task have a single *step*. Meeting the contact is the first step, but it is not the final one."

Assassins. Goddess, they were the scum of the scum, in Nevan's opinion. Willing to kill for something as mundane and unimportant as *money*. And now, because his stupid impulsiveness had gotten the better of him, he'd be just as culpable even if he wasn't the one to strike the fatal blow.

"What do they look like?" he asked through clenched teeth.

"How would I know? It's a standard guild contract. I submitted my requirements, they posted the job, somebody accepted the terms. The guild, as the intermediary, handles all the details."

"Do you even know how many assassins I'm looking for? What's the term for a group of assassins? A dagger? A melee? An excrescence?"

"You know, I was going to give you a little water before you left, but with that attitude, you've lost the privilege." Yvo tossed the bottle in the air and it disappeared before it could hit the ground. "A single one. The guild always tries to upsell, but this is a one-person contract. I insisted."

Yet by involving Nevan, Yvo had already turned it into two-person job, the maths-deficient git. "So why do you need me?"

"For logistics, of course. *I* can't be seen there." He glanced furtively over his shoulder, although in the murk of the stone-walled, stone-floored chamber, Nevan didn't know what he expected to see, especially since the room seemed to have no windows or doors. He didn't even know which realm it was in, since Yvo had pulled him in through a portal in Faerie. "My enemies might suspect my plans and try to thwart me. You need to meet the assassin, provide them with their weapon, escort them to the target, and bring the prize back to me."

"What exactly is this *prize* of yours?"

When Yvo had told him, Nevan had been sick all over the flagstones.

CHAPTER 2

The sour taste of vomit still lingered in Nevan's mouth as he stood outside the Burgerville, a Starbucks visible on the southeast corner of the intersection, and the few raindrops he was able to capture weren't sufficient to banish it. *Goddess, how can I... But I must. Lulu depends on me.*

He headed for the road, but before he reached the sidewalk, he spotted the convenience store that anchored this particular strip mall and paused.

No drink, Yvo's geas had specified. While engaged on his task, Nevan could take no drink in his hand that contained water. But *drink* meant *liquid*, right?

He bared his teeth in as close to a grin as he could manage. The problem with a geas, or with any spell for that matter, was that you had to be extremely careful and precise with the language or you could shoot yourself in the foot. If Nevan was lucky—although how often had that happened lately?—he might be able to use those words to his advantage now.

The geas brand pulsed in his palm as he changed direction, a sure sign that Yvo was losing patience. The burn would grow if Nevan wasn't proceeding with proper dispatch. He could handle a little burn, but if he didn't get this taste out of his mouth and some kind of moisture into his system, he'd pass out before he made it to the coffee shop. Thank the goddess for the rain. He could absorb a little moisture through his skin, but he needed to ingest some, too.

Hoping against hope that like most of their ilk, the convenience store carried at least a nod to fresh produce, he straight-armed the door and powered inside, heading for the coolers in the rear. Milk. Soda. Beer. *Water*. Goddess, what he wouldn't give... *Ah! There*. In the last unit, on a single shelf, were a few apples, an anemic tomato or two, and—*yes!*—a pair of oranges.

Nevan took them both, their coolness easing the burn in his palm just a trifle, and strode up to the counter. The bored-looking clerk popped their gum and said, "That'll be two fifty-eight."

A ridiculous price for two rather shriveled fruits, but Nevan passed over the cash without comment, his throat working as he recalled *why* he had human money in his pocket. As soon as he was outside, he tore a hole in the rind of one orange, held it to his mouth, and squeezed, moaning as the first sweet-tart juice hit his tongue. He sucked the first fruit dry by the time he crossed to the parking lot in front of Starbucks. He attacked the other as he stood in the rain, and although it wasn't as juicy as the first, it was better than random raindrops.

Of course, now his hands were sticky. Would the geas allow him to wash his hands in the coffee shop restroom? Any water out of the tap wouldn't be wild: Humans were fanatical about treating their sources of public water, taming it and dosing it and filtering it until its personality was extinguished and it could no longer *speak*. Just touching it made Nevan feel as though he were attending a death bed, and prolonged contact raised welts on his skin. Goddess only knew what would happen if he tried to *drink* it. But a quick wash wouldn't burn any worse than the geas brand, and at least he'd be clean.

Before he got his soul so dirty, he'd be soiled beyond redemption.

He tossed the orange rinds into a trash bin on his way into the shop. The restroom was free, thank the goddess, and the geas didn't appear to object to hand washing, at least in city-treated water, a fact he filed away under *loopholes.*

As the water trickled through his fingers, the temptation to cup his palms and bring them to his lips was almost too great to resist, just to moisten his mouth and tongue. *Surely it wouldn't be too poisonous.* Yet he couldn't take the chance. His own discomfort was immaterial, but he couldn't risk violating the geas terms. Not if it endangered Lulu.

He resolutely pushed aside the thought of who else he was endangering and dried his hands. When he stepped out of the restroom, he made his way slowly toward the counter, scanning the other customers as he passed. Was his contact already here? He doubted it was the spike-haired teen in the purple hoodie, slouched in the armchair in the corner with his gaze riveted to a hand-held gaming device. Or one of the women at the table by the window, chatting and sharing a cinnamon roll. What in all the hells did an assassin look like, anyway?

He caught a brief glimpse of his reflection in the window and snorted. *Probably like me.* Rough-hewn, enveloped in black leather, scowl permanently fixed. So large as to seem out of proportion to the surroundings. Threatening.

Although… Wouldn't assassins prefer to fly under the radar? Remain unobtrusive, the better to get close to their targets? If that was the case, the businessman in the gray suit, frowning at his cell phone as he sipped from a to-go cup, would be a prime candidate.

Nevan winced. Everyone who was seated already had their beverage of choice. Yvo had told him that he'd be able to recognize the assassin because they'd order a grande sugar cookie almond milk latte with a caramel shot and no whip but extra sprinkles to go. What if his detour into the convenience store meant he'd missed that already?

He joined the line, surreptitiously checking the cup size of everyone who was already seated. The iced drinks he could discount, as well as anyone with a personal cup, or a tall or venti sized drink. That still left three possibilities, but maybe fate would take pity on him for once in his life—all right, twice, since the first time was when he'd found Lulu and claimed her for his sister—and the assassin had yet to arrive.

Waiting for his turn, Nevan kept his ears attuned to the customers in front of him as they placed their orders. Granted, his hearing was better under water, but it was still more acute than a human's. He perked up when a man in workout gear said, "Grande," but deflated when he followed up with, "Americano." The next customer ordered a chai tea latte, and the next, a weary looking woman in scrubs, a triple-shot espresso. Suddenly, there was no one ahead of him.

"What can we get started for you?" the smiling clerk asked.

"Uh..." Shite, he hadn't thought this through. He couldn't order a beverage. If he took it in his hand, that might constitute a forfeit. "A... a bagel. Please."

"We're out of plain. Is everything okay?"

Nevan blinked. Did he really look so wrecked that cashiers needed to check his condition? "Yes. Fine."

She nodded and touched the register screen. "Warmed?"

"No, thank you."

"Butter or cream cheese?"

"What? No. Just plain. Thank you."

She gave him a quizzical look, which was understandable. Who in their right mind would go to a coffee shop only to order a bagel and no coffee? Nevertheless, she rang him up anyway and handed him the small bag with the mermaid logo—which looked absolutely *nothing* like any water-natured being Nevan had ever encountered.

He grabbed a couple of napkins from the condiment station and took a seat at one of the stools lining the high counter next to the window, where he could keep an eye on the whole shop, spot any new arrivals, and listen for the telltale order.

After a minute or so of sitting with his bag clutched in his fist, he noted the baristas giving him sidelong glances. *Right.* Big guy scoping out their store and not even pretending to eat his pastry. Definitely dodgy.

Fumbling the bag open, Nevan drew out the bagel, only to have a shower of seeds from its top patter onto his leather pants. He was about to brush them off irritably when he caught the cashier's narrowed eyes.

Got it. Don't make more work for the staff.

He sighed and collected the detritus as best he could with his hands and napkins. After he tossed the soiled napkins into the trash, he grabbed a couple more and settled back onto his stool, this time taking better care to look nonthreatening. *Nothing to see here. Just a fellow hunched over a bagel, trying to choke down a few bites when his mouth feels like the Gobi desert.*

A tall, grim-faced man with close-cropped hair, his scruff dark against his tanned skin, entered and Nevan's attention sharpened. Grim Man was clearly fit under his tight Henley and moved with the loose-limbed grace of a trained athlete. *Prime assassin material, if ever I've seen it.* He held the door for another customer—a man with wavy dark hair and umber skin, whose bulky backpack caught on the door.

"Oh. Sorry. I just..." He managed to free the pack in time to step out of the way and allow a pink-cheeked woman with a brown-skinned baby on her hip to enter. "Sorry!"

Another woman in an impeccable beige business suit, her blond hair in a sleek updo and her makeup perfect, followed him in, but as he turned, his pack hit the gray-suited businessman's cup and knocked it off his table, dislodging its lid, and spraying dark liquid over the woman's skirt.

"Oh, goodness. I'm *so* sorry. I didn't mean…" He scurried for the napkins, his pack bouncing on his back and no doubt endangering all the other cups—not to mention heads—in the place.

She smiled at him rather thinly. "Think nothing of it. It was an accident, after all."

He gestured toward her skirt with a handful of napkins. "Please. Let me…"

"No need." She patted a large, expensive-looking handbag the same shade as her suit. "I always carry stain remover with me. If you'll excuse me." She headed for the restroom, her matching stilettos clicking against the tile floor.

The man heaved a sigh and glanced around with a shame-faced smile. "Sorry, folks." He slipped the pack off his shoulders and dangled it at his side by one strap. "I'll just, um, remove the weapon of mass destruction, shall I?"

Despite Nevan's growing physical discomfort and mental anxiety, the guy drew his gaze, a flame to Nevan's tattered moth, sparking a smile. He was so… cute. Bright. Sunny. Joyful.

The exact opposite of me.

While Nevan kept his main focus on Grim Man, who'd retreated to a corner and was himself keeping an eye on the door in between glances at his cell phone, he nevertheless tracked Sunny Guy's progress.

Sunny Guy didn't immediately get in line. Instead, he chatted with the woman with the baby who'd entered after him, yielding his place to her. She smiled at him, the baby giggling at the funny faces he made, raising and lowering his wire-framed spectacles to play an odd game of peekaboo.

The door swung open again, catching the attention of both Sunny Guy and Grim Man. When a pair of women entered, one pushing a wide stroller containing twin toddlers, both men's shoulders eased, and they sported nearly identical expressions of disappointment.

Nevan, on the other hand, tensed further. *Children.* His gorge rose, and he pressed his fist against his mouth. *How can I do this? How can I sacrifice one child for the sake of another?*

Lulu was his responsibility, his family, his joy, but couldn't the same be said for any child? If he obeyed Yvo's orders, conducted the assassin to the target, watched the deed play out, and then—his belly tumbled—*conveyed* the results back to Yvo, he'd save his sister. But another sibling, another parent, another friend would be devastated.

Yet if he didn't, the geas terms meant that Yvo would have full control over Lulu. Twist her trusting nature, her innocence, her boundless wonder. *Groom* her into a being as evil and corrupt as he was. And if he was unable to turn her, might he cut his losses instead and sacrifice her in another of his depraved spells?

Likewise, Yvo would have full control over Nevan himself. What would that mean? Would he refuse him drink, refuse him the touch of wild water, let him wither, waste away, disappear like so many other fae had done over the years?

Or would he order Nevan to shift and exercise the worst part of his nature, his monstrous side, the side that would lure travelers to his back for a gallop through the clouds, only to dissipate into mist over the rocks and send them, screaming, to their deaths far below? Yvo had already intimated that he had enemies. To what ends would he go to eliminate them?

At this point, Nevan didn't know whether he'd be classed with the enemies or with the weapons at Yvo's disposal.

The woman with the baby placed her order—a cappuccino and biscotti, which she gave to the baby, who began to gum it. He hadn't seriously considered her to be the assassin, in any case. No professional who was targeting a child would bring their own child on a job. At the notion of assassins—particularly those who murdered children for hire—having their own offspring, heat grew behind Nevan's eyes, a heat he couldn't quench by a dive into his lake.

The women with the twins stepped up to the counter next,

and Nevan frowned. Shouldn't Sunny Guy have been next? As the women ordered tea and breakfast sandwiches, Nevan scanned the shop. Sunny Guy wasn't even in line. Instead, he was approaching Grim Man, his smile a little tentative. He said something too low for Nevan to hear. Grim Man scowled and shook his head. Sunny Guy's shoulders drooped, but he nodded and stepped back.

His gaze traveled around the shop, a slight frown puckering his wide brow. His gaze caught on Nevan's and he blinked. Was that a shiver? If so, he wouldn't be the first one to have that reaction. Nevan had heard one of the dryads in Faerie refer to his usual expression as "resting monster face," so he wasn't surprised when Sunny Guy's gaze slipped away.

Grim Man still hadn't gotten in line, nor had Sunny Guy, even though several more customers had entered and joined the line, and the woman in the beige suit had finally emerged from the restroom. Sunny Guy immediately rushed over to her, clearly apologizing again. He gestured to her skirt, which showed no hint of stain, and then to the counter, obviously offering to buy her a beverage. She made some low-voiced remark and shook her head before heading to the high counter facing the front parking lot and pulling a slim laptop out of her handbag. Sunny Guy glumly took his place at the back of the line.

Nevan's palm pulsed and burned with Yvo's frustrated impatience. *Time is running out.* Shouldn't assassins be punctual? Had Yvo dumped him here too early? Nevan kicked himself for not asking for more information, such as what precise time the contract was to take place. He frowned, searching his memory. He'd heard *something* about the Assassin's Guild once. Something about how they ensured their members' safety by *not* allowing explicit appointment times. They insisted on a range, to enable their members to arrive and assess the security of the situation—and, presumably, to avoid ambushes by the associates of former victims.

Nevan was pretty sure now that Grim Man was his contact. As soon as he got in line and ordered his revolting beverage, Nevan could finally discover to what lengths he himself was willing to go.

Over in the corner, Grim Man straightened and tucked his phone in the rear pocket of his jeans, his gaze riveted on the door. *Stop watching the door, mate. I'm waiting for you over here.*

But when a slender man with a face as angelic as a transformed zenko kitsune hurried in, Grim Man's expression relaxed into a wide smile, and he strode forward to take the newcomer in his arms and plant a kiss on his mouth. "You're late," he said. "I was starting to worry."

Shite. Nevan slumped on his stool. He should know better by now than to let appearances color his perceptions. But he'd been so sure, so sure he hadn't paid enough attention to the other customers who'd arrived in the last twenty minutes.

Then he heard it.

"A grande sugar cookie almond milk latte with a caramel shot and no whip but extra sprinkles. To go, please."

His belly made another leap for this throat. *Goddess, no. It can't be. Not him.*

Nevan turned his head slowly, still trying to deny the truth, because he'd recognized the voice.

"I promise not to spill it." Sunny Guy handed the cashier his card with a smile. "Although there are no guarantees."

Nevan crossed his arms, the better to contain the fury and disappointment threatening to burst out in a glass-rattling roar. That kind of thing might go unnoticed in Faerie, but in a Hillsboro Starbucks it was bound to draw attention. And now that he'd identified the assassin, attention was the last thing either of them could afford.

So he waited, scowling, hoping that maybe, just maybe, he'd heard wrong. But when the barista called out, "Grande sugar cookie almond milk latte for Seb," and Sunny Guy picked it up with an infectious smile that made Nevan grind his teeth, he couldn't deny it anymore.

The cute guy who'd played peekaboo with a baby, who'd smiled at twin toddlers, who'd joked with the whole shop about his clumsiness—which was probably just a pretense too—was a despicable, cold-blooded murderer.

Of children.

CHAPTER 3

*S*eb stared at the stupidly sweet beverage in his hand and grimaced. Just its aroma made his teeth ache. His mouth had gotten progressively dryer every time somebody arrived who definitely *wasn't* his contact. He was tempted to pull his water bottle out of his pack, but it would probably be frowned on in here. Should he buy a bottle instead? If he had to wait much longer, he'd probably give in.

How long was he supposed to wait anyway? He wished the agency had been more forthcoming with details about the meeting, but they'd said with a client this high-profile, they couldn't release any specifics, not until the client's representative had arrived to conduct Seb to the site where he'd finally meet the child. Or children. The agency hadn't even told him that.

He trudged toward the counter that lined the front window, then changed direction at the last moment because the poor woman whose skirt he'd spilled on was involved in some kind of intense conversation on her phone and clearly didn't need a distraction. He didn't want to take up a table—this shop was busier than he'd imagined it would be, and tables should be kept for people who weren't alone.

Alone. Like me. Yeah, that was the thing, wasn't it? But according to his ex, Seb had nobody to blame for his aloneness but himself. Jase had made that opinion crystal clear: He'd objected strongly to Seb's chosen profession—many times, and at increasing decibel levels—throughout Seb's training.

"I'm a lawyer," Jase had boomed. "You don't have to work at all, let alone *this* kind of work. What if somebody at the firm finds out? How will it look?"

"But I'm good at it and I enjoy it," Seb had explained, time and time again. "It's what I want to do. What I've always wanted to do."

"Even when you were a kid yourself?" Jase demanded.

Seb had laughed. "Oh, trust me. *Especially* then."

"On your head be it, then."

Seb had thought that meant Jase would stop arguing with him about it. Instead, it meant that Jase had broken off their three-year relationship with a *Call me if you ever come to your senses.*

But because he *was* alone, Seb was free to consider this assignment. He sighed. Assuming the assignment ever materialized. What did a representative from a high-end client look like, anyway? He'd thought at first that it might be the woman he'd spilled on, which would be one heck of a first impression to make. Maybe she was even now contacting the agency and expressing her doubts that Seb was up to the job.

Heck, if he were in her place, he'd probably do the same.

The tall guy in the Henley had seemed like he was waiting for somebody, so Seb had finally approached him and asked point-blank if he was the client's rep. He'd said no, and when he scooped that guy who looked like a K-Pop idol into his arms, Seb got the picture.

Seb settled on a stool at the opposite end from his spill victim, hooking his feet on the rungs and tucking his bulky backpack between them. His trainers were new for the occasion and more expensive than he could really afford, which was another reason he was anxious for this job. It paid really freaking well.

He wrapped both hands around the cup, glad for the warmth. It was early June in Portland, which meant cool and drizzly, and although he was wearing his North Face anorak, Seb's hands were still cold. They always were when he got nervous.

"You here for the job?" growled a low voice in his ear.

Seb jolted, nearly spilling the latte, and swiveled around on the stool. His eyes widened and he gulped, because the enormous man behind him didn't fit Seb's idea of a high-end client rep. For one thing, he looked as though he'd been standing in the rain without an umbrella for half an hour because his curly black hair was soaked, and even the dark skin of his cheeks was dotted with moisture. Didn't rich clients have drivers to cart their minions around? Or at least give said minions their own transportation, so they weren't traipsing around in all weathers? Seb put it on his mental list of *things to investigate someday but not currently relevant.*

That list was getting alarmingly long. He'd started it when he was still in middle school, and to this date, had never removed a single item from it.

For another, this man looked really... rough. Not as in rough-dangerous, although with that scowl, he could definitely qualify in most people's books. But rough as in ill. His lips were dry and chapped, his dark eyes sunken, his shoulders—his *really* wide shoulders—hunched as though he were protecting a pain-shot middle. In fact, he looked like he should be in bed, with somebody feeding him homemade chicken soup, or maybe in the nearest emergency department hooked up to an IV full of nutritive fluids. Surely high-end clients should have a health plan for their employees?

For a third, his clothing: The leather duster, the linen shirt, the dark suede vest with its brass buttons, the black—*be still my heart*—knee-high boots made him look as though he were about to make a grand entrance at the nearest ComiCon and totally rock the steampunk pirate cosplay. Were high-end clients that whimsical? Or maybe they just had really lax dress codes.

"Well?" the man rasped.

"Oh. Right." He'd asked a question. "The job. Yes. Yes, I am." Seb held out his hand. "Seb Ardelean. And you are?"

The man snorted. "Like that's your real name."

"Well, I admit it's a nickname, but—"

"Come on." He turned in a swirl of black leather and strode for the door.

Seb scrambled off his stool, nearly tripping on his own pack. He grabbed it by one strap, and, tossing the futile latte in the trash as he passed—*waste of money I don't have*—hurried after him.

The man was powering through the parking lot, on a straight shot for Cornell. "Are we heading for your car?" Seb called.

"No," the guy said, not even bothering to turn, although he did lift his face to the rain once.

Fine. If there was no car, maybe this was another test. Seb flipped the hood of his jacket up and struggled to slip his arms into his pack straps as he half-ran to catch up. He had a collapsible umbrella in a side pocket—he could offer it to the guy so he wouldn't have to get so wet, if only the big jerk would slow down enough for Seb to get it out. But at this pace, he'd have no chance.

Just before they reached the sidewalk, the man whirled toward him, his face a mask of fury, his teeth bared. "So you really do this? Handle kids?"

Seb bridled a little. Was this guy really questioning his credentials here? In the rain? "I assure you, I'm qualified. I have a copy of my CV if you—"

"What?" His face twisted with revulsion. "Goddess, no!"

Taking a firm grip on his patience, Seb said, "Look. The agency wouldn't have sent me if they didn't believe I was a good fit for this job. Can you at least tell me the child's age and gender? Their name?" He brightened. "Or are there more than one?"

"Shite," he muttered and turned to march down the sidewalk.

"Wait!" Seb puffed after him, his pack bouncing on his back. "Could you at least tell me *your* name?"

For a moment, Seb didn't think he would answer. Then his big shoulders rose and fell—seriously, did anyone outside Dwayne Johnson have shoulders *that* wide?—and he said, "Quirke. Nevan Quirke."

Progress. "Pleased to meet you, Nevan."

"Can't say the same," he grumbled, and doubled his pace.

Broad shoulders *and* long legs. Jeez, Seb was all of five-ten—okay, five nine and a half—but he felt like a Munchkin next to Nevan. He had to trot to keep up now, and since the sidewalk was *right next to* the street, every car whizzing by kicked up dirty water like vehicular blood spatter. By the time they'd made it beyond the airport, Seb's formerly pristine chinos looked like overripe bananas. *Soggy* overripe bananas. He would have sighed, except he couldn't catch enough breath to do it.

He was puffing and panting, wincing with every step as his pack thumped against his back—and what was that sharp thing that hit the same exact spot above his hip with every thump? True, Seb had probably over-packed, but with so little information about the assignment, he'd wanted to be prepared for any eventuality. He grimaced as that sharp-whatever-it-was poked his hip again. *Next time, I'll arrange things more carefully.*

Nevan put on another burst of speed and Seb wheezed as he tried to keep up. Several of his instructors had warned him that this profession was more physically demanding than many people realized and had recommended—some more tactfully than others—that Seb spend more time in the gym. Right about now, Seb seriously regretted not taking their advice.

A small prop plane buzzed past overhead. As Seb glanced up to track its progress over the road toward the airfield, his hood fell back slightly, sending raindrops across his forehead and dotting his glasses. With the hood no longer blocking his peripheral vision, he caught sight of a row of bright tents beyond the fairground fence on their right, the shrieks and laughter of fairgoers mostly muffled by the sound of traffic.

Beyond the fairgrounds, there was nothing for at least another mile, nothing until past Brookfield Parkway, where several restaurants, a vet practice, and a Kindercare clustered together across from Costco. Were they headed there? Seb hoped they weren't going any farther, because his new trainers, despite having great traction on the wet sidewalk, were raising a blister on his heel.

He hitched the strap of his pack further onto his shoulder and tried to shift it so the pokey bit was at least hitting a different spot. The agency, while not being exactly specific, had assured Seb that certain intermediary steps were standard for this type of job, but they'd said nothing about having to train for them like he was embarking on a half marathon. No matter what happened with the client, he was definitely reporting this to his handler.

Seb tugged his hood forward again, put his head down, and slogged onward, only to run headfirst into an extremely broad, extremely muscular, extremely *solid*—if his forehead was any judge—chest.

"Ow." He rubbed his forehead. "Maybe warn a guy next time?"

Nevan just grunted. "This way."

Seb looked around. They were at the fairground's entrance. "A carnival? This kind of environment is more chaotic than I'd like. I usually prefer to meet prospective charges privately. One on one, if possible."

Nevan snorted. "I'll wager you do." He took off toward the carnival entrance, where a red and white banner with the words *Welcome Traveler* in that classic circus font was suspended between two massive posts. "Wait," he said and rooted through his pockets as though searching for something.

"Oookay." *I'll take the opportunity to get my lungs functioning again.* Seb gulped in air and peered through the gate.

The carnival seemed moderately busy, with kids racing about, pointing at the massive carousel, or holding nearly as massive cones of cotton candy, with their adult attendants either smiling indulgently or trudging after them with ill-concealed fatigue. Was one of them his charge?

Interestingly enough, in the manner of Oregon's quirky weather, everyone beyond the gates seemed perfectly dry. Now that he finally had breath to do so, Seb chuckled, remembering instances in his childhood where it had been raining on one side of his house, but sunny on the other, with a rainbow arching over the trees.

Then he saw them.

Clowns.

They boiled out of a big, bright orange tent, and Seb's horror grew as he counted them. *One, two, three, four...* jeez, there were *nine* of the things. Surely no carnival needed more than one, although if Seb had his way, zero would be the absolute maximum.

He scowled at the ticket booth next to the gate. A tall man with skin about Seb's own color stood next to it, impassively observing the crowd, including Seb, with shrewd black eyes. Judging by his outfit—similar to Nevan's, only with less leather and more velvet—he was probably a carnival employee. *Good.* Because Seb needed to speak to someone with authority.

The carnival should post a *trigger warning*, for Pete's sake. The nightmares engendered by clowns... Seb shuddered. Why anybody had ever thought flat white foundation, fright wigs in colors not found in nature, alarmingly oversized shoes, and accessories in clashing, eye-searing colors that may or may not shoot water at you were *funny* was seriously disturbed.

He marched toward the man, prepared to express himself

with *very* stern language, but before he'd gone more than three paces, Nevan stepped in front of him.

"Here." He thrust a pasteboard rectangle the size of a business card at Seb.

Seb peered down at it. One side displayed a stylized version of the red and white big top at the far end of the midway, emblazoned with *The Carnival of Mysteries* and *Admit One*.

"Is the child already inside?" By this time, Seb knew better than to expect anything other than a growl in response. "Very well. Lead on."

When they stepped through the gates, warmth caressed Seb's face. He sighed happily. Either the carnival had heaters deployed throughout the grounds to keep the fairgoers from getting too chilled, or else it was the sun, blessedly emerging from behind the clouds. He pushed his hood back and smiled up at Nevan, whose jaw was clenched so tightly that he looked as though he were smuggling marbles in his cheeks.

Seb was about to attempt another friendly conversation—or at least to extract a little more blood from this particular stone—when a leering dead-white face with oversized, fire engine red lips and a lime green mohawk popped up beyond Nevan's shoulder. *Ugh.*

When several more clowns capered around the pair of them, Seb pulled his hood back up and hunched his shoulders, tempted to close his eyes and chant *La la la*. If any of them had spoken, he probably would have bolted, but they didn't, although the first one edged closer and squatted down, laughing soundlessly up into Seb's face, its eyes as black and soulless as a shark's.

"What is wrong with you?" Nevan demanded.

"I don't like clowns," Seb muttered. Immediately, the clown who had been staring at him flopped over onto its back, one purple-gloved hand over its heart and the other fluttering over-dramatically to its forehead. The others collapsed on top of it, one after the other, until it looked as though Seb were standing next to an animate pile of extremely unfortunate laundry. "Can we move this along, please?"

"Fine."

Nevan strode off down the midway. Seb scurried after him, thankfully leaving the clowns in his rear view.

CHAPTER 4

*I*n another stroke of Nevan's phenomenal bad luck, the rain stopped the instant he'd led the assassin through the carnival gates. But it wasn't bad enough that he had *led an assassin* through fecking *carnival gates*. *Goddess, I hate irony.* Because not only was he abetting a murder in an amusement park, he was also courting permanent dehydration in the process.

"Where are we going?" the assassin asked after they'd left the clowns in a heap. If Nevan didn't know what kind of soul-dead monster Seb was, he'd have called that tone plaintive.

Nevan glanced around at the tents that bracketed the midway.

"Turquoise," Yvo had said. "The knife thrower's tent."

Nevan had snorted. "Knife thrower? A little on the nose, don't you think?"

Yvo had shrugged. "You can't carry the weapon in with you, and he possesses several blades suitable for my purposes. Convenience, nothing more."

Nevan spotted the turquoise tent. "There." He strode off toward its open flap.

"Will there be more clowns?" Seb asked.

Unbelievable. Nevan shook his head in disgust. This man had the stones to murder children for money, yet he was terrified of clowns.

He paused and glanced up at the banner over the tent's entrance. It read *Gentleman Jim* and below it, *Master of Knives*. He shuddered at that. Yvo had vowed that the knife thrower wasn't aware of the spell he'd had cast on his blade, and that Nevan would have no trouble both identifying the bespelled weapon and removing it from the tent undetected. But Nevan knew to his cost that Yvo wasn't the most trustworthy person. He assumed, since it would be in Yvo's best interests, that he'd been truthful this time.

He ducked inside the tent, Seb crowding his heels to follow him. The show was in full swing, with Gentleman Jim at the far side of the tent, opposite a set of risers nearly full of fairgoers. He was garbed like a gunslinger from the American Old West, his canvas duster similar in cut to Nevan's leather one. He was hatless, although a Stetson hung on a hat stand next to a display rack arrayed with an astonishing number of knives and old-fashioned guns.

Nevan ground his teeth. He hoped *Gentleman Jim* had the sense not to have loaded firearms in a public carnival where anyone—including a child—might get their hands on one.

At the moment, Gentleman Jim was juggling three long-bladed knives, blindfolded. Then he whirled and launched them, one after the other, toward a red-haired woman in a sparkly, corseted outfit reminiscent of a dance hall girl. She was posed against a round wooden panel perhaps seven feet in diameter, painted with a starburst of dusty gold and orange, and held her smile—although to Nevan's eyes it was rather forced—as the knives *thunk*ed into the wood above her head and next to either ear.

Nevan took the opportunity of the audience *oooh*ing and clapping to grab Seb's arm and pull him back out the tent flap.

"*Now* where are we going? When will I meet the child?"

"Shut up," Nevan growled. He kept his grip on Seb's elbow and towed him around the tent, stepping over its guy ropes, until they reached the rear, where a shorter, smaller tent was laced to the main canvas with a double row of grommets. Nevan had spotted its entrance from the main tent behind Gentleman Jim's weapons display, but as he expected, it didn't have an external flap. He pulled a couple of tent pegs from the ground and lifted the canvas. "In here."

Seb balked. "Are you sure that's okay? I mean, the ticket grants admission to all the shows, but this seems like a private space."

"Oh, now you're worried about rules? Get the fuck inside. Now."

Seb's eyes widened. "I… I'm not sure I'm the—"

"I said," Nevan forced out between his teeth, "get in. Now." He grinned evilly. "Before the clowns find us."

That did it. Seb scuttled inside. Nevan didn't kick his backside, although he was tempted. He glanced around, but nobody was in sight. Here, the carnival backed up to the rest of the fairgrounds, which seemed deserted, and nobody else was lurking behind the row of tents. He ducked under the canvas and let it drop behind him. From beyond the flap that led to the main tent, several more *thwaps* signaled that Gentleman Jim was once more threatening his assistant with a few unplanned piercings. *Good.* The show was still in progress.

It was dimmer in here without the stage lights. The space was lit only by a small faux-kerosene lantern, its glow reflected in the mirror over a tiny makeup table. At least Nevan hoped it was faux. Because fire and carnival tents did *not* go well together.

A cabinet made of some dark wood and banded in metal, about as high as Nevan's shoulder, stood on the opposite side of the little space. It was secured with a laughably tiny padlock. Nevan would have been outraged—look how easy it had been for him and the assassin to slip in—if he hadn't detected the shimmer of magic around the hasp.

He took the two steps past Seb, who was gaping at every-thing as though he'd never seen such things as spare costumes and— *Oh.* He was staring at a First Aid kit the size of a foot-locker. Nevan buried a snort. Apparently, Gentleman Jim's blades didn't always fly true.

The burst of amusement shriveled in his chest because Yvo had assured Nevan that the spell he'd cast on the borrowed knife, combined with the assassin's own skill, would ensure that it flew true and fulfilled his fecking *quest.*

Nevan closed his fingers around the lock with the hand sporting the geas brand. If his own power hadn't been hobbled, he'd have been able to rip the damned thing off in a breath. Yvo, of course, hadn't been willing to allow him even that much strength.

"Besides," he'd said, "your type of brute force leaves far too many telltale footprints in its wake. Finesse, my friend. Finesse and stealth, that's our byword." Instead, he'd imbued the geas brand with what he'd called a *simple neutralizing charm.* He'd waggled his thrice-damned finger again, making Nevan long to shift into his water horse form and bite it off. "Don't get any brilliant ideas about trying it on anything else. It's expressly for the needs of my quest."

So Nevan gripped the bloody lock. For an instant, it flared hotter than his brand had ever burned, but Nevan's fingers were clamped in place, and he could do nothing but clench his teeth and bear it.

Fecking mage. The pain probably wasn't necessary at all. It was probably just another one of Yvo's *incentives* to hurry Nevan along.

"Jeez, is that lock *glowing?*" Seb edged closer, and the scent of damp hair and mint and citrus that Nevan hadn't previously noticed distracted him from the agony in his hand. "Is it *hot?* For goodness' sake, let go!"

Nevan didn't bother to say anything because just then, the lock clicked and the shank parted from the body, enabling him to release his hold.

"Let me see that." Seb grabbed Nevan's hand and held it, palm up. He peered at it in the dim light. "You've definitely got a burn. You need something on it." His finger hovered above the black of the geas brand. "Is that— No, that's an intentional design." He glanced at the First Aid trunk. "A First Aid kit that big is bound to have something for burns." He chuckled a little weakly. "Although it's probably got a bigger stock of cut-related treatments, right?"

Although Nevan had been momentarily mesmerized by the gentleness of Seb's fingers on his skin, he jerked his hand away, furious with himself for forgetting in that moment of unexpected solicitude what the man's profession was, what they were here to do. "Never mind. It'll be all right in a while."

"Are you sure? I mean—"

"I said, never mind." Nevan turned resolutely away. He slipped the lock from the staple, flipped the hasp, and opened the cabinet.

"Whoa," Seb breathed. "I haven't seen that many sharp things in one place since Jase and I watched *Knives Out* on Netflix."

Nevan ignored him, scanning the sunburst of meticulously polished blades for the one that carried the taint of Yvo's magic. Yvo had boasted about his cleverness in insinuating the spell into the carnival, although Nevan wasn't sure why it was such an impressive feat. He hadn't cared enough to ask, and perhaps he should have. His impulsiveness, his failure to demand the full details of the geas, was what had gotten him in this predicament in the first place.

Ah. There. A blade near the outer edge of the display pulsed with a sullen, bilious glow. Nevan reached into the cabinet and gingerly extracted it with his left hand. Again, Yvo had guaranteed that Nevan couldn't improvise on the job by informing him, just in case he was planning a little impromptu bloodshed of his own when he returned with Yvo's *item*, that he'd be unable to remove any knife but the one destined for the *quest*.

"Are you sure you should be doing that?" Seb's tone held a combination of nerves and shock. "This is *stealing*."

"*You're* squeamish about stealing?" With his right hand, Nevan closed the cabinet and re-engaged the lock.

"Of course! What kind of example does that set for kids?"

Heat beat behind Nevan's eyes, in his throat, in his chest. "Example? Who the *fuck* are you to bleat about examples? Here." He thrust the knife, hilt first, at Seb. "Take it."

"What?" Seb snatched his hands away and backpedaled across the tent until he fetched up against the turquoise canvas. "I'm not *touching* that."

Nevan huffed. "How do you expect to do your job without it?"

"My job?" He shook his head wildly. "My job doesn't need a blade the length of my forearm for anything."

"No? Then how do you expect to hit Mario Gallier with it in the middle of his trapeze act? How do you expect to carve out his heart? How do you expect me to deliver his heart to the fecking *mage* if you don't have this fecking *blade*?"

"Carve out a heart?" Seb's eyes had grown even wider, the whites showing around their dark irises. "I don't carve *anything*. I don't even buy whole *chickens*."

Nevan controlled his temper. Barely. By the pulsing of his geas brand, time was running out. They had to catch Mario while he was in flight. "You took the job. You knew what it entailed. Take the fecking knife. What kind of bloody assassin are you, anyway?"

"Assassin?" Seb squeaked. "For heaven's sake, I'm not an *assassin*. I'm a *nanny*."

CHAPTER 5

*I*f Seb hadn't been hyperventilating, he'd have laughed at Nevan's dumbfounded expression. But laughter was completely beyond his capability right now. *Assassin?* Seriously? There really *were* such things? "Y-you're not from Mrs. Macclesfield, are you?"

"Macclesfield?" Nevan's tone was a blend of uncertainty and accusation. "Is that your contact at the Assassin's Guild?"

"There's a *guild?*" Seb's voice rose. He couldn't help it. A *guild?* Full of *assassins?*

Nevan clapped his hand—the one without the knife in it, thank goodness—over Seb's mouth. "Quiet! Let me think. I've got to *think.*"

Seb nodded his acquiescence, because he really had no desire to be discovered. He'd been leery of their sketchy entrance in the first place. Now he was certain they had no business here.

He smothered a moan. If he were arrested for breaking and entering—was it technically B & E if you crawled under a tent? —his chances of landing a live-in nanny position with a high-end client would vanish. No way would Mrs. Macclesfield hire somebody with a police record to watch her children.

Assuming Seb hadn't already completely trashed his chances

by mistaking Nevan, a man who wanted to hire an *assassin*, for Mrs. Macclesfield's assistant.

On the other side of the tent wall, the audience gasped and then broke out into cheers and applause. Nevan spared a sidelong glance toward the noise, and although his eyes were bleak, his jaw was set determinedly. "The show must be over. We've got to go." He strode over to the spot where they'd entered and lifted the canvas. "Out."

Out. Yes. Out was good. Seb scuttled across the tent and ducked out into the wan sunshine. When Nevan followed him, he still had the knife in his hand. Scandalized, Seb pointed at it. "You can't take that. It doesn't belong to you."

Nevan glared at him. "I can hardly put it back now. The knife thrower or his assistant will pop in there as soon as they've taken their bows. Come on."

He grabbed Seb's elbow—*ow, that was gonna leave a bruise*—and towed him along behind the row of tents. Nevan could easily step over the guy ropes, but Seb managed to catch his foot on every single one. Which was the only reason he was grateful for Nevan's grip: It kept him from face-planting on the sparse grass.

They reached the rear of a huge red and white striped tent where the sounds of applause and cheers from inside, coupled with the whir of an enormous generator, created a sort of cone of privacy, if only because nobody could hear them above the other noise.

Nevan let go of Seb's elbow, but still loomed over him. "Now. The truth. Who sent you?"

Seb kept a wary eye on the knife still clutched in Nevan's hand. Could he reach his cell phone? Call 9-1-1?

Who am I kidding? He's not quite twice as big as I am, but his muscles probably weigh as much as I do soaking wet.

Besides, Seb had seen how fast the man could move. He'd have no chance to call for help before Nevan could stop him. And for a carnival that had seemed so busy and populated when they'd entered, this spot was completely deserted. At this point, Seb would have even been grateful for a clown or two. Okay, maybe not two. But one, anyway. He could handle one.

Probably.

In the meantime, the best he could hope for was to cooperate. De-escalate. Negotiate. After all, he'd talked three-year-olds out of second cookies multiple times. He could totally do this.

"Letitia. My handler—"

"Handler?"

Seb laughed weakly. "That's our little joke. She's the employment specialist I work with at Northwest Nurture and Nannies."

"Shite," Nevan muttered, running his free hand through his hair. "So you didn't accept this contract from the guild?"

"In the first place..." Although Seb tried to keep his voice calm and level, it shook a little. He cleared his throat and tried again. "In the first place, I've never heard of an assassin's guild outside a D & D campaign."

Nevan's brows bunched together. "D & D?"

"Dungeons and Dragons."

"Oh, thank the goddess." While Nevan didn't precisely smile, his face relaxed a smidge. "You know about us, then." He chuckled a little weakly. "I was afraid I'd have the supe council on my arse for Secrecy Pact violations on top of whatever the thrice-damned earth mage has up his sleeve for me. You're an ally of the dragon queen?"

Oookay. So not only was Nevan in serious need of some anger management therapy and at least a gallon of water—if Seb was reading the signs of severe dehydration right—but he was also delusional or else taking this cosplay a little *too* far. Stealing a knife from a carnival was one thing, but mages? Surely he couldn't believe Seb was referring to *actual* dragons, could he? Heck, even though D & D wasn't as popular as it had been, Seb didn't think anybody in the English-speaking world hadn't seen *Stranger Things.*

So, should he humor the guy? Or set him straight? Seb didn't like to mislead anyone, but there was that knife to consider.

"I'm afraid you might be under a misapprehension." Seb tried to smile reassuringly. "Letitia had arranged for me to meet Mrs. Macclesfield's representative at Starbucks to conduct me to my first encounter with Mrs. Macclesfield's child." He winced. "Or children. Since Mrs. Macclesfield is such a high-profile client, and committed to the privacy and security of her family, I had no information about who my prospective charges were to be."

Nevan's expression had morphed from shock to anger to gray devastation as Seb spoke. "But I asked you if you were there for the job. For the child. And you said yes."

"Because I was. For *Mrs. Macclesfield's* job. Taking care of *her* child. Or children. As their *nanny*." Seb tried another smile, but it didn't mitigate Nevan's obvious distress. "Although some refer to men in that job as mannies, I've never seen the distinction as important."

Jase had certainly spent plenty of time sneering over both job titles: He could never acknowledge that childcare was one of the most important jobs—perhaps *the* most important job—anyone could do. What was more critical to creating a better world than guiding children? Teaching them? Caring for them? Keeping them safe and happy?

"But… But you ordered that latte."

"Yes." Seb wrinkled his nose. "I did. Which was a mistake, I admit." He smiled with what he hoped was enough sympathy and encouragement to pull Nevan off the ledge. "But I think the role-playing has gone on long enough, don't you? D & D is just a game, after all. There's no dragon queen. There are no mages. There's no—"

"Wait. You're…" Nevan swallowed several times. "…*human?*" He said the word *human* as though it were synonymous with *Ebola* or *albino parasitic blood worms from space.*

"Nevan." Seb took a deep breath. Time to bring this delusion to an end. "We're all human. We all have rights, hopes, dreams.

Fears. And sometimes, we might need a little help." Greatly daring, he rested his hand on Nevan's forearm—the one without a knife at the end of it. "Is there someone I can call for you? Someone who can take care of you?" Nevan's eyes were bleak. Seb had heard the term *thousand-yard stare* before, but he'd never witnessed it until now. "Nevan?"

"What have I done?" Nevan's voice was barely audible over the grumble of the generator.

Seb tightened his grip in what he hoped read as reassurance. "Nothing that can't be fixed, I'm sure. We can put the knife back. Maybe just slide it under the tent during the next show for the knife thrower or his assistant to find, and no harm done."

"No harm?" Nevan barked out a harsh laugh. "You have no idea."

"Then why don't you tell me? I'm a good listener."

Nevan's gaze finally focused on Seb's face. "I've already said too much." Suddenly, his head came up, and he glanced around wildly. "How long has it been?"

"Since when?"

"Since we left the coffee shop. How long?"

Under Seb's hand, Nevan's arm muscles tensed. Seb had no hope of restraining a man this size with sheer physical force, so he let go. "I don't know. Maybe half an hour? A little more?"

"It might not be too late." Nevan's eyes took on a feverish glow, glinting in the sun, which made them look as though light actually glittered in their dark depths. "The assassin might still be there. I can still—"

"Whoa, there, bucko." Despite their size difference, and the certainty that Nevan could probably plow right over Seb if he chose, Seb planted himself in Nevan's path. "If you think I'll let you go when you're still stuck on this whole assassin scenario, you're more delusional than I thought."

"You don't understand." Nevan's tone was pleading, and, much to Seb's relief, he didn't make any effort to bulldoze his way past or use the knife in his hand to eliminate the, er, immediate obstacle. "I *must* meet the assassin. If I— *Augh!*" Nevan doubled over, his arms crossed over his middle, panting as though he were in agony.

"Nevan?" Jeez, this man endured a blistering burn with nothing more than a wince. If he was hurting enough to scream now, the pain must be excruciating. "What's wrong?"

He shook his head, teeth clenched. After a few moments, he began to breathe more easily, and so did Seb. "I've got to go back. There could still be a chance to set this right."

"If setting things right involves the murder of a child, I can't let you do that." It was Seb's turn to set his jaw. "If you take one step out of this carnival with that knife in your hand, I'm calling the police."

Nevan glanced at the knife, then at Seb, and then at the tent behind them. He held the knife out, hilt first. "Take it."

"What? No!" Seb stumbled back, barely keeping his balance when his calves encountered a guy rope. "That's stolen property. I'm not going to *touch* it."

Nevan uncurled his fingers and the knife dropped. The blade drove into the ground as though the hard-packed earth with its rough grass were no more substantial than a Jell-O mold. "Then here it will stay until I return for it."

When he put it that way... Seb slipped his pack off his back and knelt to unzip one side pocket. Gingerly taking the knife handle between thumb and forefinger, he wiggled it until he could extract it from the earth and slid it behind his spare aluminum water bottle. He'd figure out what to do with it later. Maybe he could approach the knife thrower and say he'd found it? With evidence of the break-in—duck-in?—Gentleman Jim was bound to believe him. Right?

Above him, Nevan swayed on his feet. Seb stood quickly, shouldering his pack. "Do you need to sit down? You don't look well."

Nevan's mouth stretched, more rictus than smile. "That's because I'm a dead man."

CHAPTER 6

*I*f not for that trifling detail Nevan had forgotten—that nobody under a geas could divulge its particulars to anyone who didn't already know about it—he might have betrayed more of the supernatural community's secrets to Seb. *To the human.* He was almost grateful for the pain that had nearly torn him in two when he'd started to blather about his task.

Because he'd well and truly violated the Secrecy Pact already, hadn't he? *"Are you an ally of the dragon queen?"* Bloody hells, he *deserved* to have his arse handed to him by the council for being so utterly fecking gormless.

Bad enough that he'd mistaken an innocent human—a *nanny*, for the love of the gods—for the assassin and exposed him to Nevan's shameful actions. He'd also failed to contact the *real* assassin, who'd probably given up and logged Nevan's no-show, resulting in the forfeit of Yvo's fees—and if there was one thing mages cared about more than power, it was money. The instant Yvo got the notification from the Guild, he'd have Nevan's arse on a platter.

Not to mention what he might do to Lulu.

There was no point in taking the knife with him to pass it to the guild assassin, since they wouldn't be able to bring it back through the carnival gates. When he glanced back to where he'd dropped it, the knife was gone, anyway, and since Seb was fussing with his backpack, it didn't take an oracle to figure out he'd tucked it away. *Safely out of my wicked hands.*

If Nevan expected to fulfill his geas and free Lulu and himself, he'd have to somehow convince Yvo to bespell another one of Gentleman Jim's daggers. But could the mage even do it? He'd chortled so about his cleverness in managing the first spell, but that was another thing about mages: Most of them were such narcissistic arseholes that they had a far higher opinion of their own abilities than was warranted.

Maybe… Nevan chewed on his lower lip, tasting the metallic tang of his own blood when the dry skin cracked under his teeth. If he played on that same narcissism, perhaps he could cajole Yvo into a second spell from flattery alone, even though it would nearly choke him to do so.

Yes. He might still be able to salvage the situation. If he recalled Guild regulations, for only a small penalty, a contractee could request a second meeting without forfeiting the entire contract, provided the request occurred within twenty-four hours. He'd go back to Starbucks. Ask the barista if she'd served anyone else that revolting drink. If not, he'd wait there all day long if he had to. If she had, he'd grovel as much as necessary when Yvo contacted him. That Yvo *would* contact him wasn't even in question.

"Nevan?" Seb's worried face swam into focus. "I mean it. I can't let you hurt a child, but I also think you need medical attention. There's a hospital not far from here. I'll call an Uber. You can be there in—"

"No. I can't. I—" Nevan's geas brand began to heat again, pulsing quickly, the signal that Yvo was about to initiate communication and that Nevan had better get to a private area soon or face the consequences.

He spun and raced around the big top to the midway.

"Nevan!" Seb called.

Nevan ignored him as he glanced around wildly. He needed a quiet place. A secluded place. A place devoid of humans. For the most part, the crowd on the midway was heading for the big top. *Of course they are.* The Flying Galliers were about to start their show, a show that, if Nevan had done his duty, would have been interrupted by the sudden midair death of their youngest member.

Well, that wouldn't happen, not at this performance. But there would be other performances, other opportunities. He growled, causing a nearby couple with two small children to side-eye him and veer away.

Could he wait until the show started? From the rapid pulse of his brand, its growing heat, he didn't have time. Anyway, not everyone was headed for the big top. Some were still riding the carousel, watching a marionette show, lining up for the giant swings, or trickling into the other midway tents.

Ah. There. The Fun House sat in a sort of carnival no-man's-land, nobody within yards of its gaping clown maw entrance. Nevan threaded his way through the crowd—*now I know what spawning salmon feel like*—until he could race across the empty grass in front of the Fun House and lunge through the clown's smile, directly into a rotating tunnel low enough that he had to bend double to avoid decapitating himself.

The brand's pulse sped up until it was nearly a continuous thrum, like a hummingbird's heart. Clearly, Yvo was rapidly losing patience. But when Nevan took his first step out of the tunnel, the floor shifted under his feet, tilting at a near forty-degree angle and knocking him off balance. As soon as he put his other foot down to steady himself, the floor tilted the other way.

"Fuck this shite," he growled, and dove for the crooked doorway on the other side of the tilt-a-floor. Once through it—he had to twist his body into a near pretzel to fit through the zig-zag opening—he found himself in one of those thrice-damned mirrored rooms, his reflection multiplied hundreds of times. On the right, he caught sight of his hair, standing wildly around his head; on the left, the sheen of sweat on his dark skin, moisture he couldn't afford to lose; and on into infinity, his shoulders hunched in despair.

The burst of heat in his palm dropped Nevan to his knees and naturally—*naturally*—this was where Yvo's communication simulacrum materialized. Because one Yvo wasn't enough. One Nevan huddled at his feet wasn't enough. No, the fates had decreed that Nevan's humiliation, his subjugation, should surround him, multiplied countless times.

The air shivered and writhed in front of Nevan until Yvo's transparent image appeared, hovering a foot above the floor.

"Nevan," he said, his tone deceptively solicitous, "imagine my disappointment when I received a notification from the Guild that my contract was in danger of forfeiture." His voice hardened. "Because my incompetent *pack mule* failed to connect with the assassin."

I will not cower. I will not. He lifted his chin and met Yvo's empty eyes squarely. "There were... complications."

"Complications? *Complications?*" Yvo sounded more like a harpy than a mage. "I'll tell you about complications. A complication would be me losing an absolutely exorbitant fee, not to mention an equally extortionate penalty to the Guild for noncompliance. A complication would be the Guild sanctioning me and preventing me from using their services for an entire *year.*" His ghostly shoulders rose and his nostrils flared. "A *complication* would be me losing the optimal moment to secure the central component for my spell. A *complication* would be the failure of my quest." His image rose another foot, although Nevan sincerely doubted he was actually levitating in his fecking secret stronghold. He was just indulging in his usual brand of overdone theatrics. "And don't get me started on the complications for you and your sister."

"Is Lulu all right?" Nevan clenched his fists on his thighs to keep from launching himself at Yvo. It wouldn't do any good.

The bastard wasn't really here. "You haven't hurt her, have you? You can't. Not without breaking your side of the geas."

"Little Luljeta is perfectly unharmed, although perhaps a trifle bored." Yvo's giggle sent anger spearing through Nevan's gut. "She is in... time-out, as you might say."

"What's that supposed to mean?"

The simulacrum waved an airy transparent hand. "Never mind. Merely a little whimsy on my part. I do love whimsy, don't you?"

"No." What Nevan would love was to get his hands around Yvo's throat and squeeze Lulu's location out of him. "Why are you doing this?"

"Why?" Yvo's expression darkened. On a more formidable mage, it might have been threatening. On him, it just looked petulant. "The ridiculous supe council wants to *bind* us, *restrict* us, *control* us. Because they're envious. Envious that mages aren't constrained by such ludicrous limitations as *balance* or *natural consequences* or some archaic magical nature. Look at you." He shook his head and *tsk*ed. "Drop a bridle over your head and you're helpless. Tell me." He leaned forward, lips stretched in a leer. "Does that work when you're in human form, too?"

"No," Nevan growled.

"Are you sure?" With a ridiculous flourish that caused the bell sleeves of his mud-brown gown to puddle around his elbows, Yvo conjured a leather contraption which, given the ball gag, was more BDSM dungeon than Faerie stable. "We could experiment."

"I told you. No. Only from my back when I'm airborne in water horse form." He bared his teeth. "And trust me, I'd transform into mist and drop you onto the bloody rocks before you got anywhere near my head with a bridle."

Yvo cocked his head. "We'll see." The stupid headgear disappeared. "Now. Let's discuss your abysmal failure, shall we?"

"It wasn't my fault," Nevan mumbled. "He ordered the drink.

He responded to the question. He did everything you told me would flag the assassin."

"Then he *was* the assassin!" Yvo bellowed, actually stamping his foot, which had less impact considering the floor under him wasn't visible. "My spells could not fail!"

"Well, they did. We got all the way to the carnival. Retrieved the knife. But he wouldn't take it."

"He must! It's in the contract!"

"He'd never heard of that contract. He ordered that drink by chance."

"Impossible. *Nobody* would voluntarily order something like that." He paced back and forth, apparently in the air. Then his head shot up. "He's lying to you." He jabbed his forefinger at Nevan. "It's a test. I'm told that the Guild deploys those randomly."

"I don't think so. He was absolutely horrified by the idea of gutting a child." *As am I.* Nevan attempted to swallow as his gorge rose, but his dry mouth and parched throat made it impossible. "Not only that, but he's human."

Yvo scoffed. "Also impossible. You'd never have been able to approach a human. The geas bond would have prevented it."

"Are you sure? For all you know, the Guild employs humans. Since they're so fecking *secure*, nobody knows anything about them."

Yvo frowned, crossing his arms and slipping his hands beneath his sleeves. "They couldn't. Their contracts involve magic. To employ humans would put them in violation of the Secrecy Pact."

"They're an *assassin's* guild! Why the bloody hells would they care about the Secrecy Pact? *You* don't."

"Hmmm. You may have a point."

"Bloody right, I have a point." Nevan took a breath through his nose and exhaled slowly, still trying to control his nausea. "The human has the knife. You'll have to bespell another one."

Yvo stared at him for a moment before he threw back his

head and laughed, that stupid *bwahahaha* that all evil buggers seem to learn, maybe at villain school.

"I knew it. If he kept the weapon, then he's the assassin. He's probably out right this minute, fulfilling his contract." Yvo glared at him. "Which means *you* need to get off your ass and collect my goods."

Nevan's belly jolted—not a good thing—and he pressed his fist against his mouth. Could that be true? Had Nevan played right into Seb's hands? Could he be *that* good an actor? He'd seemed sincerely appalled. Yet, despite declaring he wouldn't, he'd taken the knife. Would a nanny do that?

Nevan lurched to his feet. The Galliers had to be in the middle of their act by now. Would he be in time? Would poor Mario die for nothing? Would he and Lulu be destined to be Yvo's unwilling minions forever?

"That's right," Yvo said. "You understand now. My spells are *never* at fault. So go. Quickly. Otherwise, I'll be forced to provide further *incentives*." The simulacrum dissipated with a theatrical green flash.

Nevan closed his eyes against a wave of dizziness and snorted. One sure way to avoid eternal servitude to Yvo was to die from water deprivation, both internal and external. If this *quest* didn't wrap up soon, Nevan would be as dead as—

"Who's Luljeta?" said a soft voice behind him. Nevan's eyes popped open, and there, endlessly reflected in the surrounding mirrors, was Seb.

Shite.

CHAPTER 7

*U*ntil a few minutes ago, Seb would have chalked up Nevan's comments about magic and dragons and assassins as the ravings of a homicidal sociopath. But that guy in the clichéd wizard's robe, floating in midair, as transparent as a *Star Wars* hologram? He definitely hadn't been a Fun House special effect. For one thing, he'd carried on a conversation with Nevan in real time. Discussing *Seb*.

Oh, brother, I'm really not in Kansas anymore. Not that he ever had been, but still.

Nevan swayed in the middle of the room as Seb walked toward him. In this wonky light, he looked more ill than he had outside. His Adam's apple bobbed in his throat. "How much of that did you hear?"

"A lot. He was already, you know"—Seb waved one hand—"*broadcasting* when I got here, so I probably missed the overture and opening number." He tucked his hands in his jacket pockets. "You didn't answer my question. Who's Luljeta?"

Nevan glanced down at his palm, the one with the intricate black tattoo. "I'm not sure I can say."

"Try," Seb said softly.

He closed his fist and looked up. "My sister." He sucked in a breath and held it, clenching his eyes shut. After a moment, he cracked one eyelid and peered down at his hand again.

"Let me guess. No reaction?"

"No. I don't understand. When I tried to say something before, the pain was..." He closed his eye again and shook his head.

"Well, according the literature—"

Both Nevan's eyes popped open. "What literature?"

"Mythology. Fairy tales. Legends. I've got a minor in folklore to go along with my degree in early childhood development." He shrugged. "Sue me. I've always loved stories full of possibility and wonder."

"So what does this... literature tell you?"

"That a binding curse only prevents its victim from discussing its terms with people who aren't already aware of them." He pointed to the spot where the guy had floated in the air. "Mr. Smug and Evil pretty much gave everything away just now, so I suspect that whatever he bloviated about is fair game for us to discuss. And incidentally, whatever this guy thinks, I am *not* an assassin. I never have been and I never will be."

"Noted," Nevan said somberly.

Seb wrinkled his nose. "What's this guy's name, anyway?" When Nevan hesitated, Seb said, "Look, this joker doesn't seem like a guy who'd ever hide his light under a bushel. Give it a shot. But if you feel any discomfort at all, stop." Seb grinned. "Because I'm sure we can come up with a colorful code name for him with no trouble at all."

Nevan's lips quirked. He let his hands fall to his sides and said, "Yvo Offerman." When nothing apparently hurt him, he threw back his head and shouted, "Yvo Offerman is a bloody fecking arsehole with delusions of grandeur and... and... a hideous, putrid dick!"

Seb blinked. "Do you, er, have personal knowledge of that last part?"

"No, thank the goddess. But it stands to reason he's got to be compensating for something."

"Good point. So Luljeta is your sister. Younger? Older? Twin?"

"Younger. I call her Lulu." Nevan's expression softened. "She's still a child, really. In fact, she'd probably be a prime candidate for someone with your job. Hasn't started school yet, but she's ready." He shook his head. "She's so smart. Bright. Curious. I knew I couldn't keep her hidden at my lake for much longer. She needs to meet other children her age. Teachers. Role models."

"If you don't mind my saying, I think she's got a pretty good role model already."

Nevan's face scrunched into a scowl that made his previous frowns look like practice throwaways. "I'm not. It's my fault that Yvo got his claws in her in the first place. If I hadn't kept her isolated for so long... But I was afraid that someone would come for her." He scoffed. "And since someone did, I was—"

"Wait. Isolated? Someone coming for her? Where are her parents?"

His smile was wry. "Our sort doesn't always have parents. Not in the way you humans do."

Seb's eyes widened. "Y-your sort?"

He spread his arms. "Supernatural beings. Supes, we call ourselves."

"Wow," Seb breathed. "So all the tales are *true*?"

"Maybe not all. But probably a good percentage. After all, human imagination can't be *that* good. You all have a strong propensity to repeat what you've heard or seen and then embellish it until it's nearly unrecognizable." He dropped his chin, staring at his clasped hands for a moment before peering up at Seb from beneath his brows. "Although, I should tell you. We keep ourselves strictly under the radar. I'll be arse-deep in shit with the council for disclosing our existence to you." He winced. "Assuming Yvo doesn't do for me first. He's probably already champing at the bit because I haven't rushed off to do his bidding."

"There's hardly a point, right?" A faint breeze lifted the hair on Seb's forehead. "You and I both know there's no assassination happening, even if he doesn't."

"Yes, but that doesn't mean..." Nevan's brows drew together, and he squinted at the edges of the room.

Seb followed his gaze. The breeze, probably from that awful clown mouth entrance—*ugh*, he'd barely forced himself to walk inside—was stirring the dust on the floor, sending it skittering across the rough boards and... *wait*. No way was the breeze strong enough to make dust devils, but the dirt was spiraling into the air, nearly as high as Seb's head.

"Shite!" Nevan said. "Run!"

Seb glanced around wildly, staggering in a circle, his pack knocking him off balance. The dust devil was taller than Nevan now, and—Seb gulped—it had *friends*. His and Nevan's reflections in the mirrored walls were nearly obscured by the dirt twisters circling them like so many Looney Tunes Tasmanian devils. "Where? I can't see the door!"

Nevan grabbed Seb's wrist and yanked him directly at a mirror.

"Look out!" Seb cried. But instead of crashing into the wall in a shatter of glass, they passed into a corridor that had been nearly invisible, since its walls were also mirrored.

"Shite." Nevan halted and Seb ran into his back. "It's a fecking maze."

"Can we go back the way we came?"

Nevan shook his head. "Not with golems on our arse."

"G-golems?"

Nevan nodded grimly. "Yvo's an earth mage. He's got an affinity for dirt. At this point, the only way out is through." He darted right, hauling Seb along behind him. "Golems don't have any free will or intelligence of their own. They're magical constructs, obedient to the spell that raised them. They won't be able to negotiate the maze."

"Will we?" Seb squeaked as they came to another dead end.

"We stand a better chance than animate dirt."

"Not exactly a ringing endorsement," Seb muttered as Nevan backtracked and took the opposite turn at the last junction.

"Perhaps, but it's all we've got." They reached another intersection. Nevan glanced right and left. "This can't be too extensive. The Fun House footprint wasn't that big and there's all the other shite to fit in here." His eyes narrowed. "Mazes usually have a pattern. We just have to figure out what it is."

Seb glanced at his feet, where dust was beginning to swirl up over his ankles. "Figure it out fast. I think they're gaining on us."

Nevan swore under his breath and took the right-hand fork. Seb cringed when they broke out into a narrow corridor lined with those horrible distorting mirrors. With his wrist still locked in Nevan's grip, Seb stumbled along as they seemed to be joined by distorted images of themselves, first impossibly tall and thin, then ridiculously squat and wide. They burst through the door at the end of the hall into a room with almost palpable darkness.

"Nevan? Where— *Augh!*"

A flash of brilliant green assaulted them, accompanied by an ear-piercing shriek and the whiff of ozone. Fiendish laughter seemed to echo from every direction at once before three more flash pots erupted in quick succession—orange, yellow, blue— their afterimages the only thing dancing in Seb's vision.

Blinking rapidly—not that it did any good—Seb stuck close to Nevan, hoping he at least could see where they were going.

"*Shite! Fuck!*"

Nevan's shout was all the warning Seb had before he was suddenly airborne, only to land on both feet, hard, and lurched forward, his vision still wonky from the flash pots. He flailed, trying to keep his balance, but he stumbled again, loose gravel shifting under his feet and then his shins barked against something solid and rough and he was *flying*, only to splash facedown into water that was really freaking *cold*.

Arms flailing, he managed to lift his head above water and suck in a breath. Although his glasses were still hooked around his ears, thank goodness, his vision hadn't cleared properly, and his feet—once he got them under him—didn't touch bottom as a strong current swept him downstream.

Downstream? Downstream *where*? The Fun House had been in the fairgrounds, and the closest stream to the fairgrounds was... was... Seb didn't even know what it was, but it definitely couldn't be this deep and wide and *here*.

"Help!" he called. If he could just *see*, he could at least figure out where the bank was, but until then he'd be as likely to move farther away from the safety of dry land as toward it. "Nevan? Where are you? Are you okay? Can you reach me?"

No answer. Okay, then. He hadn't taught years' worth of preschool swim classes for nothing, so he kicked his feet, treading water as he pushed his hair back. The flash pot afterimages finally faded enough that he could see the riverbank blearily through the water coating his glasses.

The. River. Bank.

Because, yes, he was in an actual *river*, probably the width of the Tualatin during the summer, when rainfall and snowmelt hadn't caused it to leap its banks. The water was clear enough that he could see the boulders beneath his feet—*way* beneath his feet—which was unusual for Oregon, where rivers tended to pick up mud and silt as they flowed.

The current dragged at Seb's backpack, which, while waterproof—technically—was still freaking heavy. His wet clothing weighed him down, too. He needed to get out of the water before his strength failed or he was carried away from Nevan.

Nevan. *Crap.* Where was he? Had he fallen in the river too? Seb pushed at the water with cupped palms so he could turn in a circle. He didn't spy anyone else in the water, which he *hoped* was a good sign and not a catastrophe. He squinted through his spotty lenses, trying to make out objects on the river's edge. Trees, brush, big-ass boulders. *No, wait.* That wasn't a boulder. It was Nevan, huddled face down on the shore.

"Nevan!" Seb struck out for the spot, which was *hard* because Nevan was upstream and unmoving, and the current fought Seb with every stroke. "Nevan, are you all right?" Maybe he'd hurt himself when they'd fallen out of the Fun House, which... was nowhere in sight. "Nevan!"

Nevan raised his head at last. He didn't say anything, but at least he was conscious. He stared at Seb dully.

Seb flailed another few strokes closer and held out his hand. "Help me out?"

Nevan pressed his lips into a flat line and turned his face away. "No."

CHAPTER 8

The utter betrayal on Seb's face cut Nevan to the quick. He wanted nothing more than to dive into that river —wild and clean and tempting—and pull Seb to safety. But he couldn't. As much as his heart yearned for the water and his principles cried for him to help, the risk was too great.

Nevan had no idea where they were. The terrain was shrouded in mist and generic enough that it could be anywhere —the Outer World, Faerie, or some realm Nevan had never heard of before. All he knew was that Lulu's time—his time— was running out.

His geas brand didn't burn, but that didn't mean it was inactive. Seb would think he was an arsehole—and he was—but he had no choice.

"You can do it," he said, keeping well clear of Seb's splashes. "You're almost there. A few more steps."

Seb glared at him as he struggled to his feet in the rocky shallows. "Thanks so much for the encouragement." He shrugged his pack off. "Could you at least take this?"

Nevan stood, swaying on his feet, and reached out. He'd give his left arm to step off the bank and let the water flow over him, reinvigorate him, but he couldn't, not according to the terms of the geas. He strained, but couldn't quite reach.

"Oh, for Pete's sake," Seb grumbled. "Here."

Seb heaved the pack at him. Nevan managed to catch it, although its momentum sent him staggering back to arse-plant on a tuft of brilliant green grass.

Goddess, he must be closer to his limits than he'd feared. Seb's backpack was hefty, but it would have been a feather-weight to Nevan at his full strength. It was wet and dripping, and he ached to hug it to his chest, but he quickly set it aside, lest holding it could be construed as *taking water into his hand*. Then he huddled on the ground, willing his head to quit spinning, as Seb made his way toward the bank, arms windmilling to keep his balance as rocks shifted under his feet.

When Seb finally stepped onshore, he squelched over to Nevan and glared down at him, hands fisted on his hips. "Look. I know we've had our little misunderstandings, but I thought we'd at least come to a sort of detente. Would it have *killed* you to help me out of the river? I mean"—he pointed from his sodden trainers to Nevan's boots—"your footwear looks more able to withstand a dunking than mine does. For all you knew, I couldn't swim!"

"Sorry," Nevan mumbled. While his eyes had recovered from that last hellish room in the Fun House, black spots were starting to dance at the edge of his vision. "I... I couldn't."

"Fine. Whatever." Seb sighed gustily. "I'm guessing that has something to do with your curse, right?"

Steeling himself, Nevan nodded. No pain shot through his middle and his geas brand remained inert. Perhaps Seb was right —since he'd discovered the geas through Yvo's own words, Nevan was free to acknowledge it as well. But did that only apply to what Yvo had actually revealed? What had he said exactly? Nevan rubbed his aching forehead. If only he could *think*.

"It is... forbidden."

Seb frowned, peering down at him. "If you don't mind my saying so, you look even worse than before. Did you injure yourself when we… did whatever we did and landed here in the misty mist of the dusky dusk? Though, is it dusk, or just cloudy? It was only midmorning when we entered the clown maw. Maybe 10:30?"

Nevan cast a listless glance at the gray sky. "I don't know. Daylight, though, I think."

"And where the heck are we, anyway? Because this?" Seb spread his arms, water dripping from his sleeves. "This is not the Washington County Fairgrounds. That"—he pointed at the opposite side of the river, where trees crowded the bank—"is not the Hillsboro Airport." He glanced down at himself as water sheeted down his legs. "And North Face raincoats are absolute *shit* at keeping water off you from the *inside*."

Despite the tremors that Nevan couldn't control, he chuckled. "I suspect you aren't wearing it in the recommended manner."

"No shit, Sherlock." He plopped down next to Nevan and shifted from one arse cheek to the other. "Man, I think the river gave me a wedgie."

"I have noted," Nevan said, trying to remain conscious, "that your language has taken a somewhat saltier turn."

Seb gestured to the river. "Can you blame me?" He started to peel his coat off his arms. "Besides, there are no kids around to be corrupted and no parents around to be scandalized. Unless…" He looked at Nevan, one arm still in his waterlogged jacket. "You're not scandalized, are you?"

Despite himself, Nevan leaned toward Seb and closed his eyes, the better to breathe in the intoxicating scent of wild water on Seb's skin. He shook his head. "Not even a little." If he tilted his head just a bit, he could brush his cheek against Seb's shoulder. His cheek was not his hand. Surely that wouldn't violate the terms of the—

"So. Golems?" Nevan opened his eyes and overbalanced,

nearly sending himself into Seb's lap. "Whoa, there." Seb caught Nevan's shoulder and steadied him. "You okay?"

If he said he wasn't, would Seb pillow his head in his lap? Would Seb stroke his hair? Would a stray drop of water trickle from Seb's sleeve and wander across Nevan's skin? Would Seb's lips taste of—

"Nevan?"

Nevan straightened, as much as he was able. "Sorry. Yes. Golems."

"Could they have hurt us if they'd caught us?"

Nevan looked down at his hands, the thumb of his right kneading the geas brand on his left palm. "Those were the dry, unformed type. If they had managed to surround us, they could have suffocated us, blocked our mouths and noses with dust."

Seb's eyes widened. "Do they have other types?"

Nevan nodded tiredly. "Formed dry. In that state, they're like hardened mud, nearly as impenetrable as rock. Unformed wet." He gestured to the riverbank. "Like mounds of mud. And formed wet." He smiled crookedly. "Mud with arms and legs."

Seb's eyes got even wider. "Do we need to get to dryer ground?"

"It wouldn't matter." Nevan patted the lush grass between them. "Unless you're in the desert or on a glacier, there's always mud somewhere below." He let his gaze drift to the river. *So close, yet out of reach.* "But I don't think Yvo intended to kill me back there. Just..." He made a shooing motion with both hands. "Move me along."

"Is that what he meant by *incentives*? *Tormenting* you?"

Nevan chuckled at the outrage in Seb's tone. "Nothing he could do to me would matter if it keeps Lulu safe. I'm not sure..." He dropped his gaze to the brand again. "I'm not sure I can trust him to keep his word."

"You think?" Seb's tone was heavy with sarcasm. "He hired an assassin to kill a child. That doesn't exactly scream stand-up, trustworthy guy to me."

"You're not wrong." Nevan sighed. "But I was the fool who told him I'd give anything to get her back, so I'm not sure what that says about me."

Seb rolled to his knees and faced Nevan, his eyes intense behind his glasses. "It says you're a good brother. It says you love your sister." He bit his lip, and Nevan noted water still beading the scruff on his chin. "Is there any way to get out of the deal?"

Nevan shook his head. "Not until Yvo releases me, or the task I bargained for is complete." He choked out a sour laugh. "I should have demanded a few more details before I took the vow."

I could lick those drops off. My tongue is not my hand either. But would Seb take it the wrong way?

Nevan ducked his head, clenching his fists. Of *course*, he'd take it the wrong way. Nevan was the wanker who'd signed on to abet an assassination. Even if Seb found him attractive at all, that would surely be a deal-breaker.

Seb firmed his lips, determination flickering over his face. "There's got to be some way. In the literature, there's *always* a way."

"Hate to tell you this, mate, but this isn't your literature. It's reality." He glanced sidelong at Seb. "Although I've got to say, you're taking this remarkably well, considering."

Seb shrugged. "When you work with children, you learn to accept pretty much any scenario with outward aplomb, even if you're silently screaming inside."

"And are you? Silently screaming?"

Seb tilted his head, brow wrinkled in thought. "I suppose I should be. But no." The corner of his mouth lifted in a wry smile. "I guess I never lost my childhood belief that magic was real, that you only had to look in the right place to find it." He leaned closer, sending that seductive water-and-Seb scent wafting over Nevan again. "As a kid, I had an imaginary friend."

"That's standard fare, isn't it?"

"Yes, but most kids' imaginary friends are other children, or unicorns, or talking animals. Mine was an old man who smelled of peppermint and pipe tobacco and had a truly unfortunate collection of baggy cardigans." Seb sighed. "But he made me feel safe at a time when I was alone and frightened, so I suppose his appearance didn't matter." He studied Nevan speculatively. "If it's not impertinent, may I ask..." He bit his lip again.

Nevan made a rolling gesture with one hand. "Go on. We've weathered a golem attack together. We're practically soul mates. What's an awkward question or two?"

"You mentioned that Lulu doesn't have other family. That her kind doesn't have parents as humans do. What exactly *is* her kind?"

Nevan winced. "I probably shouldn't tell you."

"Because of the curse?"

"No. Because of the Secrecy Pact. Supes are forbidden from revealing our existence to humans."

Seb held up one palm. "Cat." He held up the other. "Bag." Then made a *poof* gesture. "It's out."

"She's an ora."

"A what now?"

"An ora. Albanian protective spirit. They usually attach to a child at birth and sort of watch over them throughout their lives."

"You mean like a guardian angel? Are you an ora too?"

"No. I'm not." Nevan chuckled. "And guardian angel isn't exactly right. An ora can't be classified as good or evil, but their personality can change, take on qualities of the person they're connected to. And some ora are"—he made a vague gesture—"unattached. Wandering. I found Lulu near an Albanian lake when some wanker was trying to kill her as part of a quest on his own hero's journey. He didn't care that she was a child herself, that she needed companionship, guidance. He just saw her as an easy target."

"So..." Seb lifted his eyebrows. "What did you do to the guy?"

Nevan smiled grimly. "I took him for a little ride."

"I'm guessing you're not talking about a road trip."

"No." He glanced at Seb and then dropped his gaze. "I am a ceffyl dŵr."

CHAPTER 9

Seb studied Nevan's bowed head and counted to three. Slowly. "If you imagine you've just neatly explained everything, you're wrong. What's a ceffyl dŵr?"

Nevan took a shaky breath, his shoulders rising, but he didn't lift his head. "A Welsh water horse. A shapeshifter. We're often likened to the Scottish kelpies, but we're not usually so blood-thirsty."

"Except when somebody threatens a loved one, I take it? What kind of ride are we talking about?"

"My kind are creatures of wild water. Lakes, rivers, streams —they are our joy as well as our need, but we can also ride the air like mist. Our horse forms can have fish tails for swimming, four legs for galloping on land, or wings for taking to the sky." He laced his fingers together, knuckles whitening, so this was obviously tough for him to talk about. "Only a brave soul will mount the back of a ceffyl dŵr when invited, for we've been known to shift back into mist while high above the ground, letting our rider fall screaming to earth."

"Oh, right! You said you'd do that to Yvo, when he was going all pervy on you with the BDSM gear." When Nevan flinched, Seb gave himself a mental bitch-slap. *Note to self: This may be academic to you, but it's* personal *for him.* Seb gentled his tone. "Is that what you did to the guy who was threatening Lulu?"

Nevan nodded. "Not all heroes complete their journeys. Particularly when they're villains at heart and not heroes at all. Now I think it's time to go." He pushed himself to his feet and waggled the hand with the black tattoo. "Yvo hasn't nudged me yet, but he's not known for his patience."

Seb scrambled up, too. "You know where we are?"

"No. But I know how to get out." He shoved a hand into the pocket of his duster and pulled out... an oak leaf?

"Um... How does a leaf get us out of here?"

Although his skin was even grayer than before, Nevan's eyes crinkled at the edges in a mischievous expression that made Seb's heart stutter. "Magic." He leaned forward and whispered. "Don't tell anyone."

"I won't— Whoa!"

When Nevan *kept* leaning, Seb braced his feet and grabbed him around the waist, taking most of Nevan's weight against his chest. Nevan sighed and rubbed his cheek against Seb's shoulder. For a moment, Seb couldn't move because *something*, some feeling, some want, some *desire*, washed through him.

And not sexual desire, even though Nevan was hotter than anyone Seb had ever met. No, the desire to *protect* him, to *care* for him, to make sure he was safe and happy and content. Ordinarily, Seb only felt like that for his charges. When had Nevan— big and muscular and *magical*—become vulnerable in Seb's eyes?

Maybe when I witnessed that Yvo asshole threaten him with nonconsensual bondage.

His heart gave that little stutter again, because apparently Nevan was seeking comfort and consolation. *From me!* Usually, only children considered Seb a source of strength and solace. Adults, even his erstwhile boyfriend? Not so much.

Seb couldn't remember the last time Jase had *nestled* against him like this, as though being close to Seb *everywhere* was the place he most wished to be. So Seb leaned into the moment and stroked Nevan's hair with a trembling hand, earning another sigh as Nevan snuggled closer, despite Seb's soaked clothing, as if the contact were *necessary.*

He itched to feel Nevan's hands on his sides, his back, his hips, for Nevan to return Seb's embrace, but his arms remained maddeningly relaxed at his sides. *Maybe he doesn't like the feel of wet cloth under his fingers. Maybe if I—*

Seb's belly dropped. *Of course it's* necessary, *you nitwit.*

Because Nevan's closeness had nothing to do with attraction to Seb personally, or a desire to initiate one of those stupid *Let's stop and have sex even though the bad guys are practically on our ass* moments from every bad romantic suspense book ever.

Nevan was plastered against him because Seb was dripping wet, and Nevan was a ceffyl dŵr who was somehow prohibited from diving in the river himself. *No wonder he didn't hug me back —he couldn't resist the residual wild water, but probably didn't want to give me the wrong idea.*

Fine. Message received. Seb patted Nevan's back and eased away until he could look up into those dark eyes. "You okay?"

"Yes." Nevan stepped back, although Seb noted that he was still unsteady on his feet. "It'll just be a moment and we'll be on our way."

Seb nodded and picked up his sopping—*eww!*—raincoat and looped his backpack over one shoulder. "Ready."

Nevan peered down at the oak leaf as though he were trying to bring it into focus. There was some kind of gold figure embossed on its surface. Seb didn't have a chance to look at it closely before Nevan pressed his thumb over it and croaked, "*Cludo.*"

When nothing happened immediately, Seb peered around, although the mist still clouded their surroundings. "What do we do next?"

Nevan frowned. "We shouldn't have to do anything. Our driver should be here by now."

"Driver?"

"Well, our FTA escort." When Seb raised his eyebrows, Nevan said, "Fae Transportation Association. 'Drivers' are the fae who contract to lead people—well, to lead supes—through Faerie."

Seb stared at him, slack-jawed. "We're going to *Faerie*? Like *actual* Faerie?"

Nevan's frowned deepened. "That's the general notion. But the FTA mandate requires drivers to appear within six seconds, provided the rider is in a secluded location, out of sight of humans." He flung out an arm. "We'll not get more secluded than this. I haven't seen a sign of life anywhere."

Seb grimaced. "Do you, um, think it might be my fault? I mean"—he pointed to his chest with both forefingers—"human. Maybe it's not working because you're within my sight. Or I'm in yours, although I suppose this is one of those things like math calculation rules where it doesn't matter which side of the equation you're on, the result is still the same."

"I don't..." Nevan pinched the bridge of his nose, eyes clenched. "It could be, I suppose. I'm not... I can't *think*."

"What about this? I'll get out of sight." Seb glanced around and spotted an oak tree, its diameter wider than Seb was tall. "Behind that tree. Then you can try again."

Nevan squinted, shaking his head. "No. I can't leave you here."

Seb squeezed Nevan's biceps—his *really big* biceps. "You won't. All you need to do is get the driver to show up. Then you can say you've got an extra passenger." He bit his lip, which was starting to feel raw from the number of times he'd chewed it in the last hour alone. "That won't get you in trouble, will it? Bringing a human with you?"

Nevan's lips twitched. "Faerie's portals are not barred against humans. We fae have a rather unfortunate history of spiriting your kind away, although our King and Queen have enforced strict rules about consent of late. And as you said, supe existence is well and truly out of the bag as far as you're concerned. It's worth a try." He peered down at the leaf.

"Except…" He lifted it closer, squinting harder. "My eyes are… Can you see the rune?"

Seb took the leaf from Nevan's shaking fingers. It was already starting to turn brown around the edges. He flipped it over. Both sides were free of anything other than its network of veins. "It's not there."

"What?" Nevan snatched the leaf back. "It has to be."

"Maybe you're getting charged for the failed pickup, like what happens with human ride shares. Have you got another one?"

Nevan scrabbled at his duster pocket, relief flickering over his face when he drew out another leaf. "Yes." He laid it in his palm, his thumb hovering over it, but Seb grabbed his wrist.

"Don't touch it! Not until I'm out of sight."

"Yes. Of course. Thank you."

Seb hurried for the tree and ducked around its enormous bole. "Okay." As he waited for the all clear from Nevan, he noticed something fluttering amid the foliage. He took a step away from the trunk, taking care not to put himself into view. Was that… Yes, it was. A linen shirt, similar in cut to Nevan's Renfaire style, was draped over a low-hanging branch. He looked closer. Pants, like Regency pantaloons with a fall front. A vest, although not a waistcoat like Nevan's. More like a long bolero, with no buttons.

He glanced down at his soggy clothes and back at the clearly clean and dry outfit in front of him. Could he take them? That would be stealing, wouldn't it? Even though this… wherever it was seemed completely unpopulated at the moment, *somebody* had to have left the clothes here.

He shook his head resolutely. He and Nevan would be gone soon. *Into Faerie*. Seb shivered in anticipation. Granted, it would be more pleasant to walk through a place *literally* out of his dreams without water tricking down his neck or his pants clinging clammily to his thighs, but he couldn't really justify swiping some other poor guy's clothes.

They would be home presently. Wouldn't they? Seb scrunched up his face. *Home* had its own share of problems, including that he'd failed to meet Mrs. Macclesfield's representative and had probably trashed his reputation with Northwest Nurture and Nannies. That seemed insignificant next to the reality of two children in serious peril from Mage Evil's murky plans.

But then, I'm supposed to be the assassin. I even still have the weapon. And Seb had no intention of using it anytime, anywhere, on anybody. So probably this Mario person was safe. But Lulu—and Nevan—were threatened by that douchecanoe mage, so the sooner they got out of this Nowhereland and made a plan, the better.

Seb held perfectly still as he strained to hear any sound from the other side of the tree. Surely it had been more than six seconds? His breath stalled as ice pooled in his middle. Nevan wouldn't leave him here, would he? Maybe not intentionally—Seb didn't believe Nevan was that kind of man, er, ceffyl dŵr. But what if the driver refused to wait? What if the driver wouldn't escort a human? Or worse, what if *Mage Evil* sent someone after Nevan?

Seb turned and hugged the tree trunk, slowly leaning to one side until he could peer around it to where he'd left Nevan on the riverbank. Nevan was still there, huddled in a miserable lump, his head down on his knees.

Alone.

Seb ducked back into his hiding place. "Nevan?" he called. "Is it safe to come out?" No answer. "Nevan?" When there was still nothing, Seb crept out from behind the tree. "Crap!" Nevan wasn't just huddled on the ground anymore. He was lying on the riverbank, curled into a fetal position with his back to Seb.

Seb dropped his jacket and pack and raced to Nevan's side. He fell to his knees and laid two fingers along Nevan's neck, under his jaw, feeling for the pulse. It fluttered rapidly under his touch, but weak, *so* weak. "Nevan, can you hear me?"

No response. Seb's insides were tipping and whirling like one of those freaky carnival rides now, but he was a nanny, dammit. First Aid was practically knitted into his DNA.

He scrambled to his feet and raced to retrieve his pack. He always carried supplies with him, because you never knew when a kid might fall or swallow the wrong way or cut themselves on a random sharp object.

Seb hurried back to where Nevan lay, yanking open the main zipper as he ran. He peered inside and blew an exasperated breath. While the contents appeared to be dry, they were in a total jumble thanks to all the time he'd spent hoofing after Nevan, not to mention their unceremonious exit from the Fun House.

"Screw it." He upended the pack and shook it briskly, scattering its contents on the ground next to Nevan. Once the main pocket was empty, he knelt and started sorting through the jumble.

Eric Carle board books. Nope, don't need those. He tossed them aside. *Extra socks.* Useful for feet and as sock puppets, but not relevant. He pushed those out of the way too, dislodging several oranges that rolled down the bank but stopped short of the water.

"Where the heck is my— *Aha!*" He grabbed the First Aid kit from under a box of baby wipes—useful for all sorts of cleanups —and a fairy tale book, which was probably what had been poking him in the back all day. But then he froze, gaze flicking from the standard Red Cross box in his hand to Nevan.

He's not human. And it wasn't as though a couple of Band-Aids and some children's Tylenol would fix whatever was the matter with him. *What is the matter with him?*

Seb sat back on his haunches. *Assess. Assess.* Nevan was suffering from the curse, yes, but what were the *symptoms* of the curse?

Dry skin, sunken eyes, dizziness, probably headache, since he seemed to have trouble concentrating. All symptoms of serious dehydration, which was so obvious Seb should have seen it at a glance.

He gave himself a mental kick in the pants and exhaled in a rush. He reached for his pack to pull out his water bottle, but froze with his hand on the strap. Nevan had said his kind needed *wild* water, and Seb seriously doubted his tap water counted, especially with the extra filter he'd installed.

A soft plop called Seb's attention to the river, as though it was saying, *"Seriously, dude. I'm right here."*

Well, Seb knew from recent immersive experience that the river was definitely the opposite of tame, so...

Let's give this a try.

CHAPTER 10

*W*ater. *Blessed, life-giving water, so cold it almost hurt, bathing his cracked lips, moistening his parched mouth, soothing his dry throat.*

Nevan sighed contentedly, nestling further into the lovely damp softness under his cheek.

"That's it," crooned a voice that Nevan felt he ought to know but couldn't quite place, a voice that cradled him like the pool under his waterfall, supported him like air under his wings, calmed him like the sough of a breeze through the rushes. "A little more."

Something firm and rounded pressed against his lower lip—*a cup?*—and there it was again: the trickle of water across his tongue. He opened wider, wanting more, wanting it now, because he yearned for it, needed it, *craved* it.

A warm chuckle from that voice. "Not so fast. You can have as much as you like, but I think you should take it slow. You're seriously dehydrated."

Dehydrated?

The geas.

Yvo.

Lulu.

"No!" Nevan knocked the cup away. He *couldn't* give in to temptation. He *mustn't*. Everything depended on it. He flailed, and his elbow connected with something that resulted in a pained *Ooof* from overhead. He rolled away from the softness and comfort to land face down in the grass. Should he try to retch? Bring up whatever he'd swallowed?

I don't think I can. It was probably already too late, anyway. His eyes prickled and burned, but as dried out as he was, he couldn't shed a tear. Instead, he pounded the ground with both fists. "No. No no no."

"Nevan." A warm hand caressed his spine. "Take it easy."

Memory swam back through Nevan's fuzzy brain and he pegged that voice.

Seb.

"What have you done?" Nevan croaked. His hands flexed and he clenched his fists, uprooting clumps of grass and filling his palms with their blessed coolness.

"Nevan." Seb's voice lost its cajoling tone and took on a sharp, authoritative edge. "That's enough. Give me your hand."

Without thinking, Nevan uncurled one fist, released the grass, and held out his arm. Then he frowned. *Why did I do that?* He turned his head and Seb's face swam into view, sideways. "Wha...?"

Seb smiled. "The no-nonsense nanny voice. Never fails." He gently nudged Nevan's shoulder. "Although I think this would be easier if you rolled over onto your back."

"What would be easier?" Nevan's voice was a thread, but he did as instructed, because what was the point of anything anymore?

He blinked up at the featureless gray sky. Any minute now, Yvo would call him back. Any minute now, the pain would rip through him. Any minute now, his geas brand would... would... He lifted his left hand and stared at his palm. The brand was still there, black and baleful, but he felt *nothing* from it. "What's going on?"

"Now, *that*," Seb said, grasping Nevan's hand and pulling him up into a sitting position, "is the million-dollar question, isn't it?" He let go and met Nevan's gaze, his hands bunched on his thighs where he knelt in the grass. "One I've been asking myself continually since I followed you out of that Starbucks."

Nevan gingerly touched his lips with his right hand. They were still cracked, still dry, but the sensation of coolness remained. "I dreamed... I thought I was drinking. Water." He glowered at Seb. "But I can't. You *made* me break my vow!"

Seb cocked his head. "Did I?"

"Yes! I said I'd do anything to save Lulu." He pointed at the geas brand. "This is the mark of my oath, of Yvo's chains on my soul."

"And how does it feel now?"

Nevan touched it with a shaking finger. "Inert. Quiescent. Not gone, but as though it's... it's..."

"In time-out?" Seb asked.

"I suppose."

Seb changed his position and sat, tailor fashion, down the bank from Nevan. "Tell me this. Apparently, you're not able to dunk yourself in the river as part of the curse. I get that. But why the heck have you let yourself get dehydrated enough to pass out?" When Nevan looked away, Seb tapped his knee with his fist. "Hey. Cat. Bag. Remember? What exactly are you avoiding?"

Nevan ducked his chin, staring at the geas brand. "Yvo laid it on me that I'd not be able to take any drink from my hand, nothing with a trace of water, until I'd fulfilled the terms of the geas."

"That's it? His exact words?"

Nevan glanced irritably at Seb, who had the gall to *grin* at Nevan's torment. "Isn't it enough?"

Seb's grin grew. "Then we've got him." His tone was positively gleeful.

"What do you mean?"

"You can't drink *from your hand*. You didn't." Seb leaned over and grabbed a peculiar cup that looked as though it were constructed of concentric rings of semi-transparent purple plastic. "You drank from *mine*. I held the cup to your lips. Your hands were nowhere near it. And since you said before that your kind need wild water, I scooped it from the river, not my water bottle."

Nevan's eyes widened. "Merciful goddess." He glanced down at his palm again. There was a chance, of course, that the geas was just storing up infractions until they were back in the Outer World, but Nevan himself had sidestepped the literal terms of the geas with those oranges, hadn't he? And speaking of oranges...

He pointed to the three flame-bright globes, practically glowing against the grass. "Would it be all right..." He swallowed, his throat still dry but not nearly as mummified as it had been. "Might I have an orange?"

Seb smiled at him, and Nevan was positive that he'd never seen anything so beautiful—including those oranges—and certainly never anything as kind. "You can have them all. But first, I think you should drink a little more water, don't you?"

Nevan's lips trembled. He couldn't have uttered a word if Govannon himself were to burst from the ground and threaten to drag him to the forge if he didn't speak. So he nodded.

"Good." Seb rose to his feet, not fluidly or gracefully, and winced as he picked at the inseam of his still-wet trousers. "Crap, this is uncomfortable. Good thing we'll be leaving soon, huh?"

Guilt cramped Nevan's stomach as he watched Seb wade into the shallows, and he couldn't force out any words for an entirely different reason. *I'm sorry. I'm so sorry. Sorry, Seb. Sorry, Lulu. Sorry for everything.*

He didn't reserve any sympathy for himself, because he'd bolluxed everything up from the very beginning, when he'd kept Lulu close and avoided building up an appropriate support system. When he'd left Lulu vulnerable to Yvo's machinations.

When he'd leaped into the bargain with Yvo without demanding all the details.

When he'd mistaken Seb for an assassin.

And somehow he'd bolluxed things up in such a spectacular fashion that he'd trapped them both on some kind of alternate plane where even the FTA couldn't find him.

And the FTA could find any fae *anywhere*. It was baked into its spells, born of the will of the King and Queen, that no fae should ever be stranded, alone and helpless, with no way home.

Nevan had tried the other two FTA vouchers he carried with him. He knew they'd activated when he pronounced the proper trigger word because the runes had disappeared. But nothing had happened. *How can I tell him we're trapped here?* Those oranges might very well be the only food they had, because Nevan still hadn't seen evidence of any habitation.

Seb smiled at him as he paced back up the bank, the cup cradled carefully in his hands. "I thought about using my inverted umbrella to carry more water at one time, but I doubt it's made of food-grade material, and who knows what kind of bacteria might lurk under there?" He lowered himself to his knees at Nevan's side. "This cup is safe. It was shrink-wrapped until I opened it after you collapsed." He held it to Nevan's lips. "Drink."

Nevan rolled his lips in, firming them against the rim of the cup. He didn't deserve this. Didn't deserve Seb's kindness. He shook his head.

"Nevan." There was that tone of command again. "Drink. You'll be no good to Lulu or anybody else if you don't take care of yourself first." He bumped the cup against Nevan's lips again. "Come on."

"Why are you being so nice to me?" Nevan mumbled. "I was horrible to you." Although he'd barely moved his lips, Seb managed to tip a few drops into Nevan's mouth. Nevan closed his eyes and moaned. *So good.* When Nevan opened his eyes again, Seb was gazing at him intently. "What?"

"I have never in my life known an instance where cruelty in response to cruelty solved anything. And you weren't precisely cruel, anyway." He shrugged. "Just misinformed."

When he tipped the cup again, Nevan didn't resist anymore. He guzzled the rest of the water, and then closed his eyes and blurted, "It didn't work."

"What didn't work?"

"The FTA vouchers. I tried two more and nothing happened." He cracked an eyelid. "We're trapped here. I don't know for how long because I don't know where we are or how we got here or why we can't get out, and it's my fault. All of it."

"I'm guessing there's not another option? That we can't just click our heels together three times and chant 'There's no place like home?'"

"No."

Seb's eyebrows drew together, but his expression wasn't angry so much as thoughtful. "In that case, we've got several problems to solve. But our two top priorities are getting you healthy, or at least ambulatory again, and"—he plucked at his wet shirt with a grimace—"me changing into dry clothes."

"But—"

"*Then*," Seb said as he stood, "we'll tackle the next problem. But aside from the fact that multi-tasking is a *total* myth, trying to accomplish more than one thing at a time really well? Recipe for accomplishing nothing at all, or, best case, accomplishing everything poorly."

He trotted down the bank and scooped up the oranges. When he returned, he held them out to Nevan. "Since you asked for these, I assume you can wrangle them yourself?" Nevan nodded and took the fruit. "Good. You do you, and I'll see about me." He exhaled gustily, staring down at his shoes, which were wet and muddy. He toed them off and scooped up a pair of socks, muttering something that sounded like, "I just hope that tree grows boots."

But that couldn't be right. Nevan had probably misheard

because his belly was rumbling so loudly as he rolled the first orange between his palms to release the juice. He barely registered Seb walking away as he tore a tiny piece of rind from the stem end and held it to his mouth, squeezing the first bright, blessed mouthful onto his tongue. He whimpered, lying back, eyes closed as he sucked up every. Last. Drop.

CHAPTER 11

*B*efore he ducked behind the oak tree, Seb glanced back at Nevan once more. He could tell from Nevan's reaction that, aside from blaming himself for their predicament—which was entirely Yvo's fault, in Seb's opinion— he was uncomfortable with Seb seeing him this vulnerable. Ashamed, even.

Seb had seen it before, that same stolid, stoic facade, in kids who'd experienced any kind of trauma, or whose parents had drilled into them that *big kids don't cry*, probably because they were out of touch with their *own* emotions. Or that if they were some unspecific flavor of *good* that they'd earn some equally unspecific reward, which led to kids believing that any bad things that happened were *their* fault because they hadn't been *good* enough.

For that reason, more even than the desire to get out of these wet clothes, Seb decided to give him privacy.

He stripped off his waterlogged socks. The buttons on his shirt fought back when he tried to undo them, so slippery that he finally gave up, grabbed the collar at the back, and wrestled it over his head, knocking his glasses askew in the process. As for removing his soggy chinos? *Way* too reminiscent of peeling a banana.

As he stood, debating whether to ditch his briefs too, a breeze kicked up and swirled around his body. He sighed in relief for a moment because it was warm and dried his skin nicely. Then his belly dropped to his toes. *Wind from nowhere?* The last time that had happened, dust monsters had followed.

Seb hunkered down, forehead to his knees, protecting his head with his arms. He could swear he heard a faint laugh—more a mischievous giggle than a sinister snicker—but that was probably only the rustle of leaves overhead. When nothing else happened, he uncovered his head and peered around.

No dust devils. The emerald-green grass was as undisturbed as it had been, so no mud monsters either, with or without appendages. He stood slowly, shivering not from cold, because the warm breeze continued to dance around him, but because he was seriously considering mud monsters and dust devils as possible dangers, like drunk drivers or yogurt past its expiration date.

"My life is *awesome*," he murmured happily. When he glanced down at his middle, he noticed the breeze had dried out his briefs. "*Seriously* awesome." Since there was nobody in sight, he didn't feel at all ridiculous murmuring, "Thank you."

He glanced at the clothes hanging on the branch and bit his lip. Now he felt a little bad about taking them. If he'd left his own clothes on, maybe the breeze would have dried them too. There was no going back now, though, not immediately, because he seriously doubted he could wrestle his sodden pants back on inside of half an hour, and Nevan needed him.

That's my story and I'm sticking to it. Besides, he was well on the way down this particular yellow brick road, and if he were honest with himself, he didn't want to go back. *So I might as well look the part.*

Fair was fair, though. He arranged his own shirt and pants on the limb for the next person who might wander by. They weren't anywhere near the same quality, but they were his best interview clothes, so maybe the intent would count in whatever karmic ledger was recording Seb's latest actions.

Since the dry clothes hung on the lowest part of the branch, about level with Seb's shoulders, they were easily accessible. He had few illusions about them, however. He could accept the existence of magic way more easily than he could accept that the single outfit available to him here in Nowhereland would fit perfectly. He rarely managed *that* when he had literal *racks* of stuff to choose from at Target or JCPenney or—if he was feeling especially fancy and flush with cash—Nordstrom. He just prayed they weren't too small to wiggle into.

He freed the shirt from the branch and pulled it over his head. It draped around him, the linen as soft as a caress, and although it didn't fit like his slim-cut button-down, it wasn't huge. The armhole seams hit just below his shoulder joint, and the sleeves, when he fastened the cuff buttons, were full but not balloonish.

He waved his arm experimentally, smiling at the way the fabric whispered against his skin. "I could get used to this."

Of course, shirts were a lot more forgiving than trousers, and these looked like they'd have outlined Mr. Darcy's package in a way to make Elizabeth Bennet swoon, or at least ply her fan briskly. He took a deep breath, plucked them off the limb, and sat down to work them over his feet. When he stood to pull them up—which, yeah, they were snug—they were the right length, and when he fastened the double row of buttons on the fall front, the garment hugged his waist and his butt perfectly.

"Huh." He held up the hem of the shirt and peered down at himself. "Go figure."

He tucked the shirt into the trousers and reached for the vest. As he lifted it, a glint caught his eye, and he peered at the garment more closely.

Intricate gold embroidery nearly two inches deep embellished all its edges. He nearly put it back, because it was clearly unique. Special. Way more valuable than anything he'd left in its place.

After all, he didn't *need* it to cover himself. The shirt and trousers were sufficient, and *surely* the vest had been important to whoever had left it here, although they must have had a super good reason for abandoning it, because who the heck took off their clothes in the middle of... of *nowhere* and hung them on a tree?

He eyed his own shirt as it fluttered in the breeze. "Apparently, that would be me."

But as he was about to carefully return the vest to the branch, a warm gust of wind snatched it out of Seb's hand and plastered it to his face and chest.

"Okay, okay," he said, laughing, "message received." He shrugged into the vest and smoothed its open front down over his chest, smiling at the glittering golden decoration.

He freaking *loved* it.

Seb had always been a sucker for fantasy movie costumes, imagining as he watched Legolas slide down an oliphaunt's trunk, or Inigo Montoya swashbuckle his way through the duel with the Dread Pirate Roberts, what it would be like to wear clothing that was so... so *fantastical*.

That was why he always participated enthusiastically when any of his charges wanted to play dress-up, going so far as to wear his own costumes home at times.

Jase had always sneered at him, telling him to get with twenty-first century fashion. "Hugo Boss or Tom Ford, *not* that airy fairy crap. For god's sake, Seb, you're not a child or a fricking *elf*."

This though? He traced the intricate embroidery with one finger. *This* wasn't a costume. This was *real*, and it made him feel... *magical*.

"Given where I am at the moment—wherever that actually is —and that I'm in company with a bona fide supernatural being,

I'm fully justified in dressing the part." He mentally thumbed his nose at his ex. "So there, Jase."

He snatched his soggy socks off the grass—they were his favorites, royal blue with rainbow cupcakes—and as he draped them over a couple of convenient twigs, he caught sight of something thin and brown, dangling in the leaves overhead. His belly jolted as his lizard brain immediately jumped to *snake*! But he swallowed and looked closer.

Not a snake. Shoelaces.

"You're kidding me." He started to laugh. "This tree really *does* grow boots!

He lifted onto his tiptoes, grabbed the dangling strings, and tugged. The boots—shin-high lace-ups in soft brown leather—dropped into his arms. With a delighted whoop, he sat down and donned his spare socks. Color him *so* not surprised when the boots fit him perfectly.

He stood up, grinning down at his feet as he wiggled his toes. "Like magic."

Now, dry and dressed like someone out of his favorite tales, Seb felt ready to tackle the next problem. He peered around the oak's trunk. Nevan was sitting cross-legged, the orange rinds next to him as flat as deflated balloons, as he ran something through his fingers.

When Seb approached cautiously, he saw that it was a length of sheer, spangled gold ribbon.

"Nevan? What's that?"

Nevan's big shoulders rose and fell. "For Lulu's birthday, I promised her new clothes." One corner of his mouth lifted. "She had a very specific outfit in mind: 'Leggings and boots and a floofy skirt and a Minnie Mouse T-shirt and wings and a golden sword and a matching hair ribbon.' So I took her out of Faerie for the first time since I brought her to live with me. I wasn't familiar with the town, so I asked someone the way to the nearest children's store." The half smile fell away. "I should have been suspicious that a charming little boutique was practically around the corner, but I didn't question it, not even when the salesperson was able to meet every one of Lulu's requests."

"What happened then?"

"I'd noticed an odd sensation when we walked in the door, but I chalked that up to my usual discomfort in enclosed areas, which was my next mistake. But when Lulu emerged from the dressing room decked out in her finery, grinning so wide, black curls bouncing, with joy practically sparking from her, I let my guard drop completely. Then"—Nevan swallowed convulsively —"when I went to pay, the cash register transformed into a mossy boulder and the salesperson vanished. I raced back to the dressing room, but Lulu was gone." He held up the ribbon. "This was all that was left."

"Oh, Nevan," Seb murmured.

"And then Yvo materialized in the dressing room mirror and I made my impulsive offer to do anything to get Lulu back." He smoothed the ribbon on his knee. "And you know where that led."

Since Nevan seemed about to sink into flat despair, Seb clearly needed to *redirect*. He cleared his throat and held out his arms. "What do you think? I feel kind of like a walk-on in a big budget revival of *The Pirates of Penzance*."

Nevan looked up, expression bleak. He clearly tried to smile, but it was the *worst* attempt Seb had ever seen. "You look nice." He fumbled with the ribbon and shoved it into his duster pocket. Then he lowered his brows in obvious confusion as he eyed the jumble from Seb's pack. "Did you bring those clothes with you?"

"No. I found them hanging in that tree over there." Seb bit his lip as he stroked the soft linen sleeve. "I hope it's okay that I'm borrowing them. I hung mine up in their place, so once they dry out, I can always swap them back." *I won't want to, but I will.*

For an instant, Nevan's face went slack, but then it was as though a light turned on behind his eyes. "You know what this means?"

"That alfresco laundry is a thing?"

"No!" Nevan surged to his feet, and although he looked better than he had when they'd arrived, he still had to take a step to catch his balance. "It means that somebody else has been here. And since they're not here now, there has to be a way to get out."

Seb grinned, bouncing on his toes as excitement chased along his veins. "So all we have to do—"

"Is find it!" they said together.

Nevan swayed again and Seb darted forward to fit his shoulder under Nevan's arm. "Easy there. Why don't you sit back down?"

"No. We have to look. We have to—" Nevan's knees buckled and since Seb was still half-supporting him, they did a sort of slow, partnered butt-plant, accompanied by more than a little flailing and *ooofs* from both of them.

Nevan rubbed his hands across his face. "I'm sorry."

"Don't be. Why don't I get you some more water?" He glanced at his pack jumble. The snacks he'd brought were more suitable for the preschool crowd, but they were at least nutritious, and it wasn't as though they had a lot of choices. "I'm guessing since you handled the oranges with no trouble, that Mage Evil didn't block you from *eating* from your own hand, too."

"Technically, I didn't eat the oranges. I *drank* from them." Nevan's brow pleated in the way that Seb was beginning to recognize as a combination of pain and difficulty concentrating. "But no. Not... not in so many words."

"In any words?"

After a moment, Nevan's frown vanished. "No. He didn't mention food at all. I just assumed... To be honest, I haven't had much appetite since I've been barred from the water." His longing as he gazed at the river burbling past not ten feet away was almost palpable.

Seb rummaged in the pile until he found the Tupperware container of homemade granola bars. "Oats, pecans, a little maple syrup, sea salt. Can you eat those?" When Nevan thrust out his hand, Seb laughed. "I guess that's a yes." He popped the lid and passed the box to Nevan. "They can be a little dry, so I'll get that water now."

By the time Seb returned with the brimming cup, Nevan had consumed two of the bars. "These are wonderful," he mumbled around a third.

"Thanks." He held out the cup. "My own recipe."

"You made these?"

Heat crept up Seb's throat. Nevan's tone of wonder would have been more appropriate if Seb had leaped a tall building in a single bound. "Don't give me too much credit. It's not that hard."

Nevan reached out, but instead of taking a drink, his fingers closed around Seb's wrist, the touch gentle, almost featherlight. "You have sustained me with food and drink from your own hand, asking nothing in return. Trust me. That is something we fae do not take lightly."

The heat reached Seb's cheeks. *Yep, blushing like an embarrassed five-year-old.* Because apparently that was something he would never outgrow. "Um, you're welcome?"

Nevan jerked his chin down in a quick nod and sipped from the cup in Seb's hand. He didn't guzzle the water this time, not like before, but it was clear he wasn't completely rehydrated.

Seb settled down next to him, set the cup on the grass between them, and wrapped his arms around his knees. "You know, you're in no shape yet to go head-to-head with Mage Evil."

"*Yvo*," Nevan said around another mouthful of granola.

"Yeah, I know. But he doesn't deserve to have me get his name right, so I'm not even going to try," Seb said crossly. "That's not important, anyway. What would it take for you to fully recover?"

Nevan snorted. "Drink another gallon or two of wild water. *Immerse* myself in wild water. Shift."

Seb squinted at the river, so clear and blue even though the sky was gray. "Yeah, well, we're working on the drink thing. You're sure you can't take a dip?"

Nevan shook his head. "I cannot seek wild water or I will be forfeit." He smiled a little slyly. "He reckoned without the rain though, and since it was he who thrust me into it—"

"You didn't *seek* it. I get it. The letter of the curse rather than the spirit. What about shifting? Is that part of the curse?"

Nevan got that inner listening look again. "I don't... He only said that he would prevent me from shifting. I could feel the binding, so I didn't try. But he didn't specify any consequences."

"Well, then?" Seb nudged Nevan's ribs with an elbow. "Why not give it a shot?"

evan's jaw sagged as he stared at Seb, the granola bar all but forgotten in his hand. "What?"

"It doesn't seem like Mage Evil can reach you here." He tapped Nevan's left hand. "You said yourself that your geas thingie was inert. So why not test it?" He smiled that sunny, inviting smile. "I always tell the kids that they'll never know what they're capable of unless they give it at least one go." Then he bit his lip, something he did often, much to Nevan's distraction. "You don't have to be in the water to shift, do you?" Nevan shook his head numbly. "Well, there you go." He held the cup to Nevan's slack lips. "But maybe have another drink and finish off that granola bar first."

Nevan gulped down the water, mouth trembling against the cup's rim. Dare he risk it? Would it work? *Could* it work? Yvo didn't *physically* prevent him from drinking from his own hand or from plunging into the river, as it called him to do, only declared that Nevan would breach the geas if he did. *I granted the arsehole that power when I agreed to the bargain, but it's still my choice whether to comply.*

However, Yvo had boasted that *he* was preventing Nevan from shifting, as though he'd forged an unbreakable shackle from his own spells rather than Nevan's vows. Nevan clenched his fists so tightly that he crushed the granola bar into crumbs.

The sodding bastard set a bridle on me after all, and I never realized.

He stood and brushed his hands off on his trousers. If he tried to shift and failed, he'd know that Yvo had stepped over the line: By council edict, no elemental mage could cast a spell on a supe without that supe's full knowledge and consent.

If he tried and succeeded? Either Yvo was blowing smoke out his arse or something about this place was neutralizing the spell. Either way, Nevan had nothing to lose.

He shrugged out of his duster and fumbled with the buttons on his waistcoat.

"Uh, Nevan? What are you doing?"

Nevan glanced down at Seb. "I don't need to immerse myself, but I must be naked to shift."

"Okay." Seb's voice broke on the word. "I'll just, you know, turn my back or duck behind the tree."

Something contracted painfully in Nevan's chest and he looked away. "Do you find me so… repulsive, then?" He wasn't certain why that mattered, but clearly his heart thought it did.

"What? Are you kidding? You're like"—Seb flapped his hands—"*you*. But we barely know each other. I thought you might like some privacy."

The tightness in his chest eased. "Few supes are concerned about nudity. Many of the lesser fae wear no clothing at all."

"Oh." Seb's eyes were huge behind his glasses. "Then by all means"—he gulped audibly—"carry on."

Nevan discarded waistcoat and shirt and then sat again to remove his boots. His fingers trembled as he untied the laces. Weakness or anticipation? He couldn't tell. He also had no notion whether he *could* shift in his current weakened state, let alone their present location, Yvo's spells notwithstanding.

Like all fae, his magic was tied to Faerie's One Tree. Could the One Tree find him here, wherever *here* was? His *calon*, the extra organ that every supe possessed—other than vampires for some reason—still thrummed below his heart, so he hoped that meant he wasn't totally divorced from his own nature.

He stood again, skinned his trousers down his legs, and kicked them aside. Seb made a strangled noise behind him.

Seb.

If this worked, Nevan would owe him more than his life. So he closed his eyes, lifted his arms, and raised his face to the sky, his second home.

His calon pulsed, and the familiar warmth raced across his skin, flowing over him from his scalp to his toes. The magic—*his* magic—tingled in his veins, ignited in his bones, and *yes!* When he dropped his arms, his front hooves hit the ground. When he took a breath, his barrel expanded. When he shook his head, his heavy mane flicked his neck. Even in this form, he wasn't at full strength yet, but he was better, better with each moment.

Nevan opened his eyes and uttered a startled whinny, because with his altered sight, the nondescript gray sky had taken on the iridescence of a soap bubble. Experimentally, he unfurled his wings. A breeze teased their thick membranes, tempting him to take to the air.

Why not? Yvo hadn't forbidden him the sky, only the water. He reared, then let his hooves thud to the ground and sprang forward to gallop along the riverbank. He snapped his wings out fully and launched off his haunches like a steeplechaser, timing the downstroke with the push, and it happened.

He was *flying*.

His heart, so much larger in this form, felt as though it were glowing as brightly as his calon, or perhaps winging along beside him as he caught an updraft and soared above the river.

He dove, catching himself well above the water—no sense tempting fate—and spiraled up again, waltzing with the playful breeze that tickled his coat and ruffled his mane.

Even from this height and with his enhanced eyesight, though, he couldn't see any farther than he could from the riverbank. There was still no sign of any other living soul, nobody who could have left that clothing on the tree.

But someone had been here. They'd search everywhere if they must, every hillock, every tree, every rock, until they found the way out. Now that Nevan knew he could fly, they could quarter the opposite bank, too. He would simply take Seb on his back and...

Seb.

Would Seb *want* to climb onto Nevan's back after hearing the fate of others who'd done the same? His heart faltered along with his wing stroke and he nearly stalled, but he recovered with an awkward flap and strained to regain height.

Seb hadn't been disgusted by Nevan's human form, but would he feel differently about *this* one? For some reason, the thought of Seb cowering in fear or turning away, lips twisted with distaste, pierced his chest like elf-shot.

If I keep flying until either my heart or my wings give out, I'll never have to see it. But if he did that, Seb might be trapped here, alone forever. No matter how much it hurt, Nevan had to face Seb's reaction. In any case, he was still too weak to make it more than a few furlongs.

So he banked in a wide curve and angled his wings to come in for a landing, hind hooves striking the ground first before he dropped into a trot and came to a stop near where Seb still sat. He dropped his head and gazed at Seb out of one eye.

Seb had fallen back onto his elbows and gazed up at Nevan with wide eyes. In this form, Nevan had difficulty assessing humanoid expressions, but he had no trouble reading Seb's body language.

Fear.

Nevan could understand that. He could. He was larger than even the largest draft horse, his hooves wider than dinner plates and easily bigger than Seb's head. Then, of course, there were the wings.

But he'd hoped that perhaps *this* time, with *this* man, the reaction would be different.

Call him irrational, craven, cowardly, but he couldn't watch the panic grow on Seb's face. Instead, Nevan turned to face the river and let his head droop nearly to his knees.

"You know." Seb's voice at his shoulder made Nevan snort and sidestep. "Sorry. Didn't mean to startle you."

Hesitantly, Nevan eyed Seb again. He didn't *seem* to be afraid anymore, but he wasn't exactly smiling. Nevan pawed the ground once and tossed his head, since he couldn't speak in this form, hoping Seb would see it as both acceptance of Seb's apology and one of Nevan's own for spooking.

"I was just thinking. While ceffyl dŵr might have wings"—he pointed to Nevan's back—"which are *awesome* by the way, more like a bat's than a bird's, right?" He flapped a hand as though waving his words away. "Sorry. Not relevant. Anyway, wings, sure, but hands? Nope. Not a single one." Seb laced his own hands behind his back and rocked from his toes to his heels. "Just thought I'd mention it."

Nevan blinked slowly, flicking his tail. *I don't have hands.* What did— Oh! He nickered, the closest he could come to laughing while shifted, and trotted down the bank. He couldn't risk actually stepping *in* the water, but luckily, there was a little pool eddying behind a fall of rocks right at the edge, so he splayed his legs as far as he could—*I must look proper ridiculous from behind*—and lowered his head to drink.

Goddess, it's glorious. But as he drank his fill, he felt a small niggle at the back of his mind. *Glorious, yes, but not as satisfying as when Seb lets me drink from his hand.*

Seb.

Nevan had never been a joiner. He'd coursed the rivers, soared over the cliffs, retreated behind his waterfall, always in solitude, and he'd been perfectly happy. Then Lulu had come into his life and become necessary to him.

Now Seb had broken through Nevan's barriers, too, with

honor and concern and care. And how would he likely be repaid for his kindness?

By the council stripping him of his memories, or putting their own geas on him or—*no*. Nevan refused to consider that the Queen's Champion might be ordered to execute Seb as the most expedient way to ensure the Secrecy Pact remained intact.

Over my *dead body.*

Nevan had no patron, no advocate, no ally in Faerie's court or on the supe council, and until this moment, he'd been perfectly happy with that. It meant everybody left him alone. But now, he regretted his reclusive tendencies for Seb's sake.

I don't know how, but somehow I'll protect him.

That little niggle was back, but Nevan ignored it. *It's for Seb's sake that I make this vow—not because I want him to remember* me.

Nevan got his legs back under him and shook his head, mane flying. Would Seb even *want* to remember him? *Time to put it to the test.*

He turned and paced toward Seb, whose eyes widened as he backed up a step. Nevan lowered his head and folded his front legs, wings locked tight against his flanks, inviting Seb to mount.

Nevan waited, his head bowed. And waited. And *waited*.

Nothing happened.

Finally, he raised his head. Seb had retreated another few feet, his hands behind his back, his eyes huge, and he was shaking his head wildly.

That tiny seed of hope that had taken hesitant root, the hope that Nevan might have found another who accepted him, accepted *all* of him, withered and died, leaving him hollow.

He pivoted on his rear hooves and sprang away, then let the shift take him in midair. Without glancing at Seb, he strode to his discarded clothing, shook out his trousers and pulled them on.

"Nevan?" Seb's tone was tentative. "Are you okay?"

Nevan snatched up his shirt and yanked it over his head. "I understand."

"Understand what?"

"Why you don't trust me." Shite, the damn shirt was on backwards. He tugged it off again and turned it around. "I don't deserve it."

"What?" Seb squawked, and suddenly he was there, in front of Nevan, eyes fairly blazing. "Are you kidding me right now?"

"It's no matter. I know myself. Know what I am." He scooped up his waistcoat. "Lulu is the only one who's ever looked at me as if I wasn't what I am. A monster."

"Now just a dang minute." Seb's voice, low and fierce, matched his glower. "In the first place, the reason I, er, refused your extremely kind offer is that I've only been on a horse once in my life and it was, shall we say, less than successful? Not only that, but I, er, have a thing about heights. So if what you were offering was a ride on your back, I figured we should at least discuss it first. In the second place"—Seb placed a hand on Nevan's arm, stopping his fumble with the waistcoat buttons— "you're not a monster. You're a *wonder*. For Pete's sake, Nevan, you're a freaking *miracle*."

Nevan blinked, unable to move lest he dislodge Seb's touch and deprive himself of the warmth that touch was sending throughout his body. "A miracle?"

His glower morphed into a smile, and Seb nodded. "One hundred percent. Although"—his smile turned crooked—"you've got granola crumbs on your lips. Not sure how those stayed put through the shift, but…" He reached up and brushed his thumb over Nevan's lower lip. "There."

Nevan met Seb's eyes and slowly, slowly, so as not to break the moment or frighten Seb away, raised his hand and caught Seb's. Never breaking their gaze, Nevan brought Seb's palm to his mouth and kissed it. Seb inhaled sharply, but didn't pull away. So, even more slowly, Nevan lowered his head and pressed his lips against Seb's.

Soft. Warm. Welcoming.

If Nevan had ever dared dream of what a kiss would be, it would be this.

When he would have pulled away, Seb's other hand came up and cupped Nevan's cheek, keeping him in place for another kiss. And another. And—

Something big and white and furry crashed into them, knocking them both off balance, and sending Nevan reeling down the bank toward the river. He barely managed to catch himself from falling forward into the water.

"Doop!" a young-sounding voice called. "Off!"

Nevan whirled, landing in a crouch, ready to launch himself at whatever was threatening Seb. But then he froze, because Seb lay prone on the grass, and over him, four enormous paws braced alongside Seb's body, massive head with its pricked red ears lowered toward Seb's face, was a Ci Annwn, one of Herne the Hunter's own pack of hellhounds.

Nevan snarled. Was the supe council taking proactive steps to neutralize the human threat? How had they found out? And why would they take such an irrevocable step without at least hearing Nevan's testimony?

Because once the Cwn Annwn were on the trail, their prey never returned alive.

CHAPTER 13

Seb stared up into the face of one of the biggest dogs he had ever seen in his life. Its golden eyes were *literally* glowing, so brightly that Seb had to squint against their brilliance. Its fluffy white fur was equally dazzling, except for the erect ears, which were a vivid Crayola red. He would have been more alarmed if its tongue weren't lolling out of its square muzzle in a doggy grin and its feathered tail weren't waving like a Pride flag.

"Doop!" A young man, tanned and rosy-cheeked, with slightly overlong brown hair, came racing up. "Off." The dog— Doop, apparently—didn't move. The man crouched and peered at Seb from under Doop's jaws. "Sorry. We're working on personal space, but so far he's having a little trouble with the concept."

Then he snapped his fingers and... did he actually growl?

The dog sighed gustily and stepped away from Seb with surprising daintiness for a canine that size, but not before he slurped a *very* wet doggy kiss up one side of Seb's face from chin to hairline.

"Doop!" The man stepped in front of the dog. "Sorry. Like I

said, personal space is still a work in progress." He held out a hand. "I'm Jordan, by the way. Jordan Tate."

"No worries." Seb grasped Jordan's offered hand and pulled himself to his feet. "Thanks. I'm Seb. Nice to meet you."

When Seb dabbed gingerly at his damp face, Jordan winced. "Again, sorry. Usually I travel with a bag that has wipes in it, but the King said this was an emergency, so I kinda forgot it."

King? Oookay.

"Like I said, no worries. I've got this covered." Seb strode over to his pile of stuff and dug through it. He held up the pack of baby wipes. "Never leave home without 'em."

Jordan's big brown eyes widened. "Wow. Do you have a dog too?"

"No. I'm a nanny. Or at least I was." Seb sighed as he extracted a wipe and cleaned dog spit off his face. Who knew what would happen to his agency rating after his no show for Mrs. Macclesfield? "But then Nevan..."

Heat rushed through Seb—moving downward instead of upward for a change—because Nevan had *kissed* him. But then Doop had knocked them over and...

Nevan.

Seb leaped up, searching the riverbank for Nevan, but he wasn't anywhere in sight.

"Nevan?" Seb called.

Could he have shifted and taken off again? But his duster was the only piece of his clothing still on the grass and the misty air was clear of awesome flying horses. Where—

"Seb!" Nevan's voice was strong but muffled and seemed to be coming from... above? "Run! Hurry, while I've got him distracted."

Distracted? What? Then Seb spotted Doop, looking up into the branches of the oak tree, tail still wagging. Seb bit the inside of his cheek, trying not to laugh.

"I think Doop might have treed my... friend."

"If he ran away, Doop probably thought he was playing. He

and my little brother play chase in our backyard all the time." Jordan smiled a little ruefully. "Is your friend Unseelie fae? Because they get kinda freaked out by Doop. See, his breed's normal diet is the, um, flesh of traitors."

Seb blinked. "I beg your pardon?"

"His *breed*. Not Doop himself. He's not officially part of Herne's pack, so he's never run with the Wild Hunt," Jordan said hurriedly. "But don't worry. Dr. MacLeod put together a diet plan for him, so he can get all his nutrients without, you know, tearing people limb from limb, and druids *always* know what they're doing."

"Druids?" Seb said faintly.

"Yeah. I mean, witches should be able to do the same thing, but you know, they're all about *natural consequences.*" Jordan made an *OMG, can you believe it?* face. "And a lot of them—not my friend Ky, he's an SMT, and he's cool—won't even *look* at Doop because he escaped from Faerie before he ever ran with his pack, and the natural consequence of that is starvation." His expression darkened. "And I am *not* okay with that. I mean, it wasn't Doop's *fault*. But anyway, druids are more about balance, not, you know, *consequences*. So they're a lot more helpful." Jordan glanced over his shoulder. "We should probably rescue your friend, though, huh?"

He trotted toward the tree, leaving Seb trying really hard not to butt-plant on the grass. Apparently, Nevan's supernatural community was a lot wider than Seb had realized. Sure, he'd accepted Nevan's nature, as well as his sister's and Mage Evil's, but they'd seemed... contained, somehow. In their own world, like Narnia or Oz or Barsoom or something.

I mean, hello? Faerie? If that wasn't its own world, what was?

Seb had noted that Nevan's clothing wasn't ordinary streetwear, and Mage Evil had looked like a sinister Friar Tuck who was spending a week at a fancy retro spa. Yeah, no way were those robes of his anything as mundane as homespun or even linen or wool. They'd draped like heavy silk and the embroidery had glinted with gold, even though it had been semi-transparent.

But Jordan? In his skinny jeans, Hunter's Moon band T-shirt, fleece jacket, and scuffed trainers, he looked like any college kid between classes. If it weren't for his boundless energy, he could pass unnoticed on the streets of Portland any day of the week.

How many other supernatural beings are passing for human? Living among us?

What kind of being was Jordan, anyway? Seb paced toward the oak and stopped a good couple of yards away as Jordan peered up into its branches.

"Hi!" Jordan said. "Don't be scared of Doop. He's not *that* kind of Cwn Annwn."

The leaves rustled. "There is only one kind," Nevan said, his tone as dark as Jordan's was bright.

"Well, yeah," Jordan said, "I mean, if you're talking about *breed*, but we're talking about *behavior*. I've been training him for *months*. We both work for Quest Investigations and he doesn't even live in the kennel with Herne's hounds anymore. He lives at the Doghouse—I mean the Portland Howling Residence—along with me and the other weres in Tanner's pack."

Weres. Seb gulped. Okay, so that answered one question. Jordan was a werewolf.

Who lived in Portland.

Wiiith other werewolves.

All righty, then.

"It's really okay to come down. Doop won't hurt you. He —*Doop!*" Doop had lifted his leg and was watering the base of the oak. "Sorry! Maybe you should come down on the other side of the tree?" Jordan glanced sheepishly at Seb. "He's still a pup, really, so he's not always, um, appropriate."

Seb smiled a little tightly, because *werewolf*. Seb had *so* many questions. "I expect canine instinct is hard to counteract, even with training."

Jordan beamed. "Exactly! But he's making awesome

progress." Doop had lowered his leg and was looking up at Jordan with obvious adoration. "He backslides sometimes, but only on the little things. He'd *never* pursue anybody without a command from me or Herne. I promise."

Jordan gazed at Seb, eyebrows pinched a little and his head on one side. He opened his mouth as if to speak, but then shook his head and turned back to peer up in the tree. "Do you need any help? Werewolves are stronger than we look."

"You swear Seb is safe?" Nevan's tone was skeptical.

"Absolutely. Pack's honor."

Jordan raised his left hand and made a quick gesture that Seb didn't catch because a heavy weight pushed against his hip. He stepped sideways to catch his balance and glanced down to see Doop sitting at his feet, leaning against him with his head nearly at Seb's armpit. Seb shivered, not from alarm, since Doop was gazing up at him with his tongue lolling and his tail beating a brisk tattoo against the ground, but because the dog was *cold*. As in ice-pack cold.

He gingerly laid a hand on Doop's head and scratched behind the red ears. "Jordan?"

Jordan, who was watching Nevan climb out of the tree, didn't glance Seb's way. "Yeah?"

"Is Doop well? Healthy, I mean? He's—"

"Cold? Yeah, it's a Cwn Annwn thing. Sometimes people call them the cold hounds. Totally normal."

Nevan swung down, a branch dipping under his weight, and dropped to the ground. "Have a care, Seb. You're petting a hellhound."

Jordan frowned. "I know you're probably still a little freaked, but we try *never* to use the H-word in a preju— performa— purg—"

"Pejorative?" Seb asked helpfully.

"Yes, that!" Jordan's frown disappeared, but his expression remained serious. "Positive reinforcement is *very* important."

Doop, his eyes half-lidded in pleasure from Seb's skritches, didn't seem unduly disturbed at being called a hellhound, but Seb got it.

"It definitely is." He smiled down at Doop. "Good boy."

Jordan beamed. "*Thank* you! Now." He dusted off his palms, turning surprisingly businesslike. "You activated an FTA token?"

"I didn't." Seb pointed at Nevan. "He did."

"Three, as it happens." Nevan crossed his arms. "They didn't work."

Jordan nodded seriously. "They sort of did. They were logged—"

"All three of them?" Nevan's gaze landed on Seb for an instant before it skittered away. "Even the first?"

Seb's hand stilled on Doop's head, and the dog, clearly objecting to lack of pets, butted his fingers insistently until Seb resumed his ministrations. What was Nevan concerned— *Ah. Got it.* The whole *not in front of humans* thing.

"Oh, yes," Jordan said. "Frang, the driver who took the call, was *very* upset when he couldn't seem to reach you. That's never happened before."

"Never?" Nevan frowned. "But if whoever calls the ride is in the presence of humans—"

"Nope." Jordan shook his head emphatically, causing his brown hair to flop over his forehead. "If the conditions aren't right for the driver to appear, the token won't activate. It's one of the fail-safes built into the system."

Nevan's eyebrows rose and he blinked twice. "I... didn't realize."

"Oh, yeah. The King was *really* careful about that when he designed the FTA spells. You know, Secrecy Pact and all that? But if the activation spell works successfully and gets logged, the driver should be able to reach the rider. I mean, you can get *anywhere* from Faerie. But Frang couldn't open a portal to reach you."

"But you could?" Nevan's skepticism was still present in his tone.

"Not me." Jordan turned and pointed. "Doop. Doop has an affri— affo— affe—"

"Affinity?" Seb asked.

"Yes! That! An affinity for hidden portals." He gazed at the dog with obvious pride. "We haven't run into one yet that he can't traverse. Although I make sure that he never tries it alone." Jordan pulled a cell phone out of his back pocket. "One of my pack mates wrote this app for me—and if you're worried about him hacking the magic grid, don't be. He's totally legit now that he's the tech consultant for Quest." He brandished the phone, its screen displaying a big purple dot. "See? This lets me know whether it's safe for us to make the jump. Green means all clear —there's room to land and nobody's around. Blue means there's people there, but they're not hostile, so it's still okay. Red means no-go." He frowned down at the screen. "This is only the second time I've seen *purple*, though. But Hector—my friend—said as long as it wasn't red, we could take the jump." He spread his arms. "And here we are." He scrunched up his face and looked around. "Wherever *here* is."

Still side-eyeing Doop, Nevan edged to Seb's side. "Can you get us out?"

"Of course. Like I said, Doop can go *anywhere*. Well, anywhere we've detected a portal, or to a place or person he knows. But we can head back to Faerie, no problem."

"Then the sooner we go, the better."

Jordan held up a finger. "There is one thing, though."

"What?" Nevan growled.

"The King wants to know how you got here and why."

Nevan flinched, cradling his left hand against his chest. Seb didn't know whether the brand had come back to life again, preventing him from disclosing the details of his geas, or whether he was just in risk-avoidance mode again. So Seb stepped into the breach—after all, *he* wasn't under a curse.

"Don't ask him for details," he told Jordan as he hurried over to begin shoving his stuff back into his pack. "He can't say."

Jordan frowned for a second and then his expression cleared, his eyebrows disappearing behind his bangs. "Oooh. I get it." He pointed at Nevan's hand. "A geas brand, right? One of my bosses had one of those once. Long story, but it worked out okay in the end, because it was my other boss's brother who—" He must have registered Nevan's scowl. "Um… not important now?"

"Probably not," Seb said.

"Anyway, I can take you wherever you need to go, no charge, but the King wants you to show me how you got here first."

"Can I say no?" Nevan growled.

Jordan widened his eyes. "He's the *King*. So yeah. No."

Nevan scooped his duster off the ground and held it in one clenched fist. "Then we'd best get on with it, hadn't we?"

CHAPTER 14

*N*evan's heart had dropped nearly to Govannon's forge when he'd realized a Ci Annwn had Seb in his sights. Even now, despite Jordan's assurances, he made sure to keep himself between Seb and the hound, tracking the giant dog in his peripheral vision as he knelt with his duster draped across his thighs to help Seb pack up his scattered belongings.

Seb poked at the orange rinds. "It's okay to leave these here, isn't it? I mean, compostable, and all that?"

Nevan nodded jerkily. "Should be."

With the translucent purple cup in his hand, Seb peered at him from narrowed eyes. "Before we leave, you need another drink."

"Seb—"

"Wait here."

He stood and headed toward the river before Nevan could grab his arm and pull him back. Doop was snuffling around the oak tree at the moment, Jordan at his side, and didn't appear to be paying attention to Seb. But he was a Ci Annwn. Surely he couldn't completely deny his compulsion to hunt, to maim, to kill. He couldn't deny his very nature.

Any more than Nevan could.

Nevan sighed, kneading his left palm with his right thumb. When they stepped into Faerie, would Yvo be able to tell what he'd done here, the boundaries he'd pushed, the risks he'd taken? Would the pain of forfeiture send him to his knees? Would the geas brand pulse and burn until he was ready to cut his own hand off?

Would Lulu still be in danger?

Time was running out, and Nevan's skin itched with the need to do *something*, although what precisely he *could* do, he wasn't sure. Seb wasn't an assassin, and sooner or later, Yvo would suss that out. When that moment arrived, what would it mean for Nevan and Lulu?

Furthermore, what would it mean for Seb?

Nevan's lips still tingled from their kisses. His first.

How ridiculous is it that I'm over two thousand years old and still a virgin?

While Lulu was obviously his first priority—and keeping himself from becoming Yvo's secret weapon a close second—Seb's safety was right up there. Whatever price the supe council chose to exact for his Secrecy Pact violation, Nevan would pay, provided they were lenient with Seb.

Since Their Fae Majesties were ranking council members and held enormous sway over the others, if Nevan wanted to turn them up sweet, complying with the King's request was probably a good first step. Certainly ignoring it would have the opposite effect.

He'd have to return to the carnival in any case to complete his task—he swallowed as his gorge rose again—so it wouldn't be precisely *inconvenient* to lead Jordan to the Fun House.

Not inside, though. Nevan was *never* stepping inside that hellish place again.

Seb returned, the cup brimming, and lowered himself care-fully to his knees without spilling a drop. "Here. Drink." He dipped his chin and glared at Nevan over the top of his spectacles. "No arguments, okay? You need your strength."

Nevan had no intention of arguing, not only because he needed the water, but because while Seb gently held the cup to his lips, Nevan could gaze into those warm, dark eyes over its rim. *That quenches another thirst altogether, although it still leaves me wanting more.*

After Nevan had drained the cup, Seb tucked it away and zipped the pack closed. "There. All set. Shall we?"

Nevan nodded and grabbed his duster, his tight grip no doubt pressing permanent creases into its leather. He stood and the two of them joined Jordan and his beast. *Doop.*

Does the young were realize dwp *means* stupid *in Welsh?*

"Ready?" Jordan asked. At their nods, he looked down at Doop. "Faerie, Doop. The ceilidh glade."

Doop bunched his rear legs and launched himself forward. When he was midair, the portal opened onto the expanse of brilliant green moss, bounded by white stones, that stood atop the tor at the heart of Faerie. He landed silently and pranced into its center before turning to face them, head cocked.

Seb's breath caught, and his hand fumbled for Nevan's. "Is that…"

Nevan nodded, daring to lace his fingers with Seb's.

"Yes." He braced himself for pain as they stepped through the portal, Jordan at their heels, but… nothing happened. He took a huge breath. *Reprieve.* At least temporarily. "Welcome to Faerie."

A hulking duergar stood on the edge of the glade, wringing his hands. He glanced sidelong at Doop and edged away, clearly ready to bolt as fast as Nevan had done. Nevan's excuse, though, was that he'd been trying to lead the hellhound away from Seb.

"You found them?" The duergar's deep voice sounded almost tearful.

Jordan trotted over to him, although Doop stayed next to Seb. He looked up at the duergar and patted his arm. "No trouble at all, Frang. It's all good."

"The King doesn't blame me?" He sidled further away.

"Not a bit. In fact, the King says you can have a drink on him." Jordan patted Frang's arm again. "Go ahead. Heilyn's got it ready for you in the Keep kitchen."

With one last glance at Doop, who lifted a decidedly sarcastic doggy eyebrow, Frang lumbered out of the glade.

Seb moved closer and nudged Nevan's arm gently. "You okay?"

"I…" Nevan's eyes prickled. Had anybody ever asked him that before? Lulu was the only person who'd ever cared about his well-being, and in her child's self-centric worldview, it would never occur to her to ask. "Yes. For the moment."

He uncurled his left hand and stared at the geas brand. It wasn't inert, as it had been by the river. He could feel it again, but it was as though it were numbed and buried under layers of gauze. Perhaps Faerie erected its own barriers to foreign magic.

Nevan gave himself a mental facepalm for not testing that angle himself, but he hadn't sought refuge at his lake in Faerie after Yvo had bound him. He hadn't dared, in case Yvo would construe it as running away and take his ire out on Lulu.

Which he still could do. Nevan's belly tumbled. How long had they been gone already? It felt like hours. Hours he didn't have, that Lulu didn't have. "We have to hurry."

"Sure thing," Jordan said. "Where to?"

"Wait." Seb held up a hand.

"Seb," Nevan said, trying to keep a tight rein on his impatience, "I know you'd like to sightsee, but you know what's at stake."

The expression on Seb's face mingled outrage with hurt, and he dropped Nevan's hand. "For Pete's sake, Nevan. You ought to know by now that I'd *never* put a child in danger for my own benefit." He turned to Jordan as Nevan's palm twitched with the need to feel Seb's against it again. "If you follow our same route, you won't be trapped like we were, will you?"

"Oh, don't worry about that," Jordan said. "I'll have Doop with me, so I can always get out again."

"All right then," Seb said. He still didn't take Nevan's hand. "We landed in that spot from a carnival."

"A carnival?" Jordan's brilliant grin bloomed. "Really? I should bring my little brother. He'd love it. Although..." He leaned forward and whispered, "Are there clowns?"

Seb closed his eyes, a visible shudder running through him. "So many clowns."

A similar shudder passed through Jordan. "Then maybe I won't mention it to him. Where is it?"

"At the Washington County Fairgrounds," Nevan said.

Jordan bit his lip. "Hmmm. That's a little exposed. Are there humans around?"

Nevan nodded. "It was quite busy when we... exited."

"So we won't be able to get Doop to open a portal for us, although, since he's never been there, he'd have had some trouble, anyway. Oh!" His expression cleared. "One of my bosses and his husband live near there, and there's a portal in the wetlands behind their house. Do you mind a little hike?"

Seb looked down at his boots. "How little? These boots fit pretty well, but they're new to me."

"A mile. Maybe two, tops."

"Shouldn't be a problem." Seb looked up at Nevan. "As long as you're feeling strong enough."

Strong enough for what? "I'll manage."

"Cool." Jordan pointed to the woods that edged the tor. "It's that way. Just down the hill and across the stream."

Nevan's left hand spasmed, and he folded his fingers over the brand. "Stream? Do I... That is, must we step in the water to cross?"

"Nope. There's stepping stones. In fact, you have to walk on them or you just end up on the other side of the stream in Faerie instead of where you're aiming for."

"Then let us go." Nevan took off for the tree line but stopped when Seb made a strangled noise behind him. "What is it?"

He pointed to his pack. "I kinda doubt I'll be able to pass the carnival gates with a big-ass dagger in my pack."

Jordan's eyes widened. "You have a big-ass dagger?"

Seb nodded. "Side pocket, behind the water bottle." He faced Nevan. "I mean, I didn't *see* any metal detectors, but there was a guy standing inside the gates who looked like security. Frankly, I was surprised he didn't ask to search my pack in the first place."

"The King doesn't want me to delay, in case this is a systemic problem," Jordan said, his eyebrows bunched with worry. Then he snapped his fingers, his smile returning. "I know! We can leave the knife at the Doghouse."

Seb glanced at Doop. "You want me to hide it in Doop's house? Have I mentioned it's a *big-ass dagger*?"

Jordan laughed. "The Doghouse isn't *Doop's* house. Well, I mean it is because he lives there. Didn't I mention it before? It's where me, my brother, and the other guys in Tanner's pack live, along with Tahmina."

"Tahmina?" Seb asked.

"Yeah. She's an honorary pack member, kinda our house mother." He chuckled. "In fact, my little brother calls her Tahmama."

"Is, um, she a werewolf too?"

"Oh, no," Jordan said breezily. "She's a djinn. Ready?"

"A djinn?" Nevan passed a hand over his forehead. "An actual djinn? I thought they'd all vanished eons ago."

"Nope." Jordan seemed completely oblivious that he'd just hit Nevan with a bombshell. "They've just"—he scrunched up his face and waggled one palm—"rebranded, I guess you could say. But don't worry. She and her sisters are really nice."

Sisters? More than one djinn? Clearly, Nevan had missed a lot while he'd sheltered in his secluded lake with nobody but Lulu for company.

I should have stayed there. If I hadn't ventured out, Yvo would never have targeted Lulu.

But raising a child in isolation wasn't fair to the child, and no matter how many times he played that *what if* game, he couldn't go back and change anything. *If only time surfing were a real thing, I could correct so many mistakes.*

"As eager as I am to meet more werewolves, not to mention a djinn," Seb said, his voice only wobbling a little, "I still question the safety of leaving this knife at a place with a small child. Do you have a secure place to store it?"

Jordan waved the concern away. "Oh, we'll just bury it in the backyard. Trust me." He lifted an eyebrow, which, for some reason, made him appear a decade older. "We have plenty of holes to choose from."

"I don't know," Seb said slowly, with a glance at Nevan. "That seems a little sketchy. Nevan? What do you think?"

Nevan wasn't sure if Yvo would be able to detect that his bespelled artifact was underground at a werewolf pack house, or how he'd react if he could. *I'm sure he'll let me know, though, in no uncertain terms.*

"As long as we can find it again later—and that you can make sure your brother won't dig it up in the meantime."

"We can always find what we bury," Jordan said.

"'We?'" Seb asked, blinking.

"Me and the other guys." He chuckled, a bit shamefaced. "Well, mostly me and Noah. And mostly Noah these days."

"What exactly *do* you bury?"

Jordan motioned for Doop, who bounded over to his side. "Oh, bones, balls, Frisbees. You know. The usual. Ready?"

Setting his jaw, Nevan determinedly took Seb's hand, which settled his nerves. Although it earned him a startled glance, Seb didn't pull away, which Nevan counted as a win. "Let's get on with it, then."

Jordan nodded decisively. "Doop, the Doghouse."

Once again, Doop settled on his haunches and leaped, this

time landing in the fenced back yard of a yellow two-story house with white shutters and a rather battered back deck. When Jordan beckoned for them to follow, they stepped out of Faerie and into the Outer World.

And Nevan sucked in his breath, dropping to his knees as pain seared his hand.

CHAPTER 15

"Nevan!" Seb knelt next to Nevan, who was doubled over on the grass, his right hand still clutching Seb's and his left cradled underneath him.

Jordan crouched next to him. "Is it the geas? Mal—my boss—said the pain could be really bad."

"I think so." Seb eased his fingers from Nevan's grip so he could stroke his hair. "I'm not sure what—"

But just then, Nevan took a deep, shuddering breath and sat back on his haunches. "I'm all right. It's fading." He grimaced. "Pay me no mind."

Seb frowned at him. "Yeah, that's not happening." He turned to Jordan. "Dang it, I should have filled my water bottle before we left Nowhereland. I don't suppose you have any natural spring water around?"

Jordan chewed on his lower lip. "I'm not sure. Tahmina does the shopping for us, because she says if she left it to us we'd buy nothing but Doritos and frozen pizza. I could ask her if—"

"Doop!" A small figure, barefoot, wearing navy sweatpants and a yellow T-shirt, erupted out of the sliding door at the back of the house. His shaggy brown hair bounced as he rocketed down the deck stairs and across the lawn, deftly leaping over the

E.J. RUSSELL

truly astonishing number of holes in the grass along with their attendant piles of dirt.

He flung himself at Doop, wrapping both arms around the dog's neck. "I've *missed* you!"

Doop, for his part, stood with his feet braced and took the boy's weight as a tall, slender woman with eastern Mediterranean features and long black hair walked toward them, holding a glass brimming with water. She handed it to Seb. "I believe you need this."

Seb shook his head. "Thank you, but it has to be—"

"Wild water. Yes, I know." She smiled. "Fresh from the oasis this morning."

Oasis? "Oookay." Seb took the water. "Thanks." He held the glass to Nevan's lips. "Here. I know it isn't everything you need, but it should help."

Nevan, his eyes closed, drank, throat working, until he'd downed three quarters of the water. "Thank you," he murmured.

"Not a problem," the woman, who must be Tahmina—*holy crap, the djinn*—said. "There's more in the crock in the kitchen if you should need it. It also might help temporarily for you to bathe his hand in it." She smiled at Seb. "Don't worry. He'll not forfeit. Not as long as you do the pouring."

Seb lifted his eyebrows but Nevan shrugged, so Seb trickled the remaining water over the geas brand on Nevan's palm. Nevan sucked in a sharp breath and Seb tilted the glass up. "Did that hurt?"

"No." Nevan's shoulders relaxed as he exhaled slowly. "No. That... helped. Thank you."

The boy let go of Doop and held out a hand to Seb. "Hi! I'm Noah Tate and I use he/him pronouns."

"Hello, Noah." Seb shook, unable to bury a smile at the boy's enthusiasm. "My name is Seb and I use he/him pronouns as well."

"This is Tahmama— I mean *Tahmina*, and she uses she/her

pronouns," Noah said. He tilted his head, peering at Nevan curiously. "Do you want to shake, or are you still feeling bad?"

Nevan smiled at Noah, and Seb's heart jolted at the tender expression. "I am feeling much better, thank you." He held out his hand. "I am Nevan Quirke, and I use he/him pronouns as you do."

Noah's nose quivered, and he pressed his lips together tightly, casting an agonized glance at his brother.

Jordan's eyebrows twitched. "What is it, Noah?"

He released Nevan's hand and snuggled into Jordan's side. "I'm not supposed to mention *you know what.*"

Jordan met Nevan's eyes and shrugged. "I think he's picking up on your scent. His teacher"—for some reason, Jordan gave Seb an up-and-down glance—"has to remind him not to discuss it in public, but Noah's just started shifting and until he gets his shifts under better control, he can't go back to school." He gave his brother a passably stern look. "And he's forgetting some of those lessons in the meantime."

"It's all right," Nevan said. He settled cross-legged on the ground. "What do you smell, pup?"

Noah sidled closer and sniffed. "He smells a little like Mr. Johnson's dock, or Dr. MacLeod's backyard. You know. Water with those rushy things that grow around it. But there's something else too. Like the stables in Faerie." He ducked his head and peered up at Nevan. "Sorry. I don't mean like the... the..."

Seb took pity on the boy, who was clearly trying to find a polite way to say *horse shit.*

"Manure?" Seb asked gently.

"Yeah! *Not* like that, but the way the horses smell when they're clean." He sniffed again, nose quivering like a rabbit's. "And maybe... cotton candy?"

Nevan smiled crookedly. "You have a good nose."

Noah looked up at Tahmina. "I've never smelled anything like him before. Wyn and Blair are sort of like that, but not really."

"Unless I miss my guess," she said, "he is ceffyl dŵr. Welsh also, and water fae like Wyn and Blair, but with other qualities they don't possess."

Noah looked up at Seb, forehead puckered. "You're even *more* confusing."

Seb chuckled. "I probably smell like somebody who needs a bath."

Noah wrinkled his nose. "Ewww!"

"Not a fan of baths?"

"Ugh. *No*. But that's not it. You smell almost like... school?"

Seb smiled down at Noah. "That's probably because I'm a nanny. It's my job to take care of children, and sometimes that includes teaching them things."

"Oh. I guess that makes sense then."

Tahmina turned to Jordan. "Are you home for a bit?"

"No, sorry. I'm kinda on a job right now. I don't *think* it'll take too long, but I'll have to report to the King when I'm done, so I might not be back before dinner time."

"I see." She placed a hand on Noah's head. "Then you and I are off to Dewton this afternoon, my lad."

"*Again?*" Noah's tone bordered on a whine. "But there's no *kids* there."

"Perhaps not." Tahmina shared an amused glance with Jordan. "But I'm sure Wanda will have cookies for you, and Shirl will let you into the back room if you ask nicely." She looked at Jordan. "I'm sorry. But I really can't delay any longer. The store's opening next week and I've only got half my stock in place."

"I get it." Jordan sighed heavily. "You've gone above and beyond for us already. You should be able to get back to your own life."

"Nonsense. You've given me just as much, my dear." She kissed his cheek. "We'll contrive something." She ruffled Noah's hair. "I can't blame him for being bored without his playmates. He really needs to go back to school."

Jordan squatted down in front of Noah. "Have you been doing your practices?"

Noah snatched his hands behind his back and gazed at his brother with wide, innocent eyes that didn't fool Seb for an instant. "Yes?"

"Noah." Jordan's tone held a ring to it that almost reverberated in the air. "Are your fingers crossed?"

Noah's shoulders slumped. "It's *hard*, Jordan. I have to *concentrate*."

"That's why practice is important."

Noah sidled over to Doop and threw his arm over the hound's back. Doop nosed the boy's ear, making him giggle. "It's funner with Doop. Can he stay with me?"

"Doop has a job today, too. Besides, when you play with him, you don't practice shifting. You just stay wolfy the whole time. And dig holes."

Noah gave Jordan the time-honored *adults are so clueless* look. "That's what I *said*. It's *funner*."

Once again, Seb had to bite the inside of his cheek. "If I may?"

Jordan lifted his eyebrows. "You've got a suggestion?"

"Well, like I said, I *am* a nanny." Seb squatted down to put himself on Noah's level. "How old are you, Noah?"

Noah puffed out his chest. "Nine!"

"Noah," Jordan said.

"Almost," Noah muttered.

Seb made certain he looked suitably impressed. "Then I'm sure you know how to read."

Noah rolled his eyes. "For just *ages*."

Seb rummaged in his pack and brought out his well-worn hardback copy of *The Phantom Tollbooth*. "Have you ever read this one?"

"I don't *think* so." Noah peered at the turquoise book jacket with Jules Feiffer's whimsical illustration. "Puh-*han*-tom. What's that?"

"Phantom." Seb pronounced it carefully. "It can be different things. It could be another word for ghost."

Noah scowled, his expression identical to Jordan's when he'd chastised Nevan for referring to Doop as a hellhound. "We don't say *ghost*. We say *untethered soul*."

"Uh... you do?"

Noah bounced on his toes. "Yep. Like Miss Pennybaker at Jordan's work." He leaned forward and lowered his voice into a kid's idea of a whisper—in other words, something clearly audible to everyone within a ten-yard radius. "Doop's scared of her, 'cause he can see her even though nobody else can." He wrinkled his nose again. "Except for Hugh. But only when he uses his camera."

Seb glanced up at Jordan, who shrugged and said, "Long story."

"Well," Seb said, "In this case, *phantom* means something that appears unexpectedly out of nowhere."

Noah touched the illustration. "Is there a dog in it?"

"Yes, there is." He handed Noah the book. "Milo, the boy in the story, goes on all sorts of adventures and visits different lands when he passes the tollbooth." Seb glanced up at Nevan with a smile. "Kind of like I've done today." He patted the book in Noah's hands. "This is one of my favorite stories. I've had this copy since I was about your age."

Jordan rested his hand on Noah's shoulder. "If it's valuable, maybe you shouldn't—"

"It's okay." Seb had noted the reverence with which Noah had taken the book. "Noah will take good care of it. Won't you?"

Noah nodded emphatically. "I *so* will."

"You want to know a really cool thing about stories?" When Noah nodded again, Seb said, "Stories aren't like cookies. No matter how many people you share them with—even if your copy of a book gets so old it falls to pieces—the *story* never gets used up. If you like this one as much as I think you will, I'll make sure you get a copy of your own, as long as you promise to share it with your friends."

Noah hugged the book to his chest. "I will. I promise. Most books don't have anything to do with *real* life, but this one sounds *awesome*." He gazed at Seb with definite puppy-dog eyes, which Seb supposed was appropriate under the circumstances. *Werewolf. Gah!* "Can I take it with me?" He cut a glance at Tahmina and grimaced. "I mean, *may* I take it with me?"

"You may. And maybe we can talk about it later."

Noah nodded enthusiastically and stroked the book cover.

Jordan turned to Seb. "Thanks for that. Let's get something to wrap the"—he mouthed *knife*—"in and then we can head to the carnival."

"Carnival?" Noah looked up. "You're going to a carnival? Can — *May* I come too?"

Jordan assumed an apologetic look. "Well, I suppose you could." He leaned down. "But there's *clowns*."

Noah's eyes widened and suddenly there was a wolf pup where he'd been standing, yellow T-shirt around his fluffy neck, briefs and sweatpants puddled around his paws. Tahmina deftly caught the book before it hit the ground as the little wolf scuttled over to cower under Doop's belly.

Tahmina chuckled as she tucked the book under one arm. "Doop." Doop obediently sidestepped so she could retrieve Noah and tuck him under her other arm. "We'll see you at dinner then. I'll bring takeout from Wanda's." She nodded at Seb. "You'll find some bath bombs on the counter next to the water crock. I'd recommend you draw a bath for Nevan in that claw-foot tub of yours and use one." She winked. "Sharing the bath is optional, of course, but I'd recommend that as well. You both need it."

Seb stared after her as she sauntered toward the house, his face flaming. "How does she know about my bathtub?"

"It's a djinn thing," Jordan said with a shrug. "They know stuff. Now that they only give people what they *need* instead of what they *want*, they don't exactly mince words either." He rolled his eyes. "And my boss claims *werewolves* have boundary issues." His smile returned. "Now, let's bury that blade and get back to work. Wanda's takeout is awesome so I want to be sure to make it home in time for dinner."

"Time?" Nevan peered up at the overcast sky. "What time is it?"

Jordan shrugged. "I don't know. Maybe around eleven?"

"Eleven?" Nevan stared at him intently. "Are you sure?"

"I just looked at my phone, and it was 10:55 then, so yeah?"

Nevan stared at his palm. "We weren't in Faerie for long, and we've only been here for a little while." He looked up and met Seb's gaze. "We were out of time."

Seb gripped Nevan's arm. "No. Mage Evil can't have done anything else. I still have the knife. If we hurry, we can—"

"No, Seb." Nevan's expression held... wonder? "I mean while we were trapped by the river, no time passed here in the Outer World. We were literally *outside* of time."

Seb blinked. "That, er, can happen?"

"Oh, yeah," Jordan said breezily. "Time passes differently all over the place. Slower in some spots, faster in others." He chuckled. "Good thing we don't charge for our services by the hour at Quest or Miss Pennybaker would get *really* cranky at billing time, and trust me, *that* would be scary."

CHAPTER 16

I'm still on track. Lulu is still safe. Yvo will never know.

Wait. *Would* Yvo know? Could he tell that Nevan had been... absent? But if no subjective time had passed between exiting the Fun House and emerging into Faerie...

Shite. Nevan rubbed the bridge of his nose with his left hand, since he refused to let go of Seb's hand with his right. *Time anomalies make my head hurt.*

"You okay?" Seb asked softly as they stood shoulder to shoulder in front of the carnival entrance with Doop leaning against Seb's hip and Jordan on the hound's other side. "Is your headache back?"

He smiled down into Seb's concerned face. "I'm grand. Tahmina's water worked a treat, although I'd like to know where it came from."

"The oasis," Jordan said absently. "It's in the back room of a second-hand store in Dewton."

Seb cast Nevan a perplexed glance. "I'm sorry. What now?"

But Jordan's attention was focused beyond the carnival gate, where a trio of clowns on unicycles were cutting figure eights around the motionless figure of the tall gate guard. "Wow. I see what you mean about the clowns."

"Trust me," Seb said darkly. "There's more."

"Good thing I left Noah with Tahmina then. He'd have night-mares for weeks." Jordan shuddered. "Heck, *I'll* have nightmares for weeks."

"Tell me about it," Seb said.

Nevan looked away. After the council got finished with him, would Seb even remember the carnival?

Will he remember me?

How much of Seb's memory would they leave intact? Was he forever destined to have nightmares he couldn't explain?

Somehow, Nevan had to protect Seb from that, but could he do it? Stonewall the council, pretend he hadn't leaked so much about their community to a human?

He sighed. With so little experience with lying—he didn't have occasion to, since he so rarely saw another person other than Lulu anymore—he might be total shite at it. If he bolluxed something up, he ordinarily admitted it and took the conse-quences. But how could he serve himself up for council punish-ment while still protecting Seb? He might end up making the situation *worse*.

Nevan glanced at Jordan, who, now that the clowns had disappeared into a bright orange tent, was peering eagerly through the gates. The young were had exposed just as much or more, although he wouldn't have done so if Nevan hadn't made the first gaffe.

I've got to warn him.

He cleared his throat. "Jordan? Could I have a word, please?"

Jordan glanced quizzically between Nevan and Seb. "Um... sure?"

Seb, of course, smiled encouragingly, no judgment in his expression at all. "I'll keep Doop company. You go ahead."

Nevan led Jordan back toward the busy street, where the traffic noise would help mask their conversation. He stopped at the edge of the sidewalk, where he could still keep Seb within sight.

"Listen, I need to tell you something. I should have told you when you first found us, but—"

"It's okay," Jordan said. "It's the geas thing. I know how those work."

"No. In this case, it's not the geas. It's Seb." Nevan inhaled, shoulders rising with his breath, and exhaled in a rush. "He's human."

Jordan stared at him for a moment, then glanced over his shoulder at Seb, who was looking down and saying something to Doop. "No."

"I can understand your distress. I promise you, I wouldn't have knowingly made you complicit in a Secrecy Pact violation but—"

"I'm not *distressed*." Jordan propped his fists on his hips. "That wasn't an *OMG, what shall we do* kind of no. I mean, no, he's not human."

"I assure you. He is. This is entirely my fault. I mistook him for someone else—"

"Nevan." Jordan's tone was more suited to an alpha than the happy-go-lucky college-age were he'd appeared until now. "I'm assuring *you*." He jerked his chin toward Seb. "Doop would *not* behave like that if Seb were entirely human. He *knows*. And besides, Seb's wearing those clothes. They look *exactly* like the ones a, um"—he blushed rosily—"*friend* wore in Faerie when another friend was presented as a new prince in the King's household." He turned so the two of them were both facing Seb and pointed. "That's *brownie embroidery* on his vest. You can't pick something like that up at the nearest Nordstrom."

Nevan's heart bounded, because if Seb *wasn't* human... But then it dropped. "Those aren't his clothes."

Jordan frowned. "What?"

"The clothes. When we arrived at that place where you found us, Seb fell in the river. His own clothing was soaked, and he changed into those when he found them hanging on a tree.

Where Jordan had been pink before, now he looked as pale as

new milk. "Please tell me you didn't see a blue-skinned woman nearby. About so high?" He held his other hand at chest height. "Gray hair, homespun skirt, laundry basket?"

Nevan's eyes widened. "Do you seriously believe a *bean-nighe* hung those clothes?"

Jordan moaned and clutched his hair. "I can't even..." He transferred his grip to Nevan's forearm. "Tell me. What happened to Seb's clothes?"

"He left them there. They were still wet and—"

"I'll bring them back to him." Jordan vibrated like a plucked harp string. "I don't know what it means that he was the one to hang them up, but I don't want to risk leaving them there where *she* might be able to get them."

Suddenly, Nevan's throat was as dry as if he hadn't drunk nearly a gallon of oasis water. "You think it could mean..."

Nevan had assumed the council was the only threat to Seb. What if there were other dangers, *worse* dangers? The council at least could be reasoned with, but others—Yvo, for instance—could not.

"Would *you* want to risk it?"

"No," Nevan croaked.

"Me neither." Jordan pulled out his cell phone, giving Nevan an apologetic half smile. "I've got to make a call. I'll join you in a sec." He turned away.

Nevan took the hint and strode back to Seb. Instead of taking his hand this time, he enfolded Seb in his arms and buried his face in Seb's neck.

"Hell-o," Seb murmured. "Not that I'm complaining, but what brought this on?"

"I don't want anything to happen to you," Nevan said. "Not on my account. I want you to be safe." He pulled back enough that he could look down into Seb's eyes. "You should go. Leave. Now. Before anything else happens."

Seb frowned. "Nevan, what's wrong?"

"You could be in danger."

Seb smiled crookedly. "From that Secrecy Pact thingie you mentioned? I'll take my chances."

Nevan gripped Seb's shoulders. "No, you don't understand. Yvo is dangerous."

Seb's expression darkened. "Yeah, I got that memo, since he hired an *assassin* to kill a *child*."

"I mean to *you*."

"He doesn't know anything about me." Seb patted Nevan's chest. "Even if I *were* the assassin—which I am most definitely not—he wouldn't know anything about me because of that whole double-blind thing the Guild has going on." He shook his head. "I still can't believe there's a *guild* for assassins."

Nevan tightened his grip. "You don't understand. These clothes—"

"Oh, god. I shouldn't have taken them, should I?" Seb bit his lip. "I only borrowed them. I'll give them back to whoever they belong to. Maybe Jordan could take them back when he follows our trail?" He shook his head. "No. I'd need something to change into first, and I don't have anything else to put on."

"That's not the point." *How can I get through to him? Make him understand?* He gripped Seb's shoulders and gazed into his eyes. "The tales. The lore. When you were studying at university, did you encounter stories of the bean-nighe?"

"Bean-nighe? Oh, right. She appears in some of the Scottish texts. Washerwoman of death, right?" When Nevan nodded slowly, Seb's jaw sagged. "Oh my god. I'm wearing a *dead man's* clothes?"

"No," Jordan said as he appeared next to them, pocketing his phone. "In fact, you may have saved someone, or at least delayed the threat to them." He flung his arms around Seb's waist in an odd, sideways hug that didn't displace Nevan's hands on Seb's shoulders. "*Thank* you." He let go and stepped back. "I'll bring your clothes back. I promise."

"Thank you," Seb said faintly. "I think."

Jordan set his jaw, eyes narrowing as he stared through the gates. "Bring on the freaking clowns. I can face anything now."

While Nevan appreciated Jordan's determination, he placed a hand on the young were's shoulder. "Jordan. You can't take a bloody great hellhound into a carnival full of humans."

When Doop whimpered and snuggled closer to Seb, Jordan turned slowly to glare at Nevan. "Remember. Positive reinforcement, please. We don't use the H-word."

"Sorry." Nevan bowed to Doop. "Please forgive me." He straightened and faced Jordan again. "You can't take a bloody great *hound* into a carnival. I doubt they allow pets, and you must confess, Doop is very hard to miss."

"In the first place," Jordan said, "Doop isn't a *pet*. He's a bona fide member of the Quest Investigations staff. Oh! I almost forgot." He dug in the back pocket of his jeans and pulled out several pieces of pasteboard that had clearly spent time against the curve of his arse. "My business cards." He handed one each to Nevan and Seb. They read *Quest Investigations, Jordan Tate, Search and Recovery Specialist.* "I wanted Doop to have cards of his own, but he doesn't really have anywhere to carry them."

Nevan tucked his away, but Seb was studying the card closely. "Quest is a private investigation firm?"

Jordan nodded. "The best." He screwed up his face. "Of course, it's also the only one catering to the supe community, so—"

"Jordan," Nevan said, a warning in his tone.

Jordan rolled his eyes. "I *told* you. It's not a problem. Anyway, in the second place, no human will see Doop in his true form."

"*I* can see him," Seb said.

Jordan patted his shoulder. "We'll talk. And in the third place"—he pointed through the gates at a smallish brown dog of indeterminate breed—"there are other dogs in there already." Doop gave a little yip and bounded forward. "Doop!" Jordan gave them a harassed smile as Doop joined the other dog and they raced off together, shoulder to shoulder. "I'd better go catch him. Where did you find that portal?"

Nevan pointed down the midway, where the Fun House's grinning maw was visible to one side of the red-and-white striped big top. "There."

Jordan grimaced. "Ugh. What is it with carnivals and clowns?"

"Past the hall of mirrors and the maze is a dark room with flash pots and screamers, so it'll disorient you, and probably Doop as well."

"He'll be fine. He can handle that kind of distraction when we're on the trail. That's the exit?"

"Yes."

Jordan nodded decisively. "Good." He patted Seb's arm. "And thank you. For taking those clothes. You may have saved the life of someone very important." He flushed. "To... um, to Noah." He turned abruptly and sprinted through the gates, flashing his ticket at the gate guard as he passed, and followed Doop's trail.

CHAPTER 17

*S*eb scratched the back of his head as he watched Jordan disappear behind a green tent. He'd never heard of saving somebody's life by stealing their clothing, but since he intended to save at least two more lives—he glanced sidelong at Nevan—or possibly three by being mistaken for an assassin, it wasn't the weirdest thing that had happened in his life.

Or today, for that matter.

"Seb."

Seb turned at the odd tone in Nevan's voice. He was gazing down at their joined hands. Seb had instinctively laced his fingers with Nevan's again when Jordan had taken off after Doop.

He let go. "Sorry. I shouldn't take liberties."

Nevan caught Seb's hand and pressed it against his chest. "No. That's not it. But this"—he uncurled his other palm, giving Seb a glimpse of that ominous black tattoo—"is not your fight. Please. I'm begging you. Go home now and forget I ever pulled you into this."

"Hey." Seb kept his tone authoritative but nonthreatening, something he'd honed to a fine art during his training and experience. It worked. Nevan met his gaze. "I'm the only person who knows what's going on." He squinted one eye. "Well, most of it, anyway, thanks to our monologuing evil mage and friendly neighborhood werewolf. Besides..." He tried to infuse a little playfulness into his tone. "If I leave, who will keep you hydrated?"

Nevan's gaze flicked away for an instant, a muscle ticking in his jaw. "I'm fine."

"Yes, for *now*." Seb nodded at Nevan's palm. "What's going on with that thing at the moment?"

"Burns," Nevan mumbled. "But it's not pulsing yet. I don't think he knows I was... absent."

Seb shook his head, smiling wryly. "An out-of-time pocket. I'm feeling decidedly Gallifreyan right now."

Nevan's brow bunched. "What?"

Okay, so apparently magical water horses who transformed into supernaturally hot men didn't binge *Dr. Who* on the regular like Seb did.

"Never mind. My point is, you need me. Furthermore, *Mario* needs me."

Nevan's frown deepened. "What do you mean?"

"I *mean* that we're marching over to that big tent and warning Mario's family that there's a credible threat against his life." He pointed to the brand. "*You* can't do it, for obvious reasons. So it's up to me."

"What will you tell them? *Excuse me, but your child is targeted for death by enchanted dagger at the behest of a megalomaniacal earth mage?* How well do you think that will go over?" Nevan flung out a hand and pointed through the gates. "These carnies are *human*." Seb heard *just like you* as loudly as if Nevan had shouted it. "They'll assume you're delusional, a crank, or what's worse, the actual threat. They'll call the police on you."

Seb dipped his chin and looked up at Nevan, one eyebrow quirked. "Since I'm the one who's supposed to be doing the deed, their assumption wouldn't be too far off the mark, other than the fact the enchanted dagger is buried in a werewolf's backyard and I'm not now nor have I ever been an assassin. Come on, Nevan, give me *some* credit. *Obviously*, I'm not going to couch it in those terms. I'll say I overheard something in the crowd. Warn them to take extra precautions. There has to be some kind of security in place here." He cut a glance at the guard, who was regarding them somberly. "That guy, for instance. If the Galliers don't seem to be taking me seriously, I'll mention it to him, too."

"Seb—"

"Aside from that, there's no way I'm leaving *you* until the threat to you and your sister is resolved. There has to be some way around Yvo's plans." He tilted his head. "After all, we've got allies now, don't we? Werewolves, djinni, hellhounds. We'll find a way."

Nevan groaned. "Seb, we have to keep your involvement secret. If the council should find out—"

"I suspect that particular ship will be leaving the dock any second, if it hasn't already sailed over the horizon. Remember, young Noah has my book, and considering his impulse control issues, he's bound to let something slip whether I bail on you now or not. And besides"—he patted his pack, where he'd stuck Jordan's business card—"we're acquainted with Quest Investigations' search and recovery specialist, and not only does *he* know who I am, but so does his canine sidekick. If the council asked, they could find me in a heartbeat. So let's set that aside, okay? What happens, happens." He squeezed Nevan's hand. "Ready to face Mario's family?"

"Are you sure I can't talk you out of letting me handle it?"

"Not to cast shade on you or your abilities, Nevan, but you *can't* handle it. Not without forfeiting to Yvo, and that *I* can't allow." Seb eyed the midway, where the clowns had spilled out of their tent again, this time doing handsprings in a complicated pattern that wouldn't be out of place in a Busby Berkeley film. "So like Jordan said, bring on the freaking clowns. They're the least of my worries."

Seb tugged Nevan through the gates, fumbling for his ticket, but the guard simply nodded at them and turned his attention elsewhere.

The midway was busier than it had been the last time they'd been here, with fairgoers lined up at the ring toss, the carousel, and some game called *Buttons of Mystery* that Seb didn't want to think about too much. He was about to veer away from the turquoise tent where he'd been a party to an inadvertent B & E when a tall, dark-haired man in a scarlet coat with more gold braid than a military review stepped outside its flap.

"Step right up," he called, his voice carrying easily across the noise of the crowd, "gentlefolk of all persuasions, and be terrified. Be awed. Be astounded by the prowess of Carnival of Mysteries' own *Gentleman Jim*." The knife thrower flung aside the canvas and emerged in a billow of brown leather duster, holding his assistant's hand aloft as he spun her to the side while the ringmaster dude continued his patter. "Gentleman Jim's feats of precision and daring will leave you breathless."

"Yeah, but *he's* not the one who's taking the risk, any more than the audience is," Seb muttered, but then slowed his roll. "Wait a minute." He frowned at the assistant. The sparkly faux-dancehall-girl outfit was identical down to the last sequin as far as he could tell, but the woman inside it was different. "Nevan, when we were here before, Gentleman Jim's assistant had red hair. This one's a blonde."

Nevan tore his attention from their big top destination with obvious difficulty. "So?"

Seb widened his eyes. "So, did you *see* the size of the First Aid kit in the rear tent? What if his other assistant was injured?" He gripped Nevan's lapels. "What if *we* caused it because we took that knife and he had to use another one that was weighted differently?" The bottom dropped out of Seb's stomach. "Oh, no, Nevan, what if she's dead? What if I *am* an assassin, even by accident?"

Nevan laid a gentle palm against Seb's cheek. "It's far more likely that the man has more than one assistant, don't you think?"

"I don't know *what* to think." He peered up at Nevan. "Should we ask? I mean, I don't want to throw *you* under that particular bus, and I don't want to confess to stealing something from his tent myself, because that *would* get the police on my trail, but—"

"Unlikely. You saw the array of knives in that cabinet. He had many to choose from."

"But—"

"Seb." Nevan's thumb traced Seb's bottom lip, causing his brain to short out for a second. "There may be no issue there at all. After all, the ringmaster, Gentleman Jim, and the assistant herself do not look concerned in any way, while we know of a real, true danger elsewhere. And you were right. We"—his smile was crooked—"that is, *you* must warn Mario's family."

Seb sighed. "Yes. Of course." He put his hand over Nevan's to hold it against his face for just that moment longer. "What can I say? Another side effect of working with children is the tendency to switch focus a little too quickly."

"Good man." Unfortunately, Nevan dropped his hand from Seb's face, but then—*score!*—laced their fingers together again. "Let us hope, since the ringmaster is out here, that the Galliers aren't in the middle of a show."

Seb's eyes widened. "Oh my word. You're right! If Mario should be mid-air—"

"He'll be perfectly safe." Nevan squeezed his hand. "Remember. The weapon isn't here, and Yvo still believes I have the assassin in my pocket."

I'd like to be in your pocket. I'd like to have you in my... *er...* *pocket.* Seb banished his lascivious thoughts. Time enough for *that* once the kids were safe. "Onward."

They headed for the big top, although they appeared to be the only ones doing so. The tent flap was closed but not laced shut.

Seb looked around at the busy midway, at fairgoers

streaming into other tents or lining up for rides and games. Maybe the reason everyone was out *here* was because nobody was in *there*. Which meant that the Galliers must be between shows.

That was... good. It meant that Seb would have a better chance of speaking to a responsible Gallier adult without alarming Mario.

Nevertheless, a lifetime of being a rule-follower had Seb hesitating at the tent entrance. "Do you suppose we can just waltz in?"

Nevan shrugged. "Our carnival admission grants us entrance to all the attractions. If they don't want us inside, someone will no doubt stop us." He held the flap aside. "After you."

Seb sidled inside, assailed at once by the scents of fresh sawdust and popcorn mingled with an earthier, slightly musty smell that must be the tent canvas. Empty bleachers ringed an oblong space defined by a white, shin-high railing. A gap in the rail opposite where they stood was probably where the performers entered and exited.

The tent itself was held up by three central poles, the middle one the highest, with platforms halfway and three-quarters of the way up the outer two. The lower pair of platforms had trapezes looped onto them. The upper two had a tightrope strung between them.

There was no net.

Seb gulped. *They let a* child *perform in this act with no safeguards?* What kind of family allowed that? Anger kindled in his middle, but he tamped it down... barely. A carnie's life was different, something many of them were born into. Chances were that young Mario was one such, but if ever they met face to face, Seb didn't think he'd be able to resist mentioning that the boy had *options*, just like everybody else.

The tent held no other people, although with the soft canvas walls, the sawdust underfoot, and the ranks of risers, the air felt almost thick, as though it would deaden any echo. A single forlorn balloon that had lost most of its helium drifted across the center of the ring at Seb's knee height, emphasizing their solitude.

As they moved forward, past the lowest bleachers and to the edge of the railing, a pale, brown-haired man in a black warmup suit with *Flying Galliers* across its front emerged from behind a curtain across from them. Between the hair, his pointed chin, and intense blue eyes, he reminded Seb a lot of a young Malcolm McDowell. He spotted them at once.

"Hello," he said with a smile. "I'm Paul. Have you come for a lesson?"

Seb glanced up at Nevan. Muscles bunched in his jaw and the divot between his eyebrows spoke of pain. *Guess it's up to me.* "Um... lesson?"

Paul gestured to a long, waist-high wooden beam at the far end of the central oval. "I can teach you to walk the beam—far wider than the tightrope and no danger to you. Although if you'd prefer to master the backflip"—he gestured to a trampoline about as big around as a manhole cover—"that can also be arranged."

"No, thank you." Seb swallowed once and lifted his chin, meeting Paul's gaze squarely. "We wanted to warn you."

For an instant, Paul's eyes glinted gold, and he looked almost... feral. "You are threatening me?"

Seb threw up one hand, since Nevan was clutching his other one in an almost painful grip. "No! But we've, um, heard of a threat. To Mario."

"Mario?" Paul's gaze sharpened. "What's the nature of this threat?"

"I can't really say, but I overheard something about him being targeted during your performance. While he was mid-air."

Paul's eyes narrowed and then—surprisingly—he laughed. "You needn't worry, then. Our performances for the rest of the day have been canceled."

Nevan sucked in a breath, and Seb said, "Really? All of them?"

"Boss's orders, and when Errante makes a decision, we've learned to listen. Our next show isn't until one o'clock tomorrow afternoon." He turned to go, but then glanced over his shoulder. "And you don't need to worry about Mario. We take care of our own."

CHAPTER 18

The burn in Nevan's brand flared hotter, and this time, instead of increasing in speed, the pulses grew in intensity, bursts of fire that nearly stole his breath. He gritted his teeth, glancing around for a secluded place for Yvo's upcoming comm manifestation.

"Well," Seb said, his tone laced with exasperation, "that didn't really go as planned. Do you think—" He looked up, and his expression morphed from exasperated to concerned. "Nevan. What is it?"

"Yvo," Nevan forced out, cradling his hand against his chest. "He wants to chat."

"How long do we have before he appears?"

"Not long. Seconds."

Seb shuddered. "We are *not* going back to that Fun House. Besides which, the midway is way too busy right now." He looked around and nodded briskly. "Come on."

He dragged Nevan back toward the entrance but then cut to the side, between the tent canvas and the rear-most rank of bleachers. "This is as good a place as any."

Nevan let Seb draw him into the shadows and backed against

the canvas so Yvo's simulacrum would be more hidden by the risers.

Seb let go of his hand and ducked, crawling under the bleachers until he couldn't go any farther. "Keep him talking."

"What?" Nevan was having a hard time focusing over the pain in his hand and middle.

"Get him monologuing again. It shouldn't be hard. Mage Evil loves to talk about himself. Ask him why he's doing this. What his plans are. Everything you can think of."

The penny dropped and Nevan almost laughed. "Because if he says it—"

"Then I'll hear it and *I'm* not bound by any curse. We can get help. For you. For Lulu." He cast an annoyed glance over his shoulder. "For Mario, even though his family doesn't think it's necessary."

The brand pounded like a red-hot drum and Nevan laid a finger across his lips. Seb nodded and curled himself into a ball, his arms around his knees as Yvo's image wavered into existence under the second row from the back, safely between Nevan and Seb.

Yvo crossed his arms, smirking. "I expected better from you. Did you truly believe you could hide from me in Faerie?"

Although the pain had lessened once Yvo materialized, Nevan still struggled to focus. "Faerie?"

"Don't try to deny it. I felt the kink in your tether when you passed its threshold." He chuckled. "You aren't as stalwart as you want to believe if my little pets could send you running for cover."

"The dust devils, you mean?"

"Of course. There are more where those came from, so best you keep that in mind. At least you had the sense not to linger in Faerie for more than a few minutes before making your way back to the carnival." He dusted off his palms and tucked his hands into his sleeves. "Well?"

Nevan frowned, trying to make sense of Yvo's words. *He*

thinks I crossed directly into Faerie. He doesn't know about the river-side. About my shift. About the time pocket.

Yvo tapped his foot, the curly toes of his velvet slippers bunching the hem of his robes. "Nevan. I am *waiting* for your report. Do you need further *incentive?*"

The fabric of Yvo's sleeve shifted as the mage bunched his fist, and Nevan had only a fraction of a second to brace himself against the wave of pain that crashed through his belly. He doubled over with a gasp. From the corner of his eye, he spotted Seb uncurling as though to launch himself forward to Nevan's aid. He shook his head to warn Seb to stand down—which he did, a worried frown clouding his face—although Yvo took it as an answer to his question.

"Good." The sleeve smoothed out again as Yvo unclenched his fist and the pain ebbed enough for Nevan to stand upright. "Proceed."

"There's been a further... complication."

"What have I told you about *complications?* You have a job to do. Do it or suffer the consequences." He drew one hand from his sleeve and raised it as though to sever the connection.

"Wait! This is none of our doing."

"'Our' doing?"

Nevan buried a wince. "Mine and the... assassin's."

Yvo's gaze sharpened. "Is the assassin privy to this conversation?"

"No." Which was technically the truth, since Seb wasn't the assassin.

Yvo nodded. "Since your geas constrains you to tell me the truth, I'll accept that. What is this *complication* of which you speak?"

"The Galliers' performances are canceled for the rest of today."

"What?" Yvo shrieked. "They can't be! Errante wouldn't allow it. They're the star attraction."

"If Errante is the carnival boss, apparently he ordered it

himself. The Galliers had no choice." Nevan caught Seb making a rolling motion with his hands. "If you want the assassin to target Mario today—"

"No! The dagger must fly when he is mid-air or the spell won't work and all my preparation will be for naught."

"Why does it make a difference? We've got the opportunity now. If we wait until tomorrow—"

"I told you, no."

"The assassin is going to want details," Nevan said, earning a nod and a smile from Seb through Yvo's transparent form. "They're already asking questions. I told them you knew what you were doing, but..." He shrugged.

"Too right." Yvo's expression turned smug. "Everyone assumes that mages can master only one element. That we must forge *alliances*"—he practically spat out the word—"to gain the cooperation of others. That's why the supe council thinks we're hobbled, restricted, *finite*." He spread his arms wide. "But *I. I* have discovered the secret. The secret of mastery over all!"

A chill skittered across Nevan's skin, although Seb's eyeroll and accompanying grimace did much to straighten his spine. "Over all? What do you mean?"

Yvo scoffed. "Over *everything*, fool. With Mario's heart, I shall conquer air, the most difficult as it is earth's opposite." His expression turned sly. "With the most powerful fire mage captive in Govannon's forge, I shall have little trouble obtaining an artifact from his mansion, not when I can fly over his pathetic stone wall and land on his very doorstep." His self-satisfied smirk made Nevan grind his molars. "When your sister joins me, I'll have spirit under my control as well."

Nevan couldn't help taking a stride forward, even though he couldn't throttle Yvo as he wished. "When the council finds out what you did—"

"How? *You* can't tell anyone. The assassin can't either. Assuming they wanted to risk prosecution—which no assassin worth their salt would do—the Guild contract binds them just as securely as it does me, as securely as your vow binds you. And once the council suspects, it will be too late. I'll have mastery over even the King and Queen of Faerie, because *my* magic will not be restricted by anything so paltry as my nature."

"You—"

Yvo held both palms up and pain shot through Nevan's belly again. His knees gave out, and he crumpled as Yvo laughed. "Remember your place, horse. I expect results tomorrow at the first performance. Any further delay and you'll be sorry." He slashed his arms through the air and disappeared.

The instant Yvo vanished, Seb rushed over to crouch next to Nevan. "Are you all right?"

Nevan shook his head, unable to get a word out over the waves of pain in both his chest and his hand. Seb wrestled his pack off his back. He pulled out an aluminum water bottle and flipped up its spout. "Here. I filled this from Tahmina's crock. Drink." He held the spout to Nevan's lips. "Clamp your teeth around it and suck."

Nevan met Seb's gaze as the water bathed his tongue and parched mouth.

What would it be like to suck on Seb?

From the way Seb's cheeks pinked, he was imagining other scenarios as well. Would his opinion change if he knew that Nevan had never... sucked on anyone before?

Some people were put off by inexperienced sexual partners, or so Nevan had heard. Others sought to take advantage. Seb, though...

Nevan didn't believe either was true of him, although for his sake, Nevan ought to banish such thoughts. *To save him from me, even if I can't save him from the council.*

Nevan let go of the spout. "Thank you."

Seb frowned at him. "Are you sure that's enough? You didn't take more than a mouthful."

"It will do for now." He stroked Seb's cheek. "You cared for me quite well earlier. I am good for a fair bit." He pushed himself to his feet.

Seb looked uncertain. "If you say so." He tucked the bottle back in the side pocket of his pack, a grin breaking out and making his dark eyes sparkle as he stood. "You did a *fantastic* job with Yvo. I mean, he couldn't have spilled any more if he'd been hit with truth serum. He told you *everything*."

Nevan frowned. "I'm not sure how that helps."

"Are you kidding? Not only do we have time—until tomorrow at one—but we've got information to share with our allies. We can go to the powers that be and let them know what Yvo has up his very OTT sleeve. Didn't you threaten him with the council, whoever they are?"

Nevan gripped Seb's shoulders. "We can't go to the council."

"Why not? They're the ones with the power to stop him, right? They're who he's trying to circumvent, after all. Along with other mages, of course, but if they're as bananapants as he is, I'm not as concerned. You don't have to say a word. Since I heard everything, I can tell them all about it."

Nevan bowed his head, resting his forehead against Seb's. "We can't go to the council because it's illegal for you to know what you know."

Seb frowned. "You mean because of the curse?"

"No. I mean it's illegal for humans to know about the supe community. Any supe who reveals our existence is punished. Severely."

"So you mean you…" Nevan nodded. "And Jordan?" He nodded again. "Tahmina? Noah?" Seb ran both hands through his hair. "But it's not their fault."

"We're not the only ones. Humans who discover our existence are likewise… affected."

"Affected how?"

"At the very least, your memory would be wiped. At the worst?" He winced. "I've heard of extreme cases in the past, including torture and even death. I don't know what steps they'd be likely to take now."

Seb chewed on his lower lip, turning it red and swollen, and making Nevan want to soothe it. With his tongue.

"We don't have to decide this minute. Come back to my place with me. We'll have dinner." He winked. "You can hydrate some more. Try out Tahmina's bath bombs. Then, when we're both feeling better—"

"May I kiss you?" Nevan blurted.

Seb blinked, and his smile turned shy. "We can put that on the agenda. I'd like that. Very much, in fact."

"No." Nevan licked his lips, which weren't as dry as they had been—*thanks to Seb*. "I mean now. May I kiss you now?"

CHAPTER 19

Seb's belly fluttered, and he squealed internally like one of his charges at a bouncy castle.

A man as beautiful as Nevan—a magical being out of *folklore*, for goodness' sake—wanted to kiss him. Again.

He laid his palm against Nevan's cheek. "Yes."

Nevan's smile bloomed but then it wobbled and instead of leaning in for a kiss, he listed sideways and started to topple.

"Whoa!" Seb managed to dodge around and brace Nevan before his center of gravity shifted too far: If he'd actually tipped over that balance point, Seb would never have been able to prop him up.

"I… I'm sorry." Nevan frowned, his brows pinched together and unmistakable pain in his eyes, as he leaned heavily against Seb. "I don't know what's the matter."

"I think I do," Seb said darkly. "Or if not exactly, I at least know who to blame."

"What do you mean?"

Seb led Nevan over to a riser. The graceless way he collapsed onto the hard wooden plank said a lot about how horrible he must be feeling. One of the first things Seb had noticed about him was his innate, controlled grace, as though every part of his body was under his precise, conscious control.

Seb sat next to him and took his hand, and swore he could almost *feel* the skin drying under his palm. "Before we came back to the carnival—heck, before Yvo launched his supernatural Zoom meeting—you were feeling pretty good, right?"

"Yes." His crooked smile as he gazed down at Seb nearly broke Seb's heart. "Thanks to you."

"How about now?"

Nevan looked away but didn't answer immediately. He didn't have to. Seb could see it in the dullness of his hair, his sunken cheeks, his shadowed eyes, so different from his appearance when they'd walked through the carnival gates.

Finally, he exhaled slowly. "It's the geas."

"Heck yeah, it's the geas. But I think the geas doesn't just activate when you're not pursuing your given task." Seb tapped the fingers of his free hand against his knee, thinking. "How did Mage Evil know where you were just now, anyway? It's not like the space under the bleachers screams *carnival*. It's pretty dark, not to mention nondescript."

"Earth mages can scry in any clear stone or crystal. He probably looked for me that way."

Seb snorted. "Figures there would be a magical equivalent for a Find My Phone app, but I don't think that's it. That's... what do you call it? A *pull* condition. You have to *ask* for the information before you get it. He made it sound more like a *push* situation, that your data is being fed to him constantly."

"I don't understand."

"Sorry, I'm not explaining this very well." He shifted on the hard bench so he was facing Nevan more fully. "He said there was a *kink in the tether*, like he's *plugged in* to you with some kind of power cable and something happened to cut off the juice. Tell me." Seb laid his hand on Nevan's arm. "Exactly how do elemental mages power their spells?"

"They..." Nevan swallowed, his throat clicking. "They are not magical beings, not like other supes. We are magical by nature, and our strengths as well as our weaknesses are bounded by that nature from the moment we first draw breath. Mages are born with potential. An aptitude. A quality, like artistic talent or perfect pitch, and an affinity for one of the five elements."

"Five? I thought there were four. Air, fire, water, earth."

"Spirit is the fifth. Lulu is a creature of spirit." He lifted one shoulder, as though he didn't have the strength for a full-on shrug. "I suppose you could say there are six, technically."

"What's the sixth?"

Nevan glanced sidelong at Seb. "Death. But necromancers don't class themselves with the other elemental mages. They don't have an affinity for death. They simply choose its power."

"Don't tell me." Seb closed his eyes and shuddered. "I don't even want to know."

"In any case, a human with mage aptitude must still be trained, undergo certain trials, understand the artifacts of their element, and master how to manipulate them for their spells. It is those artifacts, the spell ingredients, that generate the magic, which the mage's affinity is able to harness. That affinity is what makes it impossible for a mage to master more than one element." His broken laugh morphed into a dry, hacking cough that had Seb scrabbling in his pack for the water bottle. "At least until now."

Seb held the bottle to Nevan's lips. "Drink." Nevan sighed but closed his eyes and took far too small a sip. "Nevan. *Drink*."

He shook his head. "You have little left. We must conserve. *I* must conserve."

"Bullpucky." Seb shook the bottle, the water sloshing inside. "I'll go back to the Doghouse and get more if I need to. *Drink*."

He eyed Seb. "You're very bossy."

"I'm a nanny. You ever try to get a room full of toddlers to clean up their Legos? Of course I'm bossy." He gave Nevan a mock scowl. "Do I have to break out the time-out stool?"

Nevan blinked. "You have a stool in your pack?"

"No. But a time-out stool can be anything and anywhere. Now *drink*."

Nevan sighed again, but he complied, and the almost desperate way he gulped the water told Seb he'd been right to insist.

When he finished, leaving the bottle nearly empty, he looked *marginally* better. "Thank you."

"You're welcome." Seb tucked the bottle away in his pack and took a deep breath. "Know what I think?"

A shadow of Nevan's smile trembled on his lips. "I daren't hazard a guess."

"I think Yvo's powering his spells with *you*."

Nevan's eyebrows rose. "When I swore to the geas—"

"No, not just your vow, although that probably gave him the... the *permission* to forge the connection, like inviting a vampire to cross your threshold."

"They don't need permission, although few of them would be so impolite as to enter your home without your consent."

Seb blinked. "There are *vampires?*" He held up a palm. "Never mind. Not relevant at the moment. But think about it. You felt fine *before* the call, but as soon as it was over, you felt like crap. Weaker. Because all the strength you'd managed to build up got sucked away by Yvo's little one-man show. You said mages aren't themselves magical. He has to get the juice from somewhere, and I'll bet anything you like that he's getting it from the magical being he's got under his control. In other words, you."

Comprehension flickered across Nevan's face, followed by horror. "Lulu. If he does the same with her... She's only a child, she doesn't have the strength—"

"Sweetheart," Seb said, keeping his voice calm, "at the moment, she's probably stronger than you."

He clutched Seb's hands. "We have to find her. We have to get her back. We can't let—"

"Shhh." Seb freed one hand and laid a finger across Nevan's

lips, which were now dry and cracked. "We'll find her. We'll keep both her and Mario out of Yvo's clutches."

Years of telling kids that things would *be all right* allowed Seb to keep his voice firm and confident, although he really had no clue how to accomplish either goal. But they had allies now. Options. None of which would help if Nevan collapsed.

"Let's take advantage of this reprieve, okay? For tonight, come back to my place with me. We'll see about restoring your strength with Tahmina's bath bombs, fresh squeezed orange juice, and homemade chicken soup."

For an instant, Nevan's expression coupled relief with longing, but then he set his jaw and turned away. "You'd have to spoon-feed me."

Seb placed a finger on that determined chin and turned Nevan to meet his gaze. "I don't mind if you don't." He aimed for a cheeky grin. "After all, I've had lots of practice feeding people and you'll be far less likely than my usual companions to knock the bowl on the floor or launch a spoonful of spinach at my face." He stood up, shouldered his pack, and held out a hand. "What do you say we blow this clown-infested pop stand and go home?"

Nevan grasped Seb's hand and Seb had to brace his feet to help haul him off the riser. "Before we left the Doghouse, Jordan replenished my FTA vouchers, but I'm not certain we can call a driver here. There are far too many humans about."

Seb lifted a brow. "I didn't exactly take a stroll through Faerie to meet you this morning, you know. My car is parked in the lot outside the coffee shop. Let's go—and *not* through the Fun House."

"Goddess, no," Nevan muttered. When he staggered forward a step, Seb wrapped his arm around his waist.

"Drape your arm across my shoulder."

"I'm too heavy," Nevan fretted.

"You're heavier than the average five-year-old, true, but I

don't actually have to carry you. As long as you do your part to remain ambulatory, I'll do mine to keep you upright."

So, like Seb's fantasy version of a three-legged race, they made their way out of the big top and through the milling crowds to the gates. The tall guard nodded to them as they exited, but didn't approach.

Seb had been half worried that someone would assume Nevan was drunk or otherwise impaired and interfere, but they made it all the way back down Cornell to the parking lot without anyone so much as giving them a second glance.

On the one hand, Seb was relieved that he didn't have to explain. But on the other, he was outraged.

What if I really had drugged him and was taking him off for nefarious nonconsensual purposes? Jeez, people, if you see something, say something.

Nevan stumbled to a halt, staring when Seb used the key fob to unlock the car doors. *"This* is your vehicle?"

Seb bristled a little at Nevan's bewildered tone. He was actually rather proud of his Sienna. A hybrid, because climate change was a thing, and white because it was proven to be the safest color from a visibility standpoint. He'd bought it new because he wanted the latest child-safety features, and had counted on the job with Mrs. Macclesfield to let him keep up the payments. Now that didn't look like a possibility. He swallowed. How long before he'd miss a payment and lose it?

"What can I say? Nothing like a minivan to bring all the boys to my yard."

Nevan looked down at him, his brows drawn together. "And does it?"

Seb forced a smile. "Only the ones who are clamoring for a trip to the playground or the ice cream parlor. Let's get you situated."

He supported Nevan to the front passenger door—the only option without a booster seat. After he helped Nevan climb in, he played out the seatbelt and leaned over to fasten it with a click.

"Don't worry. I don't live far from here. We'll have you feeling better soon."

Before Seb could close the door, Nevan grasped his forearm, his grip gentle. "Thank you."

As Seb gazed up into those impossibly deep, dark eyes, his middle fluttered again. "I'm happy to help."

Nevan tilted his head, a smile tugging his dry lips. "You really are, aren't you?"

"I do try."

Seb patted Nevan's shoulder before shutting the door carefully. He seriously doubted that willingness to help would be enough to foil Yvo's schemes, free Nevan and Lulu, and keep Mario safe.

He straightened his shoulders and palmed the key fob. *I'm Seb Ardelean, experienced nanny. I can withstand both tantrums and puppy-dog eyes when enforcing reasonable bedtimes.* Surely he could channel that resolve into a little anti-mage ruthlessness.

He jogged around to the driver's side. "Keep telling yourself that, Seb," he muttered, "and maybe someday it'll actually be true."

CHAPTER 20

"*N*evan. Nevan?"

The soft voice murmuring his name twined around Nevan's heart. He wanted to wrap it tighter, nestle into it forever.

"Nevan." This time, the voice was laced with unmistakable worry. "Hey." A warm hand closed on his shoulder and gave him a gentle shake. "Are you all right? Nevan. Can you hear me? Can you open your eyes?"

"Don't want to," he mumbled, trying to chase the dream that had cocooned him so sweetly, but it was slipping away, dissipating like lake mist at sunrise, until he couldn't even remember what it was about, only that its loss made his chest ache.

"I know." This time, the voice held amusement. "But we're here. And I think you'll feel better inside." The hand squeezed his shoulder. "Come on, big guy. Let's get you fed, hydrated, and in bed."

Nevan jerked, his chest colliding with a strap that held him in place, and somehow managed to lift his eyelids, even though they felt as though they were lined with sand. "Bed?"

A warm chuckle from his left tumbled him back toward that

lovely dream. "I'm not sure what to think that you homed in on that option."

Blinking furiously, Nevan fought to bring his surroundings into focus. The first thing he saw was a narrow face, light umber skin, warm brown eyes behind wire-framed spectacles, full lips curved in a smile. "Seb," he croaked, the warmth in his middle unfurling like a night-blooming waterlily.

"That's right." Seb reached down next to Nevan's hip and, after a soft *click*, the pressure across his lap and down his chest disappeared. "We're at my place. Hold on while I run around and open the door for you." Seb turned away, did something with the car door that made it swing wide, and slid out from behind the steering wheel.

"I can open my own door," Nevan grumbled.

"Uh huh." Seb bent down and peered inside. "Just wait, Nevan. Let me help you."

Nevan curled his fingers into his palms, fighting his instinct to protest. He'd never accepted help from anyone, although to be fair, nobody had ever offered. It was... an unfamiliar sensation, although not an unpleasant one.

"Very well," Nevan mumbled. Then hastily added, "Thank you," in a less defensive tone.

"Good." Seb closed his door and as he trotted around the front of the car, Nevan peered through the windshield at their surroundings.

They were parked in the short driveway of a brown-shingled bungalow. Two gracefully curved dormers centered above the two wide windows on either side of the front door made the house look as though it were raising its eyebrows, although not in a judgmental way. A herringbone-patterned brick sidewalk lined with purple and yellow pansies and flanked by neat patches of brilliant green grass led to a wide porch. The steps, also brick, curved outward, contributing to the impression that the house was smiling eagerly in welcome.

Even though the house sat on a tree-lined street, separated

from its neighbors by not more than ten feet on either side, and Nevan was accustomed to having nobody within miles of his lake, he somehow felt at home here—and he hadn't even gotten out of Seb's car yet.

Seb opened Nevan's door, snapping him out of his reverie. "Ready to come inside?"

"This is your place?" Nevan swiveled to climb out of the car, slapping a hand on its roof to catch himself when his knees threatened to buckle.

"Whoops!" Seb wrapped an arm around Nevan's waist to steady him. "Yeah, it was my bună's. That is, my grandmother's. She left it to me."

Nevan looked down into Seb's eyes. "I'm sorry for your loss. Was it recent?"

Seb grinned up at him. "Oh, she didn't die. She just moved to Germany." He eased Nevan away from the car and closed the door with a bump of his hip.

"Your family is German, then?" Nevan had to lean on Seb to make it to the porch and up the steps, and even then, he arrived ridiculously out of breath.

"Nope. Well, not really. Both my grandparents are Romanian, but moved to West Germany in the Seventies, which was *not* easy to do. My dad was their only son, and my mom was in the military, stationed over there, so we moved around with her postings. Bună and Bunic moved to Oregon when I was about six." He stopped outside the burnished oak front door, a half-circle leaded light at head height echoing the curve of the stairs and the dormers. "Think you can stand on your own while I open the door?"

When Nevan scowled, Seb squeezed his forearm. "Needing assistance isn't shameful, Nevan. It doesn't make you *less*. You're being magically mummified by Mage Evil, and even if you weren't, everybody can use a little help now and then."

Nevan heaved a sigh. "You're right." He braced a hand on the wide door frame. "There. I'll do now."

Seb's smile made Nevan's knees wobble again, but he managed to hide it. He hoped.

"Excellent. Won't be much longer." Seb hurriedly unlocked the door and pushed it wide before propping his shoulder under Nevan's arm again and leading him inside. "Let's get your bath started first so you can soak while I fix you something to eat."

"You don't have to—"

"Hey." Seb glared at Nevan over the top of his spectacles. "What did I say about accepting help?"

"Thank you," Nevan said meekly.

"That's better." He kicked the door closed with a backward swipe of his foot and supported Nevan through a cozy living room, its gleaming oak floors protected by hand-braided rag rugs in subtle rusts, browns, and golds. The long sofa and cushy-looking armchairs were upholstered in brocade fabric in the same colors. Three of the walls were painted rust, but the one with the fireplace was decorated with a mural—a forest scene at dawn, the waters of a lake just visible between the trees. Instead of a mantel, a curved niche above the fireplace held a wooden camelback clock, its brass face gleaming in the sunlight streaming in through the windows.

A set of glass-paned French doors opened into a dining room with a long trestle table that Nevan identified as cherry, two highchairs pulled up along one side. They had to turn sideways to walk down the hallway and into the bathroom.

"Here we go." Once Nevan was within reach of the vanity, Seb eased himself away. He pushed aside the shower curtain in a clatter of metal rings and turned on the taps. "Use the facilities if you need to. I'll grab my pack out of the van and collect the bath bombs." He grinned as he stood, his lenses clouded from the hot water. "Don't worry. I'll knock before I come back in."

He closed the door behind him, and Nevan absently tracked the patter of his footsteps through the house. He sighed, staring down at the huge clawfoot bathtub, which actually looked large enough for him with room to spare. He watched the steam billow and curl in a seductive dance that had him reaching out, fingers spread, an invitation for water to bead along his skin, to meld with him, to—

A knock at the door had him snatching his hand back.

"Nevan? May I come in?"

Nevan scrubbed his palms along the outside of his trousers. "Yes."

Seb slipped inside with a grin. He brandished a blue-green sphere about the size of a grapefruit. "Here's the good stuff."

"I'm not sure..." Nevan took a shaky breath. "This has the potential to be anything from useless to uncomfortable to disastrous. The risk might be too great." Although his soul *yearned* for water's caress, it was *wild* water he craved, so fiercely that his heart felt as though it might burst.

Seb glanced from Nevan to the object in his hand. "Tahmina said this would work, and since she's a djinn—" He blinked, shaking his head. "I can't believe I said that like it was as normal as saying *since she's a Republican.*" He shivered. "Although *that* would definitely be creepy. Anyway, djinn, so I suppose she knows what you need. Besides, we haven't got any alternatives other than going back through that Fun House, and I, for one, am *so* done with clowns and anything made in their image." He met Nevan's gaze, biting his lip. "Will the effect be immediate? I mean, if it *doesn't* work and the treated water starts to drain you or... What *does* it do, exactly?"

"Allergic reaction," Nevan said.

Seb's eyes grew round behind his glasses. "Anaphylactic shock?"

"I... don't know? I've never immersed myself in it before."

"I've only got stuff on hand to treat mild reactions—Benadryl and hydrocortisone cream—but does human medicine even work with your physiology?"

Nevan was three heartbeats from passing out, so he really couldn't muster the energy to care. "If not, we can call St. Stupid's."

"St. Stupid's?"

"The supe medimagical wing of United Memorial Hospital."

"There's a supe *hospital?*" Seb closed his eyes and shook his head. "Never mind. Still not relevant."

He tossed the sphere into the tub and it dissolved immediately, almost as though it were made of smoke, which, considering it came from a djinn, a creature of fire, might actually have been the case. The scents wafting up from the water had tears prickling Nevan's eyes. *Mist on mossy stones. Cattails bobbing along the shore. Willow branches tickling the lake surface.* He sighed. *Home.*

Seb sniffed appreciatively. "Wow. That's the most realistic-smelling bath bomb I've ever, um, smelled. It's like being beside a forest pool." He wiggled his hand under the tap. "Or a forest hot spring." He shook droplets off his fingers and shot a worried glance over his shoulder. "The water's pretty hot. How warm do you usually like your baths or showers?"

Nevan smiled wryly. "I've never had a warm bath. Or a shower at all, unless you count standing under a waterfall."

Seb's jaw sagged. "What? *Never?* How old are you again?"

"Old enough. But recall, I'm a creature of the water. I spend most of my days in lakes or rivers, which aren't known for their heat, especially during spring runoff."

"Do you—" Seb bit his lip around a grimace. "I don't want to be insensitive or anything, seeing as I know nothing about ceffyl dŵr mythology—or I guess it would be culture, right, since you're *clearly* not a myth—but do you *have* to stay underwater so much? Could you live more on land if you wanted?"

"I suppose. I've spent more time out of my element since I found Lulu, but before that, there was never any reason to emerge." Nevan's middle clenched and twisted, the urge to hide rolling over him. "And when I did, I invoked one of two reactions in humans: terror or avarice." He reached out and touched Seb's shoulder gently. "You're the only one whose reaction was to help, not to run or to control. I thank you for that."

Seb's smile was far too diffident for Nevan's liking—a man

with a heart that large should *never* feel inadequate. "Trust me. It was no trouble."

"Seb, I..." Black spots danced before Nevan's eyes and he swayed, but then Seb's shoulder was there, supporting him, steadying him, grounding him.

"Let's get you into the water, huh? We can talk while you eat."

Nevan squinted, trying to focus on Seb's face despite his impaired vision. "You'll eat too, correct?"

"I'm fine. I'm not the one who's been deprived of food and water for however long."

"Unacceptable," Nevan growled. "If I must be fed like a tooth-less babe, the least you can do is join me."

Seb hummed tunelessly, tapping his lips with his forefinger. "If I agree, will you get in the tub?"

"Yes."

"All right. I'll bring enough for two." He winked. "And maybe I'll let you feed *me*. It'll be a change to be on the other end of the spoon." He levered Nevan to his feet, keeping a hand on his shoulder and another on his ribs. "Can you stand? Do you need help"—he gulped, and pink infused his brown cheeks—"undressing?"

"I can manage." Nevan shrugged out of his duster, but then stared at it in his hand. Should he drop it on the floor? Was that a violation of Seb's hospitality?

"Here. I'll take that." Seb took the coat and folded it over his arm. "I'll hang it up in the closet so it won't get crumpled."

Nevan chuckled as he unbuttoned his waistcoat. "It's survived worse than wrinkles over the years. You don't need to go to the trouble."

Seb mock glared at him. "It's hardly a stretch of my abilities to hang up a freaking coat, Nevan. Give me a little credit."

Nevan reached out, intending to trace the line of Seb's jaw until he noticed the dry, flaking skin on his fingertip. *Not precisely pleasing.* "I have complete faith in your abilities, *fy annwyl.*" Nevan froze. He hadn't intended to let the endearment

E.J. RUSSELL

slip out, but Seb didn't react to being called *my dear* in Welsh. *Good.* "I simply don't want to inconvenience you."

"Then do me a favor and get in the tub before the water cools."

When Nevan grinned at Seb's bossy tone, he felt his lower lip split, so he turned quickly to hide the additional evidence of his unattractive state. "As you wish."

For some reason, that caused Seb's breath to catch, but he didn't say anything else, and as Nevan shed his waistcoat, the door clicked closed.

CHAPTER 21

"*A*s you wish," Seb muttered to himself as he stowed Nevan's duster in his coat closet. "Way to activate all my *Princess Bride* fantasies, Nevan."

Nevan was a sort of combination of the *PB* rescue team, though, wasn't he? Sure, he had Westley's steadfast loyalty, but he was also almost as tall as Fezzik the giant, had the swash-buckling vibe of Inigo Montoya, and would probably give Princess Buttercup a run for her money in the beauty department.

And I'm just a nanny. A human nanny. Who may or may not be subject to some unspecified punishment for even knowing *Nevan* existed, not to mention curses, and evil magicians, and freaking *assassin's guilds.*

He sighed and shuffled into the kitchen, its sunny yellow walls and butcher-block countertops not cheering him as they normally did. He approached the fridge, its door covered three-deep in artwork from kids he'd cared for, and peered inside. As he'd thought, he had a nice big pot of Radauti sour soup, made last night with Bună's special recipe. Plenty for two. He pulled it out and set it on the stove to reheat, hoping that his homemade stock was far enough from tap water that it would be safe for Nevan to eat.

In the meantime, though, Nevan really needed something to drink. Seb glanced through the dining room doorway, frowning at the blue ceramic fruit bowl in the middle of the table. Bananas weren't exactly juicy, and the few apples and oranges would only yield a glassful, if that. Although Seb always bought juice that wasn't made from concentrate, he couldn't be completely confident that it didn't have some kind of preservative or residue from the manufacturing process that would adversely affect Nevan. If only he'd—

The doorbell rang.

Seb inhaled sharply, pressing a hand to his chest where the sound seemed to echo, bouncing around his ribcage. He wasn't expecting anyone. Could it be someone from the agency, coming to do a surprise home visit, or to interrogate him about why he'd missed the appointment with Mrs. Macclesfield's representative? For that matter, could it be Mrs. Macclesfield's representative? Or worse, since Mage Evil could track Nevan, might he have changed his MO and sent more golems?

"Chill out, Ardelean," he muttered. "It's highly unlikely that animate dust can ring doorbells."

But Mage Evil might have other, more sentient minions under his control. After all, he had Nevan, didn't he? Seb set his jaw. *Not for much longer if I can help it.*

Still, a bit of caution made sense, so he ducked low and crept through the dining room to the living room, where he could peek through the big plate-glass window over his couch.

A mid-sized delivery truck was parked at the curb in front of the house, its company name—*Oasis*—emblazoned on its blue-green door and panels. Through the fanlight in the door, he spotted a ball cap in the same blue-green.

Okay then. He exhaled slowly, willing his heart to stop racing as he stood upright and walked to the door.

The man on the porch was dressed in what was clearly a

uniform: black trousers, a blue-green shirt that matched the hat and truck, with his name—*Bob*—embroidered above the shirt pocket. He glanced at the clipboard in his hand. "Seb Ardelean?"

"That's me."

"Sign here." Bob thrust the clipboard at Seb.

"For what?"

"I just deliver the goods, pal. You gonna sign or what?"

Oasis. That had to be a good sign, right? Seb studied the form, searching for the shipper's address and—*ah.*

The Doghouse.

Seb's heart finally settled down, and he smiled as he scrawled his name and handed the clipboard back to Bob. Bob looked at it, grunted, and then trotted back to his truck.

"Do you need any help?" Seb called.

"Nah," Bob said above the clatter of the truck's rear roller door. He slid out a metal ramp with more clatter. "I got it."

He disappeared up the ramp and then reappeared with a hand truck laden with a large box and a plastic five-gallon bottle of water. He wheeled them up the path and offloaded them in front of the porch.

"There's more in the truck. Can you take these inside while I fetch 'em?"

"Sure. No problem."

Seb hurried down the steps as Bob headed back to his truck, humming tunelessly. Seb hefted the water and staggered up the steps with it. He left it on the dining table and returned for the box. It was bulky, but when Seb lifted it, it wasn't particularly heavy. He carried it inside and set it next to the water so he could slit it open with his pocket knife.

A folded sheet of paper lay atop crumpled packing material. With a shaking hand, Seb opened it and read:

Dear Seb and Nevan,

You'll need this.

Best, Tahmina

Seb's eyes prickled. *Allies.* He and Nevan didn't have to figure this out on their own. He tossed the packing paper onto the table, exposing a blue and white crock with a spigot on the side. He knew exactly what it was—a water dispenser intended to hold a five gallon jug of water just like this one. *Perfect.*

Tucked next to the crock was a small wooden box, the carving on its lid depicting a pool surrounded by palm trees.

Seb chuckled. *Another oasis.* He flipped up the lid. A tightly folded paper lay atop a nest of tiny silver globes that looked a lot like the decorations Seb broke out when he made holiday cookies with his charges. Seb unfolded the note.

Crush and add to food for safe consumption. Note: Only works with food that has encountered fire.

Seb picked up one tiny sphere between his thumb and forefinger. Food that has encountered fire. So… Soup yes, tap water no. A tightness in Seb's belly eased. He didn't need to worry about Nevan having an adverse reaction to the stock now.

With Bob continuing to ferry more five-gallon bottles from the truck—were there actually ten of them?—Seb wouldn't have to worry about running out of water, either.

By the time Bob finished unloading and took off, Seb had the dispenser arranged on the kitchen counter and one of the bottles installed. He filled a glass and hurried down the hallway to knock on the bathroom door.

"Nevan? I have something for you to drink. May I come in?"

"Come." Nevan's voice was languid and husky, which either meant he was enjoying the bath or—*crap!*

What if Tahmina's bath bomb hadn't worked? What if Nevan was in the throes of anaphylaxis? What kind of caregiver was Seb that he hadn't waited to make sure Nevan wasn't in distress?

He flung the door open and charged in. "Are you o—" Seb's own mouth dried, because he'd forgotten several pertinent details about Nevan being in the bath.

One: The tub was big, but Nevan was bigger.

Two: The bath bomb didn't cloud the water, like *at all*.

Three: Nevan was naked.

Nevan's head was resting on the lip of the tub, his bent knees poking out above the water. He rolled his head to the side and smiled at Seb. "This feels wonderful."

"Good," Seb croaked. He thrust the glass out, causing water to slosh over the rim. "I brought water. From Tahmina. She sent more. Water. So much..." He couldn't keep his gaze from drifting over Nevan's body. "Water. So much water." He clapped a hand over his eyes. "I'm sorry. I'm staring at you like a creeper. I should give you some privacy."

Nevan's chuckle was low and warm. "If you do that, how will I drink all this water you mention?"

"Right. Drink. Yes." With his eyes still covered, Seb shuffled toward the tub.

"Seb."

"Yeah? Ow!" He flexed his toes that he'd somehow managed to stub on one of the tub's clawed feet.

"You can look at me. I don't mind."

Seb peeked through his fingers, keeping his gaze *firmly* aimed at Nevan's face. "You don't?"

"Those of us who change forms cannot be too concerned with nudity as we cannot shift while clothed. We talked of this before."

"Ah. Yes. Right. I remember." He squeaked when he felt a soft caress on the outside of his knee.

"And I would welcome your gaze on me. If"—Nevan's voice roughened, tone turning uncertain—"you don't find me monstrous."

"Are you *kidding* me right now?" Seb dropped his hand, the better to scowl—and ogle. "I'm practically *drooling*. Besides, I already told you. You're a wonder."

"But you wouldn't kiss me before." He lowered his gaze. "In the tent."

"Because you looked like you were about to pass out. Or dry up and blow away. Not to mention being in pain from Mage

Evil's little one-man show. You weren't exactly in shape to give full consent."

Nevan smiled slowly and a little shyly, although he let his knees fall open and *gah!* "I'm feeling much better now."

With monumental effort—really, Seb defied Olympic athletes, or heck, Olympic *gods* to match his determination—Seb tore his gaze away from Nevan's cock, although it was head and... well... *head* above the water and seemed to be waving at him.

"I can, um, see that." Seb blew out a breath. "But you still need to drink. And eat. And finish your bath."

"You are, of course, correct."

Nevan sat upright, sloshing water up the sides of the tub and fully submerging his cock again—not that Seb was looking. Directly. But that thing was really hard to miss, even out of the corner of his eye.

Resolutely, he held the glass to Nevan's lips, which already looked smooth and tempting, flaky no longer. He tilted the glass, careful not to tip it too far despite his trembling hand, and Nevan closed his eyes and drank.

And OMG, the *sound* that Nevan made... Not quite a moan, more like a throaty purr that tightened Seb's groin.

Cool your jets, Ardelean. He's still not completely well.

But later, after the bath, after food and water, Seb was definitely revisiting the kiss option to see if he could tease that sound out of Nevan *that* way. A lot.

Nevan finished the last of the water and smiled. "Thank you."

"I'll get more. And some soup. I made it with homemade stock." He scrambled to his feet and hugged the glass to his chest. "Although stock is made with water. But Tahmina sent along this stuff for me to sprinkle on your food to make it safe, so I'll put some of that in and bring more water and—"

"Seb?" Nevan's tone was fond. "You needn't reassure me. I trust you."

"Oh, mercy. I was babbling. Was I? Babbling? Because I'm

not used to having big, hot men in my bathtub. Jase didn't like me to come into the bathroom when he was in here, even if he was just brushing his teeth or shaving, and he wasn't, you know, *you*, so even if I *had* come in, it wouldn't have been the same as—"

"Jase?" Nevan growled, his eyebrows bunched in a frown. "Who is this Jase?"

Seb blinked. "Um. My ex? We broke up a while ago. He didn't approve of my profession."

Nevan's expression cleared, and he leaned back in the tub again. "The more fool he, then."

Warmth pooled under Seb's heart. "Why do you say that?"

"Caring for others—keeping them safe, keeping them well, keeping them happy—is our highest calling. Anyone who doesn't appreciate a person like you, a person who looks after others so beautifully"—Nevan's smile was wry—"whether those others make it easy or not, doesn't deserve that person." He lifted one hand out of the water and traced Seb's cheek. "Never doubt that, Seb. He doesn't deserve you." He let his hand fall across his belly. "I'm not certain that anyone does."

Seb narrowed his eyes. "Okay, I call bullshit on that."

"You don't think kindness and care are our first duty?"

Seb set the glass aside and reached out to capture Nevan's hand. "First, taking care of others isn't a duty to me. It's a privilege. I do it because it brings me joy, but I'm just as capable of being petty and vindictive as anybody else. I'm no saint."

Nevan squeezed his hand. "Ah, I fear we must agree to disagree about that."

"And second," Seb said, raising his voice to make his point, "*everyone* deserves that kindness and care." He frowned. "Well, maybe not *everyone*. I exempt people like Mage Evil who have lost any vestige of kindness themselves. But if you're talking about yourself, Nevan? You deserve kindness and care more than almost anyone I know. Because you are willing to do *anything* for someone you love."

167

Nevan's expression turned bleak. "But in so doing, I've condemned another. I'm just as bad as—"

"Shhh." Seb laid a finger across Nevan's lips. "You're not. Because you don't want to hurt anyone else, not by choice." He grinned. "And anyway, we're going to stop Mage Evil in his tracks and save your sister *without* hurting anybody else in the process."

"We are?" Nevan said behind Seb's finger. "How?"

"Well... I'm not sure. But I've coordinated the extracurricular activities for a family with four kids before, and if I could get a four-year-old, a seven-year-old, a ten-year-old, and a thirteen-year-old to playgroup, swimming lessons, soccer practice, and ballet class respectively on time, every time? Figuring out how to foil one narcissistic jerk with a terminal case of arrogance and tunnel vision will be a piece of cake."

CHAPTER 22

*C*ould Seb be right? Could Nevan truly be worthy of hope, of redemption, of love?

Could I be worthy of him?

Nevan wanted that, wanted that so much that his *calon* ached with it, burned for it. No, not burned—*yearned*. But how to do it? How could Nevan convince Seb that he was capable of being something other than a monster?

He steepled his fingers and tapped them against his lips. Perhaps... Perhaps he could use Seb as a model? Nevan knew of none better. If he showed Seb the same consideration that Seb had shown Nevan since they met... Yes. Yes, that would at least begin the journey.

So when Seb returned with an enormous, steaming bowl of soup, its aroma making Nevan's mouth water, Nevan sat up in a slosh of bath water. "Where is your bowl?"

Seb blinked. "What?"

"You are in need of sustenance too."

"I'm fine. You're the one with Mage Evil sucking out your essence." Seb's cheeks took on a ruddy glow. "That is, draining your energy."

Nevan crossed his arms. "I will eat if you will." When Seb

frowned, Nevan nearly laughed. He was adorable when he was cross.

"But it's liquid. I need to feed it to you. I can't—"

"Get another bowl. You can feed me, and *I* will feed *you*."

Seb blinked again, his eyebrows lifting. "Well, that's… different."

"Those are my terms. Take them or leave them."

"You are so… *Fine*." Seb stood and set the bowl on the vanity. "I'll be back." He paused at the door. "And just in case you're not up on your human cultural references, that particular phrase doesn't always end well."

"I'll take my chances." Nevan slid down to rest his head on the tub lip. "I trust you."

"Oh. Well. Good." He backed out of the room, banging his shoulder on the door frame. "I'll just, um, get that soup, then."

When he returned, he held not only another, smaller bowl, but a short wooden stool that he plopped down next to the tub. He handed the smaller bowl to Nevan, along with a spoon, all while staring fixedly at his feet.

"This one's for me. It doesn't have the special stuff in it that makes it safe for you, so be sure not to taste it." He turned away to retrieve Nevan's soup from the vanity, but stayed there, the bowl cradled to his chest. "Maybe you should have more to drink first. Do you want more to drink? I should get another glass of water. The soup's probably too hot. I could—"

"Seb."

Seb didn't turn, but he looked up and met Nevan's gaze in the mirror. "Um, yeah?"

"You're babbling."

"I am?" Seb exhaled, his shoulders sagging. "Oh, heavens. I am. I'm sorry. It's just—"

"I make you nervous."

Seb's mirrored eyes widened almost comically. "You *think*?"

The back of Nevan's throat burned. "I still frighten you."

"What?" Seb whirled, and soup slopped over the edge of the

bowl to dribble onto the floor. "No. That's not it at all. It's just..." He glanced away again. "I'm a *nanny*, Nevan. I'm trained to avoid inappropriate behavior. To *report* inappropriate behavior when I see it. But you're *naked*, and all I want to do is gawk at you like some pervy locker room lurker."

The burn faded and Nevan chuckled. "Unless you haven't noticed, I'm an adult and capable of expressing my opinions." He reached out, and while the bathroom wasn't narrow, Nevan's arm span made it easy for him to trail a finger along the lovely brown skin of Seb's forearm. "I have made no move to cover myself or to ask you to avert your gaze. In fact"—he squeezed Seb's arm gently—"I have done everything in my power to invite it."

Seb turned his head slightly, enough to peep at Nevan from the corner of his eye. "You have?"

"Hoping against all hope that I did not disgust you."

That got Seb's attention. "You could *never*. You're beautiful and honorable and protective, and just... just *wonderful*. You could have anyone you wanted."

Nevan quirked an eyebrow. "But Seb. Nobody wanted *me*. I am a monster."

"You're *not*," Seb said fiercely.

"Ceffylau dŵr were Unseelie fae before the Faerie convergence—"

"There was a *convergence*?" Seb closed his eyes. "Never mind. Not relevant."

"Before the convergence that joined the Seelie and Unseelie spheres, most Unseelie were, by definition, monstrous. That hardly mattered to me, because if you want to know the truth, I have never wanted anyone before."

Seb pivoted slowly, a frown pleating his brow. "What do you mean?"

"I mean"—Nevan released Seb's arm—"that I have never been with anyone *that way*. I have rarely spent more than an hour with anyone other than Lulu." He took the spoon in one hand.

"Usually because the only people who approached me were trying to kill me."

"So you're telling me... you're a *virgin?*" Seb plopped down rather ungracefully onto the stool. "Oh, man, now I feel even *more* like a creeper."

"I am over two thousand years old. I *welcome* your attentions, crave them to be honest. And I am fully capable of saying *no.*"

Seb met Nevan's gaze somberly. "Not to Yvo. You can't say no to Yvo."

Nevan winced. "No. I cannot. Not now."

"Well, then." Seb scooped up a spoonful of soup and held it up to Nevan's lips. "All the more reason to take him down. Because *everyone* deserves to control their own body. Everyone deserves consent."

Holding Seb's gaze, Nevan closed his lips around the spoon. But as soon as the flavors hit his tongue—silky and savory, meaty with chicken and just a hint of sourness—his eyes fluttered closed and he moaned low in his throat. "Goddess, that's the best thing I've ever tasted."

When he opened his eyes, Seb was staring at him, his eyes wide behind his glasses. "What?"

Seb squirmed on the stool and quickly held up another spoonful of soup. "Nothing. It's just the sounds you make... Well, let's say they're rather... evocative."

Seb wriggling like that was evocative, too. Nevan wanted more. So, as he accepted the soup, he moaned again, even louder, but kept his eyes on Seb.

Seb shifted again, narrowing his eyes. "Now you're just being a jerk."

"Perhaps. But I wanted to make it very clear how I feel." Nevan met Seb's gaze squarely, keeping his smile buried. "About the soup."

Seb's shoulders fell. "The soup. Right."

"The soup," Nevan murmured. "And you."

Seb peered up at Nevan from under his lashes. "Me?"

"You." He held a spoonful of soup up to Seb's mouth. "If I must keep up my strength, then so must you. Because tomorrow, we are thwarting a megalomaniacal earth mage. And tonight, I hope that I will at last get that kiss you promised, and perhaps have a chance to feel someone else's skin against mine at last."

"I'm *so* good with that." Seb's teeth clicked against the spoon, so quick was he to take it.

As they fed each other, trading spoonful for spoonful, Nevan's vitality returned, his *calon* blooming under his heart as though it had been dry and shriveled for his whole life and not simply the last few days.

Seb scraped the bottom of the bowl and held out the last mouthful. "Do you want more? I can get you seconds, or even thirds, if you're not full."

Nevan set his own empty bowl on the tiles next to the tub and surged to his feet. Water sluiced down his chest, his hips, his legs. And, of course, his cock, so hard and eager that it seemed to have a life of its own. He gazed down at Seb, who was watching him wide-eyed. "I believe I can say I am quite... full. Wouldn't you?"

"Holy *crap*," Seb breathed.

"Now I would very much like to hug you, but I don't want to get you wet." Nevan smiled wickedly. "At least not with bath water."

"Right. Right." Seb scrambled off the stool, catching his foot and nearly falling until Nevan steadied him with a hand on his shoulder. "I'll get a towel. A, um, *big* one."

He left the bowl on the counter and stumbled into the hall-way. Nevan stooped and unstoppered the tub, watching the water swirl down the drain for a moment as he uttered a brief prayer to the Goddess, thanking her as he did every day for the gift of water, the gift of his sister, and now, for the gift of Seb.

He closed his eyes, reaching for his connection to Faerie's One Tree. *Please, my lady, keep us safe. Allow us to prevail against those who would harm your people.*

"Sorry about the, um, extreme color." Nevan opened his eyes at Seb's apologetic tone. He was holding up an enormous sheet of toweling in an eye-watering shade of purple. "What can I say? Kids aren't really into earth tones and pastels. Even the ones who are going through a princess phase like things a little brighter."

Nevan stepped out onto the bathmat and took the towel from Seb's hands. "Never apologize for your calling, *cariad*."

As Nevan dried himself briskly, he considered that every choice Seb made was for others' pleasure, comfort, or safety, never for his own. Nevan had focused on Seb's comfort when he'd insisted on feeding him. He was determined to somehow ensure his safety from Yvo and the council.

But for now? Tonight? Whatever few hours they could steal for themselves? He would focus on Seb's pleasure. *His pleasure, and my own.*

He dropped the towel, letting it puddle around his feet. "I am no longer dehydrated. I am not thirsty or hungry or dirty. So Seb, cariad? May I kiss you *now*?"

"Oh heavens, *please*."

Nevan held out his arms and Seb stepped into them, raising his chin so all Nevan had to do was incline his head and then… and then…

His lips were on Seb's, and yes, it was *so* much better when his own weren't dry as grave dust, his belly wasn't cleaving to his spine, and his head spinning from want of water. And all those changes—in his lips, his belly, his very being—were all because of *this man*.

And as thrilling as it was to feel his hard cock nestle against Seb's stomach, the slight abrasion from his trousers a tantalizing hint of what was to come, that wasn't what set Nevan's *calon* singing.

As much as he would dearly love to leave his virginity behind him, he was in no hurry to move beyond this kiss. He would be happy for this kiss to go on *forever*.

And then Seb hummed and Nevan felt something else, a slight tickle against the seam of his lips and... Was that Seb's *tongue*? He inhaled sharply, and Seb's tongue darted inside his mouth to touch his own.

Nevan whimpered. He actually *whimpered*, and while he wasn't ashamed of the noise—he couldn't help it, after all—he was dismayed because it caused Seb to pull back and gaze up at Nevan worriedly.

"Oh, crap. I forgot." Seb traced Nevan's lower lip with his finger. "You probably haven't done this much."

"Other than with you at the riverside? Not at all."

Seb winced. "Right. At all. I know some people don't like—"

"I liked it." Nevan captured Seb's hand and held it against his chest. "I adored it. But I'm feeling a bit unsteady."

Immediately, Seb's expression morphed into what Nevan now recognized as his *nanny* mode. "I knew it. You need more water. More soup. More—"

Nevan stopped the flow of words by the simple expedient of covering Seb's mouth with his own, and sending his own tongue on a mission.

When he pulled away at last, Seb's eyes were a bit glassy. "Um... What was I saying?"

"Once again, you were worried about my needs. But what I truly need more of, cariad?" Nevan kissed Seb again. "Is you."

CHAPTER 23

For a moment, Seb couldn't do anything but blink up at Nevan, because for a guy who'd never done much kissing, he was a *really* fast learner. Nobody had *ever* taken Seb's wits offline that fast, nor made his knees melt like a popsicle left out in the sun.

Then, with an almost palpable *zhing*, his brain rebooted. "When you say *more*," he said cautiously, "do you mean—"

"More kisses. More skin. More touches." Nevan's dark eyes were impossibly deep, and it was almost as though something moved in their depths. "More of everything." He cradled Seb's head in both enormous hands and dropped the gentlest of kisses on his mouth. "I have been a virgin for millennia, Seb. I would prefer not to remain so for another day."

Seb's cock throbbed, pressing almost painfully against his fly. "A-all right."

Ordinarily, habit would kick in and he'd wipe down the tub, put the dishes in the dishwasher, pack the soup away.

But all that could wait.

Thank goodness I already turned off the stove.

He took Nevan's hand and led him out of the bathroom and down the hall. Long practice made it possible for him to unlatch the child-guard gate at the base of the staircase one-handed. He mounted the stairs with Nevan following a step below and emerged into the attic he'd transformed into his bedroom suite so he could use the first floor bedrooms for a nap room and a playroom.

Nevan looked around, smiling at the sun that spilled through the dormers, gleamed on the polished oak floor, picked out the colors in the braided rug, and pooled on the crazy quilt on Seb's king bed. His gaze caught on the silver picture frames that clustered atop the cherrywood dresser. "I like this room."

Seb shifted uneasily from foot to foot because they were standing *this close* to the bed and Nevan was very, very, *very* naked. "The en suite isn't big. Just a shower since the downstairs tub is so huge, but—"

"I'm not talking about the amenities, Seb." Nevan drew Seb against his chest. "I like it because it's you. Sunny and bright and full of things that speak of love and care."

Seb's knees wobbled. "Oh."

"Now, if you please?" Nevan traced the embroidery on Seb's waistcoat. "Could I undress you? I would very much like to feel your skin against mine, even if we go no further."

"I thought you said you wanted to punch your V-card."

"My what?"

"That you wanted to have, you know"—Seb widened his eyes and lowered his voice—"sex."

"Yes. I would like to. But if *you* are not ready, I can wait." His lips quirked. "I have waited this long, after all."

And that's why he shouldn't have to wait any longer. But that didn't mean Seb had to *rush*.

"I'm ready to take things as far as you'd like, but you can change your mind at *any* time." He flattened his palms against Nevan's chest—his bare, amazingly smooth chest—his fingers twitching with the need to pet and stroke. "*Any time*, understand?"

Nevan nodded gravely. "I do. I would extend you the same courtesy."

"Then we're, ah, on the same page." Seb glanced down at his boots. "I'm super happy to let you do most of the undressing, but I've learned from experience that it's best to eighty-six the footwear first. Otherwise tangled trousers, awkward face-plants, and unexpected visits to the emergency room can really kill the mood." He glared at Nevan. "Don't ask."

Nevan merely gestured to the wingback chair next to an overfull bookcase, but when Seb sat down, Nevan dropped to one knee in front of him and began unlacing the boots.

I will never be able to go to a shoe store ever again.

Seb gripped the chair arms, the brocade rough under his palms, as Nevan slipped off first one and then the other boot. He then rose and held out his hand. Seb yanked off his socks quickly before he took it and allowed Nevan to pull him to his feet.

He slipped his hands under Seb's waistcoat lapels. "May I?"

When Seb nodded, Nevan pushed the vest off Seb's shoulders and laid it on the chair. When he tugged the linen shirt out of the waistband, Seb couldn't suppress his shiver as Nevan slid his hands under the hem to skate lightly over Seb's chest. The shirt caught briefly on Seb's glasses—that *always* happened if he didn't duck his head, but he'd been too busy gawking at the heat in Nevan's gaze to remember.

The shirt joined the waistcoat, and then all that was left were the trousers. Seb glanced down at his fly. *Man, those Regency dudes had it so much easier.* Although the fall front was plenty snug, it didn't chafe his erection as much as a zipper. He intended to look up at Nevan's face again, but his gaze caught on Nevan's cock, and really, that was hardly his fault, because it was huge and hard and leaking and *impossible* to miss.

Nevan's hand intruded on Seb's line of sight to pop one fly button. Another. Seb gulped, because Nevan's fingers this close to his *own* erection were the only things that could distract him from Nevan's.

When Nevan freed the last button and the fall front... fell, Seb sucked in a breath so loudly that he nearly missed Nevan's own gasp.

Nevan's forefinger hovered above the bulge in Seb's boxer briefs. "May I..." His Adam's apple bobbed. "I have never touched another's member. I don't know what I should do."

Seb caught Nevan's hand, his own trembling only slightly, and pressed it to his groin. "If something feels good when you do it to yourself, chances are it'll feel good to me too, and if it doesn't, I'll let you know. But for now?" Seb shucked his briefs and trousers down in one go and stepped out of them. He opened his arms. "How about a hug to start things off?" Seb grinned crookedly. "At least we know we won't be bowled over by a hellhound this time."

Nevan didn't return the smile. Instead, his gaze was intense, his expression pensive as he stepped forward and wrapped his arms almost tentatively around Seb. "I can't bear it if you're hurt."

Seb tightened his arms across Nevan's broad back. "I'm pretty sturdy. You don't have to be too gentle."

With his face buried against Seb's neck, Nevan murmured, "I don't mean this, us, here. I mean the council."

"Hey." Seb smoothed Nevan's springy curls with one hand while stroking his back with the other—nannying built awesome ambidextrous capabilities. "We've talked about this. If there's council fallout, we'll deal with it when we must, and not before."

Nevan raised his head, and the devastation in his eyes made Seb's throat ache. "You don't know what they'll do to you."

"No. And neither do you. You said so yourself."

"But they're not the only danger." Nevan's arms tensed, his palms flat against Seb's spine, and Seb could almost swear that one of them burned hotter than the other. "Remember Yvo's tether? He knows where I am, Seb. Which means he knows where you live."

Even though Seb had sort of considered that before, the reminder sent a wash of ice water over his libido. Which in turn sparked anger that burned like an ember under his heart. "There is absolutely *nothing* about me that would interest Yvo."

"You've sheltered me. Fed me. Restored me. That's enough to catch his attention."

Seb cradled Nevan's face between his palms. "I don't think he's that good a magician. Heck, he still thinks I'm an assassin. I mean, he never even *checked*."

Nevan's lips curved—not much, but enough to count as a smile in Seb's book. "The guild spells prevent it."

"Yes, but I'm *not* in the guild." Seb shook his head. "I still can't believe there's a freaking *guild*. But that's another thing I've learned as a nanny. The whole *trust but verify* thing. When children's safety is at stake, you never take *anything* for granted."

"But—"

"No." Seb kissed Nevan softly and was rewarded with another one of those purrs. "I refuse to allow that jerk to add *cockblocker* to his résumé. He has no place in this room with us." He kissed Nevan's chest, directly over his heart. "No place in here."

"Seb, you don't understand." Nevan's arms tightened around him. "If he even suspects... He's willing to kill a child to master air, an element not his own. He has no boundaries. What might he do to you if he discovers you helped thwart his ambitions? And if we..." Nevan swallowed, closing his eyes briefly before inhaling slowly and leaning his forehead against Seb's. "If we fail, and he somehow succeeds in conquering air, what might he do next? To conquer fire? To conquer water?"

"Sweetheart," Seb said gently, brushing Nevan's tumbled curls off his forehead. "He's already conquered water. He's conquered *you*."

Nevan's eyes widened. "I... *Shite*."

He broke away from Seb's embrace to sit down heavily on the end of the bed and drop his head into his hands. Seb sat next to him and wrapped an arm around his waist.

"Didn't that ever occur to you?"

"I am ashamed to say that it did not." Nevan lifted his head and stared down at the geas brand in his palm. "How foolish is that? I delivered water to him when I agreed to his bargain." He met Seb's gaze, his own bleak. "He'll never release me, will he?"

"Maybe not voluntarily, because he's a complete entitled *asshole.*" That ember under Seb's heart flared brighter, brighter, brighter, filling him with a burning sense of purpose. "But you'll be free of him, Nevan. I swear."

Nevan smiled sadly as he took Seb's hand. "That is a promise you cannot keep, *cariad.*"

"No? I'm a nanny, Nevan. If I can wrangle a birthday party full of preschoolers hopped up on ice cream and cake, I can do anything."

"But Yvo still has Lulu. That means he has earth, water, and spirit under his control. He's already more powerful than any elemental mage has a right to be."

"Maybe." Seb laced his fingers with Nevan's. "But we have an advantage he doesn't know about."

"Tell me. Because right now it seems all the power is in his court, and as long as he has Lulu, I can't risk defying him." He sighed. "Not that I'm able to, anyway."

"He may *think* he has the power, but he doesn't, and that's his biggest weakness." Seb lifted Nevan's hand and kissed it. "In the first place, he still believes your geas to be secret. While he might know where I live, if he even cares, he doesn't know I know what you know. In the second place, we have allies he doesn't suspect. You're not alone anymore."

"But Lulu is. Alone with him, somewhere I can't find her."

"Ah, but you forget." Seb stood and drew Nevan to his feet. Both their erections had flagged, but that could be remedied.

"We happen to know a supernatural search and recovery specialist."

Nevan blinked, and for a moment, hope flared in his eyes. "Jordan?"

"Mmmhmmm. First thing tomorrow, we're heading to Quest Investigations."

"But—"

He laid a finger across Nevan's lips. "If you're about to invoke that secrecy thingie, forget it. We'll go and lay the whole thing out for them. But for now?" He drew Nevan beside the bed and flung back the covers. "Come to bed. I might have ruined the mood, but let me hold you. For comfort, if nothing else. And if something else should"—he glanced down at Nevan's groin—"arise during the night? Well, we'll handle it then."

Nevan's smile was more heartfelt. "You are very good at making plans, cariad."

Seb shrugged and then crawled into bed and held up his arms. "What can I say? I'm a nanny."

Nevan lay down next to him. "That's where you're wrong, cariad." Nevan scooped Seb into his arms and rolled onto his back, with Seb splayed on top of him. "You're everything."

CHAPTER 24

I *am no longer a virgin.*

Nevan lay on his side, studying the way the breaking dawn illuminated Seb's sleeping face, casting the sharp cheekbones into relief, emphasizing the fan of his dark lashes, highlighting the full lips still swollen from many, many, *many* kisses.

Because Seb had been right, of course. Despite their worry, things had *risen* again—more than once. Indeed, the night had been a revelation to Nevan in so many ways. The warmth of Seb's skin, the thrill of Seb's touch, the taste of Seb's spend—all of it had awoken something in Nevan's soul that had been slumbering all his life.

Because of his nature—not only the way most viewed ceffyl dŵr as monstrous, but the real danger that someone might capture him and bind him to their will—he'd never allowed anyone to get this *close* before, never let anyone, even Lulu, on his back before.

I let Seb on my back, though. And that had been glorious, as Seb had entered him, joining them in the most intimate of ways. The second time, though, Seb had lain Nevan out, crouched over him, and *oh, Goddess. That* ride had been as glorious as the first.

But it was afterward, as they'd held each other, all barriers gone, that Nevan's world had shifted, inexorably, fundamentally, irrevocably.

I am no longer alone.

"We have only known one another a day," he murmured softly, "but you have dwelled in my heart forever."

He couldn't say why he was so certain, only that his *calon* was flaring so brightly in his chest that it probably rivaled the rising sun to anyone with aura sight.

I am his. And he is mine. No, that wasn't quite right. *He is ours.* Because Seb hadn't displaced Lulu in Nevan's heart. Simply joined her in a totally different way, a way that made Nevan feel whole for the first time since he'd been spawned.

But that meant that, like Lulu, Seb was to be protected at all costs. And the best way to do that was to hide Seb from Yvo's perception by whatever means necessary.

He pressed a soft kiss to Seb's forehead and slowly rolled onto his back. With excruciating care, he lifted the blankets and eased to a sitting position. But as he was leaning forward, ready to stand, a warm palm landed on the base of his spine.

"I hope you're not thinking about sneaking out." Seb's playful tone nonetheless held an edge of steel.

Nevan's shoulders drooped. He propped his elbows on his knees and let his hands fall between his knees. "I'm sorry, but I cannot put you in danger. It's better if I—"

"If you what?" The bedclothes rustled behind him and then Seb was there, his warm skin pressed against Nevan's back, the point of his chin digging into Nevan's shoulder. "You can't go to Quest alone, because you can't tell them the whole story. You can't find Lulu because you don't know where to *begin* to look. And you can't confront Yvo because, hello? Even if you could find *him*, he's still got you in his clutches."

"But if you're hurt—"

"I'm willing to take that risk."

Nevan straightened, dislodging Seb's chin. "But what if I am not?"

"Then I would say that I'm an adult, not a child, and making decisions for me is a little insulting. Nevan, come on. We've got a plan, and you know it's reasonable. Maybe not terrific, but good at least." He kissed behind Nevan's ear. "But to be successful, we need to be at our best." He wrinkled his nose. "And maybe not smelling like sex."

Despite himself, Nevan grinned. "I like that smell." He swiveled on the bed enough to pull Seb into his lap and nuzzle his neck. "Just as I like the way you taste. As wild as the water in my lake."

"Wild?" Seb scoffed, but didn't push Nevan away. "I'm about as domestic as you can get."

Nevan gazed into Seb's eyes. Without his spectacles, they held hidden depths, yet sparkled like sunlight on the lake. "There are more ways than one to be wild, cariad, such as diving unhesitatingly into unknown adventure for the sake of others."

"Yes, well, hmmm." Pink tinged Seb's brown cheeks. "Never mind that. But let's focus on making a good impression at Quest and convincing them to take our case, shall we?" Much to Nevan's disappointment, Seb scrambled out of his lap. "I'll run a bath for you with another of Tahmina's bath bombs, then I'll come up here to shower."

Nevan pouted and reached out for Seb's hips. "You won't share the tub with me? It's big enough."

Seb dodged him neatly. "No, because our focus today is on finding Lulu, saving Mario, and cooking Yvo's very shady goose. We can't afford distractions."

"Has anyone ever told you that you're very bossy?"

"*So* many people, although most of them are significantly shorter than you." He kissed Nevan all too briefly. "Come down in about five minutes." He trotted across the room, and for a moment, Nevan simply stared, mesmerized by the play of muscles in Seb's backside.

After Seb vanished down the stairs, Nevan straightened the bedclothes, which took longer than it should have because he got distracted by Seb's tantalizing scent on the pillows. When he reached the hallway, Seb was already emerging from the bathroom in a cloud of steam, shirtless, but clad in a pair of soft gray sweatpants.

"It's all set in there. Fresh towel on the vanity, and your clothes hanging on the hooks behind the door." He paused to kiss Nevan's cheek. "I've laid out a new toothbrush for you, and I'll bring in a glass of water presently."

"You needn't. I can wait."

Seb smiled up at him. "It's no trouble. I like taking care of you."

If Nevan were completely honest with himself, he liked being taken care of, at least when Seb was the one doing the caring. "Very well."

So, as he bathed, Seb plied him with two glasses of water before retreating upstairs for his own shower. By the time Nevan climbed out of the tub and dressed, Seb was already in the dining room, the long table cluttered with a truly astonishing array of objects, including his open pack.

He pointed to several oranges next to a bright blue ceramic dish full of what appeared to be more homemade granola. "You can eat those on your own, right?" At Nevan's nod, Seb picked up another two oranges and stowed them in the pack. "Have a seat. I'll get everything ready to go and we can head out as soon as you've eaten."

Nevan sat down and pulled the chair in to the table. "And when *you've* eaten."

Seb waved Nevan's words away. "I already had toast. Would you like some tea?"

Nevan straightened, his mouth watering. "Tea?"

Seb chuckled. "I'll take that as a yes. I made it with Tahmina's water, just in case. Hold on."

He disappeared into the kitchen as Nevan tore into the

orange rind. By the time he returned, walking carefully with a large mug in his hand, Nevan had already consumed two of the fruits and half the granola.

"My bună used to say that the secret to not spilling your tea was not looking at it while you walked."

Nevan tilted his head, studying Seb's neat beige trousers and sky blue polo. "If that's true, why are you staring down into the cup as though you could read the future in its leaves?"

Seb glanced up, merriment sparkling in his eyes behind his spectacles. "Although I conducted *many* experiments to prove otherwise while staying with her as a child, she never accepted the data. She simply said I must have looked down at least once, and after that, the spell was broken." He chuckled as he reached Nevan's side. "I told her once that I wasn't Orpheus, and the tea wasn't Eurydice, but she just told me not to be fresh." He held the cup to Nevan's lips. "I hope it's not too hot."

Nevan didn't care if it was scalding. He hadn't had a good cup of tea since he'd made his bargain with Yvo. But when he took a sip, he moaned at the perfect temperature. "This is marvelous."

Seb beamed at him. "The company's based in Oregon. This is my favorite tea. I have it every morning."

Nevan took a deeper gulp. "If you have this to hand, why on earth did you order that horrid beverage in Starbucks?"

"Oh, that. I—" Something dinged in the kitchen. "Shoot! The toaster." He set the cup on the table. "I'll be right back to help you finish that. I just need to grab the bagels."

He hurried away, and Nevan finished his fruit and granola while eyeing the tea covetously. When Seb returned, he had three bagel halves slathered with cream cheese on a plate and a fourth clamped between his teeth. He set the plate in front of Nevan before tearing a bite out of his bagel. As he chewed, he held up the teacup again.

"I sprinkled some of Tahina's magic djinni dust on the bagels.

They're not really water based, but I wanted to make sure they were safe for you to eat."

"Thank you." Nevan picked one up. "I'm pretty certain they're no more dangerous than granola."

Seb grinned. "Excellent. While we finish eating, I'll finish getting ready. Let me know when you want another sip of tea."

He returned to his packing. Nevan watched him bemusedly as he munched on his bagel. When several plastic containers followed a restocked First Aid kit, a bunch of grapes, three bottles of water, and a couple of books, Nevan shook his head.

"I have no notion how you manage to fit all of that into a single knapsack."

"Well, it's a big pack. Lots of useful internal pockets." Seb studied the items that remained on the table and snatched up a pair of red socks dotted with little stars. "Besides, I only take what I need. Or might need." He bit his lip. "Or what might come in handy." He shot Nevan a smile. "When you're dealing with kids, you have to be prepared. I figure dealing with evil mages can't be so different." He zipped all the pockets. "Ready?"

Nevan stood. "Can I help clear away?"

"Just leave it. I want to get to Quest in plenty of time."

Nevan glanced out the window. It was barely past dawn. "It's a bit early. They might not be open."

"It's a supernatural PI agency, and I've got their business card." Seb shouldered his pack. "If they're not open, I'll call."

Since he was conscious during this trip, Nevan was able to study their surroundings as Seb piloted his vehicle through the streets. The scenery flashed by nearly as quickly as when he was flying, especially when Seb sped up in an alarming way and merged onto what he called the *freeway*.

After Seb parked along the street in a charming business district in downtown Portland, he peered through the windshield. "Quest must be doing okay if they can afford offices in the Pearl District." He cupped Nevan's cheek and dropped a kiss on his lips. "Ready?"

"As I'll ever be."

When they climbed out of the van, a savory aroma greeted them, and Nevan inhaled deeply. "What is that?"

Seb pointed to the restaurant next door to Quest's address. "Falafel. We'll have lunch there."

Nevan had to admire Seb's certainty that they'd have time for lunch, but he didn't want to dampen Seb's enthusiasm. As he reached for the handle on the glass door emblazoned with Quest's name, he noted the New Age supply on the opposite side and sniffed, detecting a telltale whiff of the supernatural underneath the tantalizing falafel scent.

Witches.

Apparently, Quest wasn't the only supernatural business in the neighborhood.

"Nevan Quirke?"

Nevan turned at the curt question. Two uniformed officers, their hands on their belts, stood on the sidewalk with Seb hovering wide-eyed behind them. "Yes?"

"You're under arrest."

"Arrest?" Nevan very carefully kept his hands within view. "For what?"

One of the officers grabbed Nevan's arm, none too gently. "The kidnapping of Luljeta Offerman."

"Offerman?" Nevan jerked in the officer's grip, which only succeeded in getting him thrust face-first against their patrol car. "Her name is Luljeta Zanash, and *I'm* not the one who kidnapped her."

"That's not what her guardian says," one of the officers said as he snapped handcuffs on Nevan's wrists. "Be advised you have the right to remain silent..."

*a*s though his feet were glued to the sidewalk and his voice was frozen, Seb couldn't move or speak as Nevan was Mirandized. But as one of the officers opened the back door of the squad car, he finally croaked, "Wait."

The officer who had his hand on Nevan's head to guide him into the rear seat looked over at him. "Are you with this man, sir?"

Seb gripped his backpack straps with both hands. "I—"

"He's not," Nevan growled, and as Seb opened his mouth to protest, he gave a tiny shake of his head. "Bad enough you're detaining me improperly. Leave random passersby alone."

The officer manhandling Nevan shoved him into the car and closed the door, although the other one was watching Seb with narrowed eyes. Nevan, on the other hand, was virtually motionless in the rear seat, his gaze focused straight ahead, jaw tight, and lips pressed into a line.

Why wouldn't he let Seb help? *I could testify that he's been with me non-stop since yesterday.* The charges were *obviously* bogus, just one more ploy by Yvo to control Nevan. But to what end? Wouldn't involving the human police force make it more difficult for Nevan to complete Yvo's revolting quest?

Nevan's whereabouts for the last twenty-four hours might not be relevant, not if Yvo claimed the kidnapping took place earlier. But why was Nevan denying their friendship, their connection? Seb could *help*.

One officer climbed into the passenger seat, although the driver was still eyeballing Seb. Nevan said something that Seb didn't catch, but it caused the officer in front of him to say something to his partner. The other officer shook his head, but climbed behind the wheel. Once their backs were to him, Nevan cut a glance—a very brief glance—at Seb with another tiny head shake.

Lights flashing but siren silent, the car pulled away from the curb.

"Holy crap, was that *Nevan* in that police car?"

Seb turned to find Jordan gaping at the disappearing tail-lights, Doop panting at his side. "Yes."

"The *human* police? What for?"

"Kidnapping. And I don't understand why he wouldn't let me tell them that we'd been together constantly since yesterday."

Jordan snorted. "Well, *that's* easy. You're a nanny. Not many people would trust their kids to a nanny who was mixed up with a kidnapping. He was probably trying to protect you."

"I don't need protection," Seb said fiercely. "*He* does. He can't prove his innocence, and if they put him in jail, he'll die."

"You think someone will attack him?" Jordan's eyes widened and his hand tightened on Doop's ruff. "I've heard human jails can be pretty rough, but Nevan's a big dude. Nobody with any sense would try anything with him."

"You underestimate the stupidity of humans with something to prove," Seb said dryly. "Some of them would attack him precisely *because* he's so big."

"Ugh." Jordan wrinkled his nose. "Small-dog complex. I get it."

"But that's not the greatest danger. Because of the geas, he can't eat or drink, not without forfeiting." Seb slapped his forehead. *"That's* why Yvo did it. He was afraid Nevan might actually succeed, and he wants to have his cake and eat it too."

Jordan brightened. "There's cake?"

"Not actual cake." Every instinct urged Seb to *hurry*, and his lungs burned as though he were already running. He tore his gaze away from the disappearing squad car to face Jordan. "I need to engage Quest's services, like *now*. Is the office open?"

"It's pretty much always open if it needs to be. Go on up and talk to Miss Pennybaker at the desk. Second floor." He patted Doop's ruff. "I've got to, um, check in with Noah's teacher, but I'll be back in a bit. Do you think Nevan will be back by then?"

Panic warred with resolve in Seb's middle. "He'd better be."

"Good, 'cause I've got some things to tell you both. We won't be long." He trotted off down the sidewalk, Doop loping along at his side.

Seb took a deep breath, opened the glass door, and stepped into a small, marble-floored entry. Wide stairs, also marble, rose in front of him, seeming to go up forever. He mounted the first flight. A sign reading *Quest Investigations*, with the same logo as on Jordan's business card, hung over an archway on his left.

"Guess this must be the place," he muttered, and, gripping his backpack straps for courage, entered a subtly lit room, its carpeting so unobtrusive that Seb had to glance twice to make sure it was actually there.

The half-dozen padded chairs that lined two of the walls were upholstered in the same earth tones as Seb's living room rug, and a subtle scent reminiscent of spring meadows hung in the air. Opposite the archway sat a long desk with a couple of big monitors, a keyboard, a multi-line phone and, for some reason, a vintage manual typewriter. There were two chairs behind the desk—a wooden ladder-back and a gray Aeron—both of them empty. In fact, the whole place seemed deserted.

Seb crept forward, peering down the darkened hallway behind the desk. Through the dimness, he could make out several doors, all of them closed, and frowned. That hall was too long for this building, surely. It hadn't seemed that wide from outside. He shook his head, dismissing the thought. Childcare and folklore were his subjects, not architecture.

Along the edge of the desk sat several business card holders, one with more of Jordan's cards. The others held cards for Mal Kendrick, Niall O'Tierney, Eleri Deilen, Zeke Oz, Hector Gonzales, and—seriously?—Hugh Mann.

"Hello? Is anybody here?" Who had Jordan told him to ask for? Oh, right. "Miss Pennybaker?"

Clack clack clackity-clack.

Seb jumped backward, nearly stumbling when his sneakers caught on the carpet. He'd heard of player pianos, but player *typewriters?*

Get over yourself, Ardelean. It's a supernatural *PI agency.* And given the trouble Nevan was in, Seb was grateful for any and all magic on offer.

He edged around the desk and looked at the paper that was rolled on the platen.

"Good morning, young man. Please wait here."

Oookay, then. "Of course."

So what if he was speaking to empty air? He had extensive experience conversing with imaginary friends, including his own. So he slipped off his pack and sat down gingerly on the edge of a chair the color of fall maple leaves with his pack on his lap.

He barely had time to draw three breaths before footsteps clattered on the stairs and a pale, bespectacled man with curly dark hair rushed in from the landing.

"I'm so sorry I wasn't here to greet you. I ordinarily arrive a bit earlier, but, um…" Pink blotches bloomed on his neck and face, but they didn't entirely camouflage what Seb recognized as a hickey on the base of his throat. "Have you been waiting long?"

"No," Seb said slowly. He could have sworn that the footsteps had come *down* the stairs, not up. But the Pearl was famous for mixed-use buildings. Maybe the man lived upstairs. "I just arrived. Jordan told me it was okay to come up and to ask for Miss Pennybaker."

The man exhaled, his shoulders easing down in a clear release of tension. "She welcomed you then. I should have known."

"Well, the *typewriter* welcomed me, which was, you know, an experience."

"Typewriter? Oh, dear." He faced the ladder-back chair. "Miss Pennybaker, is your vox spell offline again? I'll let Hector know right away. I'm sure he'll have it fixed in a heartbeat." He turned to Seb and held out his hand. "I'm Zeke Oz. Welcome to Quest Investigations. How may I..." His smile faded and his dark eyes widened behind his lenses. "Oh, my stars. This is... Could you wait here for *just* a moment longer?"

"I'm afraid a moment is all I have time for. This is kind of an emergency."

"Yes, I can see that." He pulled a cell phone out of the back pocket of his black dress trousers and punched in a code. "Don't worry. My boss will be here momentar— Ah, here he is."

An almost preternaturally beautiful man who was nearly as large as Nevan, his hair as black as Seb's but his eyes a startling cobalt blue, strode in from the landing. He was wearing black leather pants, just like Nevan's, too, although the jacket over his white T-shirt was more biker than steampunk Western pirate cosplay. This time, Seb was certain he hadn't heard the downstairs door open. He pushed his misgivings aside. Maybe they had offices upstairs, too.

"Mal," Zeke said, gesturing to Seb, "this... gentleman is in dire need of our services. Jordan referred him."

"He did, did he, the scamp," Mal said as he leaned against the edge of the desk and crossed his arms over his chest. His accent was British, but not posh, and his tone had a sardonic edge. "Why would he do that?"

"My... friend, Nevan Quirke. He's a... a ceffyl dŵr."

Mal lost his lazy smile and pushed himself upright. "You know of ceffyl dŵr?"

"Well, I know of *him*. But the thing is, he's been arrested by the Portland police."

"The *human* police?" Mal ran a hand through his hair. "Shite. What'd he do, threaten some bloke on the riverside?"

"He didn't *do* anything. The charges are completely bogus. They accused him of kidnapping, but the earth mage who filed the charges—"

"Earth mage, you say?" Mal grimaced. "Bollocks."

"Yes. Please, you have to help. Nevan's under a geas to him—"

"Say no more." Mal kneaded the palm of one hand with his other. "I know too well what that's like."

Seb blinked. "Oh. Jordan said one of his bosses was under a geas once. I guess that would be you."

Mal exchanged a glance with Zeke, and they both sighed. "Looks like Jordan might need that discretion refresher sooner rather than later, Zeke." He turned back to Seb. "So, Nevan's under a geas to this mage wanker. How do you know about it?"

"Because I overheard them. The mage did this sort of holographic Zoom call. He didn't know I was there." Seb scrunched up his nose. "He really likes the sound of his own voice."

"Bloody mages. They're all like that, the arseholes. Go on."

"The mage—"

"Excuse me," Zeke said diffidently from the Aeron chair, his fingers poised over his keyboard. "Do you happen to know this mage's name?"

"It's Offerman. Yvo Offerman."

Mal gestured for Seb to take a seat as Zeke's fingers flew over the keys so fast they blurred. "Let Zeke dig up the dirt on this earth mage while you fill me in on the rest. Usually a geas is tied to something the spell-caster wants. So what is it?"

Seb bit his lip. "Big picture, or just Nevan's specific part?"

"Let's start with Nevan's binding. What's this Yvo wanker got over him?"

"He kidnapped Nevan's little sister. Nevan can't get her back unless he... delivers."

"And what's he got to deliver?"

Seb swallowed. "The heart of a teenage aerialist who's killed by an assassin's bespelled dagger while he's midair during a circus trapeze act."

Mal blinked, his eyebrows rising toward his hairline. "Well, that's certainly specific. Where's the circus?"

"Washington County Fairgrounds. It's a technically a carnival, I guess." Seb retrieved his ticket from his pack and handed it to Mal.

Mal grimaced. "Shite. We might have trouble with jurisdiction there." He handed the ticket back. "Is Nevan the assassin?"

Heat traveled up Seb's throat and infused his cheeks as he tucked the ticket away again. "No. That was me. Well, it's *not* me. I'm just a nanny. But there was some confusion at Starbucks, and Nevan *thought* I was the assassin. The thing is, we don't have a lot of time here, not if we want to save Nevan, his sister, *and* the teenager, but Nevan's danger is most immediate."

"Too right, if he's been taken by the human police." Mal shared an inscrutable glance with Zeke and... the empty chair? "The council won't half have it in for him if he lets slip anything about the supe community."

Seb waved that away. "He won't. But the thing is, the geas doesn't let him drink anything from his own hand, he can't even *touch* wild water, and he's allergic to treated water. He was so dehydrated when we met that I thought he—"

"I get it. Ceffyl dŵr can't live without wild water and if this arsehole's blocking him from it..." He stood. "Miss Pennybaker, if you would be so good, please call Quentin Bertrand-Harrington and tell him to get his arse down here five minutes ago." He grinned down at Seb. "We've got a water horse to spring from chokey."

CHAPTER 26

*N*evan's shirt chafed where it pulled against his neck. When the uniformed officers had marched him into the police station, they'd taken his duster and waistcoat, and then searched him—intrusively—because they couldn't believe he didn't carry a wallet or a mobile phone. When they'd dumped him in this room, they'd caught his full sleeves in the shackles attached to the metal table.

Hence, the chafing.

The male detective, Taylor, paced back and forth across the small room, the harsh lights of the interrogation room gleaming on his shaven skull the same color as Nevan's own skin. But whereas Taylor's forehead was sheened with sweat, Nevan's was dry, bordering on flaky, something that Taylor seemed to find incriminating—or else personally insulting.

Taylor spun and slammed his palms on the table. "Where. Is. She?" Taylor barked.

Nevan gritted his teeth. He'd lost count of the times the two detectives had asked that question, just as he'd lost track of how many times he'd given the same answer. They'd fired questions at him for what seemed like hours, the same ones, over and over, as though his answer would somehow change, until Nevan's voice had finally given out.

"I don't know," he croaked, yet again.

Taylor jabbed his finger at Nevan's face. "That's not what Mr. Offerman says. He claims you became obsessed with his little girl, so much so that you threatened *him* with bodily harm when he denied you access to her. Did you?"

"Did I what?"

The female detective, Garnett, stared at him stonily from her seat across from him. "Threaten Mr. Offerman with bodily harm when he refused to let you see his daughter."

Nevan's palm burned and his belly writhed like a nest of eels. Despite trying to keep his mouth clamped shut, he ground out, *"Yes."* Because he had. When Yvo had announced he had Lulu in his clutches, Nevan had promised to remove his lungs. Through his arsehole. Now, it seemed as though not only couldn't he lie to Yvo, but he couldn't lie *about* Yvo.

Garnett leaned back in her chair with a satisfied smirk. "So where is she?"

They'd offered him water—the unopened bottle still sat on the table near his elbow. Since he couldn't drink it, however, they'd interpreted his refusal as intentional lack of cooperation. They'd hinted at putting him in *gen pop*, whatever that was— human law enforcement was a mystery to him—although Taylor had informed him with something like glee that criminals who victimized children didn't do well there.

Nevan was so miserable by that time that he paid little attention. His thirst and physical discomfort were almost irrelevant. His worry over Lulu knotted his belly worse than the geas.

And he missed Seb with an ache that went beyond physical.

Would Seb believe that Nevan had lied to him? That *Yvo* was the victim here? Huddled on the hard chair, cold iron circling his wrists, he buried his face in his shaking hands.

No. Seb wouldn't. He'd heard Yvo himself, and nobody who

was as kind, as caring, as perceptive as Seb could believe Yvo was anything other than a manipulative liar.

But could a kind, caring, perceptive man truly learn to love a monster? Because somewhere in the night, as Seb had cuddled close against him, his arm flung across Nevan's middle, Nevan had realized that he wanted that. Wanted Seb. Wanted Seb to be part of a family who looked out for one another, protected one another, *loved* one another. A family with Nevan and Lulu.

He'd been ready to face down every last member of the council, including the King and Queen themselves, if it meant Seb could stay. Nevan had pledged himself to less scrupulous people for stakes just as high. If Their Majesties required a sacrifice from him to make it so, he'd give it, gladly.

The only two things—two *people*—he refused to sacrifice were Lulu and Seb.

"Seems like our friend here needs a little more—"

A knock on the door interrupted Garnett's words. Taylor stopped looming over Nevan and walked over to have a murmured conversation with the officer in the corridor. When he closed the door and turned, he had a murderous expression on his face.

"Apparently," he said through gritted teeth, "our friend's lawyer has arrived."

Nevan blinked. "Lawyer?"

"Yes. And he's demanding a private chat with you." He tugged at his loosened tie, sending it askew. "We'll allow it. Five minutes. Then we'll be back. Because make no mistake, Quirke. We will find that little girl."

Nevan's shoulders slumped and he let his chin drop to his chest. The human police wouldn't be able to find Lulu any more than Nevan could, because Yvo had her. *He* knew where she was. But Nevan couldn't even say *that*. Every time he tried, the geas brand burned so hot he was surprised the skin on his palm didn't blacken and slough off onto the floor.

"Ah, Mr. Quirke."

Nevan glanced up at the cultured voice. A dark-haired man in a bespoke suit, holding a brown leather briefcase with the initials *QBH* monogrammed in gold on its gleaming surface, closed the door behind him and sat across from Nevan. He wore tortoiseshell spectacles with lenses that glinted with red sparks. Nevan knew what those were—bespelled lenses that allowed demons with Sheol-adapted sight to see in the Upper World.

"Who are you?"

"Quentin Bertrand-Harrington. Your advocate." He laid the briefcase on the table, twirled the combination under the handle, and flicked open its clasps with a double *click*. He lifted a small glass vial holding a virulent green liquid from the case's interior and pulled its cork. "Drink this."

"I can't." Nevan glanced at the video camera above the door, but its red light had gone dark. Quentin saw the direction of his gaze.

"They're not recording, if that's what you're worried about," he said. "We've got five minutes of privacy."

"Even so, I can't drink anything from my own hand. And treated water doesn't agree with me."

"Yes, yes. I know all about that. I'll hold it for you. But this is a druid potion, in any event. It will make it appear to the geas tether that you're in the same place you consumed it. I'm afraid it will taste rather nasty, but according to the druid who concocted it, improving the flavor would've taken more time. And since it's imperative that we get you out of here, and that Offerman doesn't know that you've gone, speed is of the essence."

He held the vial across the table. When Nevan leaned forward and opened his mouth, Quentin tipped it onto his tongue.

Nevan grimaced. "*Pfaugh.* That is vile."

"Perhaps, but effective." He stowed the bottle back in his briefcase and closed it with a double *snick*.

Nevan gestured to Quentin's glasses. "Are you a demon?"

"Dynastic incubus, and fully qualified advocate, in case you're concerned. Now, are you ready to depart?"

"They're not going to let me go." The taste of the potion on his tongue, like unripe sloes and rot, made Nevan long for Seb and his water bottle.

"On the contrary, they will discover that they've made a serious error and that there is, in fact, no accusation against you."

Nevan frowned. "How did you manage that? Did you put them in 'cubi thrall?"

"As an imprinted incubus, I can't seduce anybody"—he smiled wickedly—"other than my husband, but my powers of persuasion are more than adequate for our purposes. In addition, Quest employs an extremely gifted hacker who's not entirely constrained by human technology." He stood. "Are you ready to go?"

Nevan raised his wrists, the shackles *clank*ing against the metal table. "Not precisely.

Quentin sniffed. "That will be remedied in three... two..."

The door opened and Garnett walked in. Without a word, she strode over and unlocked Nevan's cuffs. She glanced at Quentin and then away, but didn't lose her game face. "He's free to go."

Nevan rubbed his wrists, where the iron content in the cuffs had raised welts on his skin. "Where are my other clothes?"

"Front desk." She turned and left without bothering to meet Nevan's gaze even once.

"I suppose an apology is too much to hope for?" he said.

Quentin raised one elegant black eyebrow. "Don't push your luck. Let's go. They're waiting for us at the Quest offices."

Nevan struggled out of the chair, catching his balance with one hand against the table. "Is Seb there?"

"I'm unaware of precisely which Avengers have assembled, as I was contacted by phone and wasted no time indulging in pointless chitchat. But the sooner we're out of here, the sooner you can discover for yourself."

Brows bunched in confusion, Nevan followed Quentin out of the room and down a brightly lit hallway. "A question?"

Quentin glanced over his shoulder at him, tilting his head slightly to indicate the officer walking toward them.

Nevan waited until the officer had passed, then leaned forward to murmur, "I know why I want vengeance, but what other avengers might be there and what would they want?"

Quentin stared at him for a moment, his lips parted as though he couldn't find a response. Then he shook his head. "Hugh is right. Most in our community are sadly unaware of human popular cultural references."

He gestured to the counter and the officer waiting behind a thick sheet of what was no doubt bulletproof glass. Nevan stepped up, and the officer pushed the bulky package of his duster and waistcoat through the gap under the window. He followed that up with a plastic bag, no doubt containing the contents of his pockets, then slid a clipboard after it. "Sign here that you've taken receipt of your belongings."

Nevan slipped the waistcoat on, but didn't button it. He peered at the bag. It contained his three FTA vouchers, and he wondered briefly what the human police made of a person carrying oak leaves around in his pockets rather than car keys and cell phone. Then he looked closer.

Lulu's ribbon was missing.

His chest constricted. Where...? He always kept it close to his heart, but it wasn't in his waistcoat pocket. When had he held it last? He couldn't— *Ah. The riverside.* He'd had it in his hand while he'd told Seb about Lulu. But afterward? Hadn't he put it back? Why couldn't he remember?

He snatched his duster and shoved his hand in each pocket, both outside and inside. Nothing.

"Something's missing," he growled at the office. "Where is—"

"*Thank* you," Quentin said and grabbed Nevan's arm, his grip tight enough to bruise—and was that the prick of his claws? He hauled Nevan away from the counter.

"But they didn't give me—"

"Shut *up*," Quentin whispered fiercely. "Whatever's missing, we'll follow up. Trust me on that. But not even my persuasive powers or Hector's hacking skills will help if you make an inter-dimensional incident out of this and make yourself *memorable*. Need I remind you of the Secrecy Pact?"

"No," Nevan said, and morosely followed Quentin out the station doors.

That ribbon was the last thing of Lulu's that Nevan had. Somehow, its loss cut nearly as deep as when she'd first gone missing. As though he'd lost his last link with her. As though he'd never find her again.

He clenched his fists at his sides, digging his nails into the geas brand, as he trailed Quentin to a sleek black sedan. *I'll get her back. I will.*

And then Yvo would pay.

CHAPTER 27

*S*eb sat on the chair in the corner of Quest's lobby with his pack clutched to his chest, gnawing his lip as the Quest staff rushed about with purpose. Zeke had disappeared upstairs, and Mal down the hallway. A round-faced man with shiny black hair and skin a shade darker than Seb's hurried in at one point. With his faded jeans, open flannel shirt over a faded navy *Space Invaders* T-shirt, and battered messenger bag, he gave off a definite college-student vibe. But instead of approaching the desk, he simply raised a hand at the empty chair.

"Hey, Miss Pennybaker. Can't stop now, but when I'm done here, I've got an upgrade for your voice synthesizer." Then he hurried down the hallway behind the desk without acknowledging Seb's presence.

Seb stared at the empty chair, which clearly wasn't empty. Apparently, Quest had an invisible receptionist. That was... inconvenient. Although he supposed that if their clientele were supernatural beings, maybe they could all see her, unlike Seb with his ordinary human vision.

"Seb?"

Seb startled at Zeke's soft voice and tore his gaze away from where Miss Pennybaker... wasn't. Zeke was standing a few feet away with a laden tray holding a fanciful teapot shaped like a rotund orange and pink dragon, a delicate china teacup and saucer painted with apple blossoms, and a plate of pastries. Seb sniffed appreciatively—*cinnamon and nutmeg.*

Zeke set the tray on the table by Seb's chair. "I thought you might like some refreshments while we're waiting. If you don't care for tea, we have coffee or water."

"Tea is lovely. Thank you."

Zeke lifted the pot. "I thought so."

He poured the steaming tea into the cup, the liquid dark and fragrant with a hint of vanilla—although *not* bergamot, thank goodness. Seb couldn't abide Earl Grey tea. To him, it smelled like vintage Wash'n Dri towelettes, and he didn't want to associate his tea with cleaning up toddler messes.

Seb set his backpack by his feet so he could accept the cup from Zeke and took an absent sip. "Can you tell me what's going on?"

"Well, to a certain extent." Zeke sank into the chair on the other side of the table. "However, since there are several issues to address—Nevan's arrest, his sister's capture, and the mage's actions, not to mention a guild assassin with a Portland-area target—I don't know the status of everything right now. But rest assured, we're working on *all* of it." He smiled, a rather impish glint in his eyes. "And our track record is excellent."

"That's, um, good to know."

Zeke held out the plate of pastries. "Scone? They're fresh."

"I…" Seb's stomach lurched, and he set the cup on its saucer with a clatter. *Nevan* wasn't enjoying tea and scones. Who knew what he might be enduring right now?

"Is it too strong?" Zeke asked. "I can brew another pot if you'd like something lighter. Perhaps an herbal infusion instead?"

"No, that's not it. I—"

A low chime sounded, followed by the click of the street door and footsteps—at least two sets—on the stairs.

And then Nevan was *there* in the archway, his duster billowing behind him as though he were standing on a windy hilltop, his waistcoat unbuttoned, and his linen shirt creased.

"Nevan!" Seb launched himself out of his chair and fairly flew across the lobby to fling himself into Nevan's arms. "Oh thank goodness." With his face pressed against Nevan's chest, his voice was muffled. "I was so worried."

Nevan stroked his hair. "Easy, cariad. I'm fine." He gripped Seb's shoulders and eased him away. Seb flushed, about to apologize for the perhaps inappropriate PDA, but then Nevan lowered his head and kissed him softly. "Thanks to you. Quentin here"—he nodded at the extremely dapper man next to him—"said you're the one who set Quest on the job." He kissed Seb again and then tucked him under his arm, tight against his side.

Quentin stepped toward the desk, inclining his head at the ladder-back chair. "Miss Pennybaker." Then he turned to Zeke. "Is Mal in his office?"

"Nah, Mal's right here." Mal strode out of the hallway, a sheaf of papers in his hand, and Seb felt Nevan tense beside him.

Quentin heaved a rather exasperated sigh. "And referring to himself in the third person, apparently."

"Just playing to the cues you feed me, mate." He winked at Quentin and then turned to Nevan. "I take it you're our ceffyl dŵr."

Nevan's arm fell away from Seb's shoulder and he dropped to his knees. "Lord Maldwyn."

Seb stared wide-eyed from Nevan's bowed head to Mal's irritated expression. "Lord Maldwyn?" he croaked.

Mal rolled his eyes. "Give over, mate. We don't stand on that kind of ceremony here." He waited until Nevan rose to his feet and then grinned. "Although I'll warn you—my business partner is Niall O'Tierney."

Nevan's eyes widened so far that the whites showed all around his irises. "The *prince*?"

"The very same. Although like I said, we don't stand on ceremony. Call him *Your Highness* and he'll throw a right strop. But never mind that." His expression turned grim. "Show me."

Seb frowned, but Nevan apparently knew what Mal meant because he held out his left hand, palm up, displaying the geas brand.

Mal whistled, long and low. "That's a nasty one. Mine wasn't nearly as bad. But that's because at its heart, it was an *unbinding*, and the bloke who cast it had pure intentions. Yours, though. Not only is it a binding spell, but the caster's intentions are as black as his own shriveled soul."

"Can you undo it?" Nevan asked, and the desperate hope in his tone tore at Seb's heart.

"Sorry, mate. Elemental mages don't work the same as fae magicians, witches, or druids." He rattled the papers in his hand. "We've got a team working on untangling it, but it'll take time, and we don't have that. Seb told us this Offerman wanker is trying to master *all* the elements?"

Nevan opened his mouth, but then gritted his teeth around a groan.

Mal winced. "Sorry. Should have known better than to ask you about it. Wasn't necessary anyway, seeing as Seb already filled us in." His wince disappeared and his blue eyes sparkled. "Which gives us more than enough to go on with. The council has been in negotiations with the elemental mages for years, trying to rein in their worst excesses. They pretend they're a united front, but this." He rattled the papers again. "This is proof that they've got dissension in their ranks, and won't *that* put a cat among the budgies."

Nevan scowled. "I don't care about the politics. I need to get my sister away from him."

"And maybe," Mal drawled, "keep yourself from becoming his unwilling tool for eternity?"

Nevan waved that away. "That's secondary. Lulu's safety is the most important. Can you find her?"

Mal frowned. "Don't you know where she is? Offerman claimed you had her."

"*He's* the one who's got her tucked away somewhere." Nevan punched his left palm—twice. "He claimed he was her *guardian*, not her captor. Said she shared his last name. Lies, all of it. He did it to punish me because I haven't moved fast enough."

"But he got the human police involved," Quentin said from his spot leaning against the desk. "That changes things in a way he might not have foreseen. If there's one thing that'll unite all the supe factions as well as the mages, it's getting humans up in their business, supes because of the Secrecy Pact, and the mages because they can't afford too much attention paid to how they source their spell ingredients."

Nevan looked from Quentin to Mal. "Can't you find her? Please?"

Mal patted Nevan's shoulder. "We will, mate. I promise. But we've got a ticking clock on another problem—the little matter of the guild assassin mucking about where they shouldn't be. That's what we've got to handle first."

"No! Please," Nevan begged, "you have to help me find Lulu. She's only six. She's got to be terrified."

"Yes, and I'm sorry about that. But terrified is not murdered."

"To a child that young, though," Seb said, snaking an arm around Nevan's waist, "terror can cause lasting trauma. Besides, Mario isn't in any danger. Yvo thinks Nevan met with the assassin as planned, but he didn't. He met *me*. I'm not about to try to kill anybody, and even if I was, the magic dagger is buried in the Doghouse back yard. Mario is perfectly safe."

"Um, guys?" They all turned to find Jordan standing on the landing, shifting nervously from foot to foot while Doop looked up at him adoringly. "That's one of the things I needed to tell you. The knife's gone."

"Gone?" Nevan said sharply. "What do you mean, gone?"

"Weellll..." Jordan screwed up his face. "Somebody sort of"—

he made a scooping motion with both hands—"dug it up overnight."

"Could it have been Noah?" Seb asked.

Jordan shook his head. "No. He never fills in the holes after he digs. This was perfectly level."

"Are you sure the knife was gone?"

"I checked. Definitely gone."

"Yvo," Nevan growled.

Seb let go of Nevan's waist and turned to face him, hands on his chest. "Let's think about that a minute, okay? How could it be Yvo? He still thinks I'm the assassin and that we can't strike until one o'clock. Why would he dig up the knife? It would prevent me—that is, if I *were* an assassin, which I'm not—from making the hit."

"I don't know how, but it was him. It had to be." Nevan's fists curled and uncurled at his sides. "If we knew where he lived, we could go over there and *make* him tell us where—"

"Oh, we know where he lives." Mal brandished the papers again. "Wanker put his address on the bloody police report. Hector checked it against our roster of known elemental mages, and it's his actual residence, all right." He shook his head. "Why do all those blighters want to live in the West Hills?"

Nevan's eyes glittered and he bared his teeth. "Then let's go."

"*You* are going nowhere," Mal said. "Too emotional, and when ceffyl dŵr lose their shit, there's no reining them in." He smirked. "Not without a bespelled bridle."

"Mal," Zeke chided. "That's not nice."

Mal shrugged. "Sorry, mate. My husband always says my snark'll be the death of me. But I'm serious about this. We're already working on an infiltration plan. You need to be patient. But in the meantime, we need to figure out where that dagger is and stop the assassin." He turned to Jordan. "Think you and Doop are up for the job?"

Jordan slid a glance at Nevan. "Yes, but—"

"Good. Come with me." Mal thrust the papers at Zeke, who

scrambled to keep them from fluttering to the ground, and strode down the hallway, Jordan at his heels.

"Doop!" Zeke set the papers on the desk and hurried over to where the giant hound was very efficiently vacuuming every scone off the plate. "Oh, my stars, Jordan is going to kill me. Those are *not* on your diet plan." He grabbed a handful of Doop's ruff and tugged. The hound didn't move.

There was a clash of keys from the typewriter and Doop yelped, then took off down the hallway with his tail between his legs.

Seb looked after him. "What just happened?"

Zeke collected the tea tray. "Miss Pennybaker can *always* get Doop to obey. I'd better tidy this away before he comes back, though." He hurried out of the lobby and up the stairs.

Seb sighed. "Well, I guess now we wait."

"I am not a fan of waiting." Nevan grinned down at him, a determined glint in his eye.

"Nevan," Seb said slowly, his belly dropping. "What are you thinking?"

Nevan strode over to the desk and scattered the papers across the desk until he held one up in triumph. "I'm thinking I'll track the arsehole down and make him tell me where my sister is. Now."

CHAPTER 28

*T*his was it. The opportunity Nevan never thought he'd get. Not only did he know where Yvo was, but Yvo only *thought* he knew where Nevan was. Thanks to that execrable druid potion, the arsehole still believed Nevan to be in jail.

He'll never see me coming.

Nevan ignored the clack of typewriter keys as he strode toward the landing. But then Seb stepped in front of him, arms outstretched.

"Stop. You heard what they said."

"But they didn't listen to what *we* said. What *you* said. The longer Lulu is in Yvo's clutches, the harder it will be for her to recover, to get back to herself. All these blokes"—he waved a hand toward the hallway—"they're focused on the assassin. Since one of them is Lord Maldwyn Kendrick, the Queen's bloody *Enforcer*, they've got skills. But there's no reason I can't get Lulu back while they're working."

"But—"

Nevan gripped Seb's shoulders. "Don't you see? They've got different priorities. Maybe I should be more worried about the political ramifications and where that dagger got off to, but from where I stand, the only person putting Lulu first is me."

Seb's frown morphed into a wobbly smile. "You're not. I'm worried about her too."

Nevan shook his head. "I can't let you come with me. It's already a problem that he knows where you live. I can't let him see your face. It's too dangerous."

Seb crossed his arms. "If you go, I go."

Nevan carded his fingers through his hair. He had an almost palpable sense of minutes—critical minutes—slipping away from him. "I don't have time to argue with you."

"Then don't. I'll hang back out of sight. But you don't know your way around Portland, nor do you have a car." He tapped one foot. "How exactly were you planning to get there? Through Faerie?"

Nevan scowled. He hadn't thought of that. If he called for an FTA driver, would the druid potion be neutralized? Druid magic and Faerie were inimical.

Tick tick tick.

"Fine. You can come." He pointed at Seb's nose. "But you'll stay back. Stay safe."

"I'll do my best, but have you forgotten?" He stroked Nevan's cheek. "Lulu isn't my only priority, sweetheart. You are too. I won't *stay* back if it means I can't *have* your back."

The typewriter clattered again. Nevan frowned at it. "What is going on with that?"

Seb cleared his throat and gestured to the chair as though announcing visiting royalty. "Nevan, may I introduce you to Miss Pennybaker, Quest's invisible receptionist?"

Clack clack clackity-clack.

Nevan winced. "So what you're saying is Lord Maldwyn and his crew will know exactly where we've gone."

Seb nodded. "May do so already."

This time, the rat-a-tat of keys was followed by the decisive ding of the carriage return. Seb held up a finger and then edged around the desk to peer at the paper.

"She says she's the office manager, not the receptionist." He glanced at the empty ladder-back chair. "I sincerely beg your pardon. I meant no disrespect." He looked back at the paper and blinked. "She, um, also says"—he glanced up at Nevan and then back down at the paper—"and I quote: *Nail the scoundrel's balls to the wall.*"

"Well, then." Nevan saluted in Miss Pennybaker's direction. "We've got our marching orders."

Seb held out his hand and waggled his fingers. "Give me the address."

Nevan handed over the paper, because Seb was right. In order to surprise Yvo and not collide with the Quest team, they had to move quickly, and Nevan needed Seb's knowledge and skills, not to mention his car, to do it.

Strike that. I just need Seb.

Seb peered at the paper. "Okay, I know where this is. I had a temporary nanny gig near there when the regular caregiver was on vacation. Come on."

They hurried toward the stairs.

"Guys?" Jordan called from the hallway. "Wait a minute."

"No time," Nevan called. "We'll be back."

They ran downstairs, burst out of the door onto the sidewalk, and sprinted to Seb's van. After they'd climbed in, buckled up, and Seb started the engine, he peered through the window at the building, biting his lip.

"Do you suppose we should have asked what Jordan wanted?"

"Not if it meant more delays. I have no idea how long this potion will last." Nevan buckled his seatbelt. "Drive." Then he winced. "Please."

Seb shot him a wry glance as he pulled away from the curb. "I appreciate the gesture, Nevan, but there's no need for unnecessary politeness between us."

Nevan rested his palm on Seb's thigh. "Cariad," he said softly, "no consideration I could offer you is ever unnecessary, even if it is only simple courtesy."

Seb blinked rapidly and then swallowed. "All right, then." He returned his gaze to the street. "Next stop, evil mage lair."

They headed out of downtown and into the winding streets above Northwest Portland. Nevan was glad Seb was driving, because he'd never have been able to find his way. "Are you certain these streets weren't laid out by weasel shifters? They make no sense whatsoever."

"Says the man who lives in a lake. These are hills. The streets have to accommodate the topography." He slowed and pulled to the side of the road, under a stand of maples. *"This* is an evil mage lair?"

"It's the address on the police report. Provided Yvo didn't lie to them, this is where he lives."

Seb turned off the engine, his eyebrows bunched in thought. "There might be a little too much gingerbread on the turrets, and that wishing well would be more in place at a Disney theme park, but the place doesn't scream evil. More like granny-who-hasn't-updated-her-aesthetic-since-1918. I mean, you'd think he'd at least have a ten-foot-high wall topped with barbed wire and a security booth at a massive iron gate. All he's got is a three-foot-high hedge." Seb wrinkled his nose. "Granted, it's the grumpiest looking hedge I've ever seen, but the driveway is completely open. Anybody could just walk up to the door."

They climbed out of the car, and immediately Nevan felt the telltale prickle on his skin.

"Not just anybody. He's got magical wards across the drive." He flicked a finger at the hedge. "And you're not wrong when you call the hedge grumpy. It's got three-inch thorns under those spiky leaves."

Seb's eyes widened. *"Three inches?* Man, that's worse than the natal plum bushes around Mr. Davis's house when I was a kid."

Nevan shrugged. "I suspect he hired a dryad to plant them, but then used his earth magic to distort them."

"Dryads?" Seb said faintly.

Nevan nodded. "Dryads. If they find out what he's done, they won't be happy." He paced toward the break in the hedge that opened onto the gravel drive. "And trust me when I say that unhappy dryads are not folk you want to face."

Seb joined Nevan at the foot of the driveway. "So now what? Do the magical walls mean we can't get in after all?"

Nevan smiled grimly. "Mages are arrogant arseholes, not to mention paranoid, but they're lazy. They get too used to leaning on their spells for their own convenience. While they depend on their magic to keep out those who don't belong, they want to make sure that *they're* not accidentally locked out."

"I guess that would be really embarrassing," Seb said, peering up at the house. "Like getting locked out of your room in nothing but a towel in a hotel full of a pre-teen dance competition."

Nevan lifted an eyebrow. "Speaking from experience?"

Seb's cheeks colored. "Shut up. I was just lucky there was a janitor's closet nearby or I could have been arrested as a sex offender, which would *not* have worked with my career objectives."

"In this case, mage laziness will work to our advantage. Unless I miss my guess, Yvo's wards will only sound the alarm if someone tries to enter who isn't a part of his household."

"So he'll know as soon as we walk past the hedge?"

Nevan held up his left hand and waggled his fingers. "You forget. I *am* a part of his household. The wards will let me pass."

Seb's eyes narrowed. "Are you sure about that?"

Nevan was tempted to lie, but this was Seb. There should be no pretense between them. "Mostly. There is still a chance that I'll be stopped. But I'm as certain as I can be."

Seb studied his face for a moment. "Thank you for not trying to downplay things." He raised on his toes and kissed Nevan's cheek. "Let's go."

Nevan blinked. "The wards might admit me, but they'll never admit you. You'll need to wait for me in the car."

Seb's pointed chin firmed in a very mulish fashion, and he grasped Nevan's arm in a firm grip. "Not a chance."

Tick tick tick.

"Seb. Please. Let me go."

"I'm guessing these famous wards don't require household people to take off all their clothes to pass."

"Since that would be exceedingly awkward, no."

"Okay then. Crouch down a bit."

"What—"

"Just bend your knees, Nevan. As you said, we're running out of time."

Nevan sighed, but did as Seb asked, huffing an *oof* when Seb jumped onto his back and wrapped his arms around Nevan's neck, his legs around Nevan's waist.

"There," Seb said. "Now I'm your backpack. Carry on."

Nevan tucked his arms under Seb's legs to keep him more firmly in place. "All right. But if this doesn't work and you're in any danger, promise me you'll run back to the car."

"I—"

"Seb. You're the only one who can bring help. Promise me."

Seb's sigh ruffled the hair at Nevan's nape. "All right. I promise."

"Good." Nevan took a deep, steadying breath. "Here goes."

Since stealth was not really an option, Nevan saw no point in hesitation. He strode past the hedge and ignored the curved gravel drive to cut straight across the wide swath of half-dead grass toward the door.

"Wait, wait," Seb said, arms tightening around Nevan's throat.

"Seb," Nevan croaked, "can't breathe."

"Oh, sorry." He released Nevan's neck and slid his legs down to stand on the ground. "Think we're still undetected?"

"We wouldn't have made it past the hedge if not."

"Good. Then I want to check out this well."

Nevan shook his head irritably. "The longer we delay, the more likely we'll be discovered. Besides, I can't be sure there isn't an inner perimeter as well."

"If Yvo is as arrogant as we know him to be, he'd never believe anybody could breach his outer defenses." Seb nudged Nevan's ribs with his elbow. "Right?"

"I suppose," Nevan said, rather grudgingly.

Seb hurried over to the well and peered over the waist-high stone wall where a rustic wooden bucket balanced. A second, larger bucket, this one of metal, hung from a rope wound around a spindle under the well's thatched roof. "I can see water. It's not very far down." He glanced back at Nevan. "Can you tell whether it's wild water or not?"

"Why?"

Seb rolled his eyes. "It's *obvious*, isn't it? Once you're face to face with Yvo, he'll be able to drain you again. We'll need a source of water to replenish you."

"'We'?"

"Yes, *we*," Seb said, his tone fierce. "If you pass out, you won't be any good to Lulu, not to mention being at Yvo's nonexistent mercy." He frowned. "I should have brought my pack. I've got extra water in there as well as some of Tahmina's magic djinni dust."

Nevan leaned over the edge and sniffed. If he wasn't so focused on Lulu—and if he wasn't on Yvo's very doorstep—the call of the wild water might have tempted him to throw himself down the well. "It's safe."

"Good." Seb grabbed the handle attached to the bucket rope and smiled a bit mischievously at Nevan. "You know, it'll go a lot faster if you help me crank."

CHAPTER 29

eb's skin itched like he'd spent all morning in a sandbox with a couple of overexcited toddlers, but when he and Nevan pulled the brimming bucket onto the well's stone ledge, he felt *marginally* better.

He dipped both hands into the water and held them out to Nevan. "Drink."

For a wonder, Nevan didn't argue. Seb wasn't sure if it was because an argument would waste more time or whether he'd accepted Seb's logic about being at full strength for the coming confrontation. *Whatever.*

After Nevan downed three double handfuls, Seb eyed both buckets. The smaller wooden one was decidedly more rustic—it looked handmade—but still serviceable, plus it had the advantage of being unattached to inconvenient ropes. It wasn't huge— maybe a couple of gallons. But a couple of gallons of water wasn't exactly a couple of gallons of feathers. While Seb had no trouble carting preschoolers around, they didn't have as great a danger of sloshing.

He made a snap decision and poured water from the metal bucket into the wooden one, but left enough airspace at the top that he could carry it without spilling.

"What are you doing?" Nevan asked.

"Insurance. Think of it as snacks for the road." Seb lifted the wooden bucket. *Ooof. This'll be awkward.* "Why would this joker have a wishing well in his front yard, anyway?"

Nevan looked down at Seb almost fondly. "To control me, of course."

"What?"

"You said it yourself, cariad. He conquered water when he bound me to his service. But I wouldn't be much use to him if I died. This way, he has a water source on hand, but one too small to allow me to shift into my most dangerous form."

Seb ground his teeth, and *not* just from the effort of hauling the bucket off the well wall. "I swear to goodness, Nevan, this guy needs to go down. *Hard.*"

"Indeed. And there is no time like the present."

Nevan strode toward the front door—which would be far more imposing if its bottle green paint weren't peeling—with Seb scuttling in his wake, listing sideways and wincing with every step when the bucket banged into his knee.

He waited on the wide porch until Seb joined him. "I'm sorry, cariad. I should have offered to carry that for you."

"Nope," Seb panted. "Taking it into your hand might have violated the terms of the curse. I'm good." He frowned at the door, which had three—*three!*—deadbolts as well as a keyhole in the ornate brass doorknob. "This could be a problem. I don't suppose you've got the keys? Or maybe a set of lock-picks?"

"No need." Nevan grinned and held up his palm. "I've got this."

He laid his geas brand atop the tarnished brass lions-head knocker, and...

Click. Snick. Thunk.

Then he turned the knob and the door opened smoothly. He didn't step inside, though. Instead, he faced Seb, grasping his shoulders gently. "I don't suppose I can convince you to stay outside?"

Seb shook his head. "Nope. But I'm not an idiot, Nevan. I'll keep out of your way." He forced a smile. "And don't forget, I have practice finding convenient closets to duck into when necessary."

"Very well. Although I'm loath to put you in danger, I can't deny that I'm more confident with you at my back." He leaned down and kissed Seb softly. "For luck."

Then he stepped inside, holding the door for Seb to follow him into the dim vestibule. The instant Seb crossed the threshold, he was assailed with the stench of stale sweat, a hint of skunk, and an odor like half-decomposed compost.

"Oh, man. *That's* a fragrance that'll never catch on."

When Nevan closed the door, all the locks re-engaged simultaneously, and Seb gulped with visions of the end of too many true crime shows dancing in his brain.

Nevan got us in. He can get us out. I hope.

An enormous grandfather clock sat to the left of the door, ticking sonorously as its cobweb-draped pendulum swung back and forth. A tall, narrow table to the right was so dusty Seb couldn't pick out the wood, and the bedraggled silk flower arrangement in its center was so faded the colors were equally unidentifiable. As they edged further inside, their feet kicked up gouts of dust.

"Ugh," Seb whispered. "This guy seriously needs a Roomba and a vat of Lemon Pledge."

Nevan glanced down at him. "I suspect it's more on the order of ammunition than housekeeping failure."

Seb blinked. "Ah. Right. Golems. Got it."

Nevan peered cautiously around the archway beyond the clock. "Parlor," he murmured. "Lots of brocade and grimy antimacassars."

Seb peeked through the doorway on the other side of the entryway. "Dining room. Dusty velvet chairs and cobwebby chandelier. Unless he's into gothic immersion, I'm guessing he doesn't spend much time here."

"If he's at odds with his fellow mages, no. There'd be no reason for him to entertain them or impress them with his wealth."

"So where do you suppose he is?" Seb nodded at the staircase that rose opposite the door in a total Feng Shui fail. "Upstairs, lounging in his four-poster, wearing another one of his stupid gowns and a tasseled nightcap?"

Nevan shook his head. "I suspect he's in his workroom. At least that's where he was the only time I was here, and where he's been during all his manifestations."

"Upstairs?"

"It has no windows, so I'm guessing basement?"

Seb nodded. "Outside, it was obvious the windows were all filthy, but they didn't look blocked off."

Nevan stalked toward a door at the other end of the vestibule, where a dozen or so waist-high granite figures sat in a disorganized jumble in the shadows under the stairs, his silence surprising for such a large man. When Seb followed him, the floor creaked under his feet, making him wince.

Nevan glanced back at him. "Will you wait here?"

Seb nodded. "But leave any doors open behind you, okay? Just in case."

Nevan shot him a quick smile and swung the door wide, propping it open with one of the granite figures, which, now that Seb looked closer, resembled a very rough-hewn, unpainted garden gnome.

As Nevan disappeared down the stairs in a swirl of leather duster, Seb studied the little statues. Could Yvo animate them as well? He shuddered. Clowns were bad enough. Rampaging garden gnomes were a step too far, even for someone as immersed in fairy tales as Seb.

He crept to the side of the room, next to the center staircase, where the floor would probably be more stable, and edged toward the open door. He peered around the frame. The narrow stairs seemed to descend into shadows thicker than winter fog. He couldn't see the bottom, let alone any sign of Nevan.

But as he was about to draw back, he heard a startled shout and then an angry roar. The roar was definitely Nevan, but the shout? That had to be Yvo.

Their voices twined, overlapping in an increasingly loud quarrel. Since there was no way they'd be able to hear him over that amount of noise, Seb didn't bother to try to mask his footsteps as he hurried downstairs as fast as he could go. Granted, that wasn't all that fast, given he was lugging a very heavy bucket of water that had started to leak onto his shoes, but he got the job done.

He found himself at the end of a long hallway, which would have been completely black if it weren't for the flickering light emanating from an open door at the far end.

Seb shuffled through more dust, staying close to the wall as he approached.

"I said, where is she?"

Seb froze, blinking. *Both* men had shouted that at the same time. Did that mean Yvo truly didn't know where Lulu was?

Hope sprouted under Seb's heart. If she was as bright as Nevan claimed she was, perhaps she'd been able to find her own way out. On the other hand, maybe Yvo was simply trying to throw Nevan off the scent while he readied another nasty spell to throw at him.

The hope shriveled.

Seb edged closer until he was right outside the door, near enough that he heard Nevan growl, "I swear, if you've hurt her, I'll—"

"You'll what?" Yvo sneered. "You've forfeited in every way possible. You've clearly consumed water, expressly against the terms of the geas, and you never connected with the assassin at all, despite *lying* to me that you had."

"I never lied," Nevan said.

"No? Are you saying you've had nothing to drink?"

There was a pause, and Seb could envision Nevan's grimace as he fought the geas. "N-no."

"Aha! As I suspected. A good thing I checked in with the guild, or your lies about the assassin could have cost me my quest. But now the *true* assassin has my dagger—"

"You found it?"

Yvo scoffed. "It was my spell. Of course I could find it, as well as send the assassin directly to its location." There was a silence broken only by the swish of cloth against a hard surface—Yvo prancing around on his workroom floor, maybe, and no doubt stirring up clouds of dust. "The contract will be fulfilled at last, and now that you belong to me forever, you'll collect my prize and return it here to me." He chortled. "And *then* you'll lead me directly to Luljeta and commend her to my care."

"I'll die first." From the strangled sound of Nevan's words, he was speaking through gritted teeth.

"You'll not die until I've no more use for you. But for now." More cloth rustling, followed by the thunk of something hitting wood. "The plants in my conservatory are a bit thirsty, and since you've got moisture to spare—expressly against your vow—your unsanctioned water will do for them."

Seb heard Nevan gasp. "What did you do?"

"Since you're not entitled to it, this little water diversion spell will siphon it off. If I'm feeling merciful"—Yvo's voice hardened to the farthest thing from merciful Seb had ever heard outside ballet studios—"I'll allow you to retain what I leave you after you complete the task. If not? We'll see."

Nevan uttered a strangled groan.

I can't let this happen. Despite Nevan's stern orders for Seb to stay hidden—and Seb's own declarations that he wasn't *foolish*—he couldn't let Nevan suffer like this. He needed water, and he needed it now.

Seb glanced down at the bucket. He had appropriate water, but could he reach Nevan without Yvo noticing? Not likely, considering Mage Evil was torturing Nevan like the Emperor zapping Luke Skywalker with the dark side of the Force.

But immersion worked, too.

Before he could second-guess himself, Seb darted through the door. He had seconds to take in his surroundings: a long, narrow room, its walls, floor, and ceiling tiled in some kind of stone; wooden benches lining the long walls to his left and right and across the far end, all of them cluttered like the playroom before clean-up time. The stench was stronger here, but Seb pushed aside thoughts of what ingredients might cause it to focus on Nevan, who was standing near the room's center.

Seb couldn't see Yvo's face—it was blocked by Nevan's body —but he glimpsed the skirt of that stupid robe between Nevan's legs amid eddies of dust.

Nevan. *Oh, mercy.* He was shuddering like an electrocution victim, and it looked as though his skin were flaking off and swirling around him.

That asshole is killing *him.*

Yvo might have declared he'd leave Nevan ambulatory enough to collect his revolting *prize*, but they'd already had evidence that the jerk wasn't as hot shit a mage as he thought.

So Seb shifted his grip on the bucket, one hand on the rim and the other on its bottom, and dashed forward. He flung the water at Nevan's exposed neck, hoping to hit as much skin as possible, but as the water left the bucket, Nevan doubled over, his arms wrapped around his middle.

The water hit Yvo square in his smirking face.

With one wide-eyed squawk, his face folded in on itself like an inside-out sock puppet—and kept folding, contracting, *shrinking* until there was nothing but a gold-spangled robe over a pile of steaming, reeking mud.

CHAPTER 30

*N*evan sucked in a full, deep breath. His mouth and throat were still dry, his skin itchy and flaky, but the pain in his middle was gone, as was...

He unclenched his eyes and stared at his left hand.

His palm was still callused, but the skin was unmarred, the geas brand vanished as though it had never been.

"I'm free," he croaked. He straightened up and spread his arms with a roar. "Free!"

A grin split his face, because now he could *do* for Yvo, force him to reveal where Lulu was, and *then*—

"Oh good grief, I *melted* him?"

Nevan spun around to find Seb clutching an empty bucket to his chest, staring down at a putrid mud mound with Yvo's robe on top.

"Seb? What did you—"

"I only wanted to keep him from hurting you." He raised wide, shocked eyes to Nevan. "I mean, yeah, I've felt like Dorothy since yesterday, but I never thought *that* would happen!"

"Shhh." Nevan took the bucket and set it on the floor so he could take Seb in his arms. "You succeeded, cariad. He can't hurt me anymore. See?" He held out his hand. "The geas is broken with the death of the mage who cast the spell."

Seb buried his face against Nevan's chest. "Oh, help. I really *am* an assassin," he wailed. "But it was an accident. I didn't *mean* to kill anybody!"

Nevan dropped a kiss on Seb's hair, even though it was dimmed with the dust that pervaded Yvo's lair. "I suspect it's only temporary. He can be reconstituted, much the same as golems are raised, to answer for his crimes."

"Temporary?" Seb drew back and glared up at him. "I'm CPR certified, but my training never covered giving mouth-to-mouth to a mud pile."

Despite Seb's obvious distress, Nevan couldn't hold back a low chuckle. "You needn't worry, cariad. That will be up to the council." He stared down at the noxious mess on the slate floor. "In fact, it's possible he might be able to raise himself once he dries out a bit."

"But why would water affect him like that? Aren't earth and water, you know, compatible elements?"

"Only to an extent. Too much water can erode earth, just as too much earth can constrain water. I suspect Yvo was more susceptible because his relationship with water was more… adversarial." Nevan nudged the crumpled gown with the toe of his boot. "Water doesn't react well to being forced into servitude. It will always look for a way."

"So, he did this to himself?" Seb said hopefully.

"No." Nevan cradled Seb's face in his hands. "He might have made himself susceptible, but you struck the blow, *fy annwyl*. And for that, I shall be forever grateful."

"I don't want *gratitude*," Seb said crossly.

"You have it, whether you do or no." He kissed Seb softly. "I'd like nothing more than to kiss you for hours, but this is neither the time nor the place."

Seb wrinkled his nose. "Definitely not the place. Ugh. It

smells like the inside of a dumpster, and that's not counting the dust, and, you know, melted evil mages."

Nevan frowned down at Yvo's remains. "We can't leave him here. He could recover on his own and who knows what havoc he could wreak? We need to take him to the council."

Seb regarded the mud doubtfully. "How?"

Tick tick tick.

"Do you think you could scoop him into that bucket if I found a shovel for you? I'd do it myself, but I need to search the house for Lulu. She's got to be here somewhere."

And the thought of Lulu imprisoned in this horrible place... Nevan wanted to simultaneously howl, put his fist through a wall, and toss every room until he found her.

Seb stroked Nevan's cheek. "Of course. It's the least I can do." His gaze strayed to the workbenches lining the walls. "There's a trowel over there." He rolled his eyes. "A golden trowel with a jewel-encrusted handle. Seriously? That can't be comfortable to hold."

"I could look for another."

Seb made shooing motions with both hands. "Go. Go. Find your sister. I'll handle this."

"If you're certain?"

"Positive." Seb kissed him. "I'm a nanny, remember? I clean up worse messes than this on a regular basis."

Nevan stole one more kiss, then ran out of the room. Once in the hallway, he looked right and left. Nothing to the right other than a rough stone wall, but several closed doors lay to the left between him and the stairs. He strode to the first, hoping it wasn't locked, since with the geas broken, he no longer belonged to the household. The knob turned easily, but the room was empty even of dust. He hurried to the next. Same situation.

The last one before the stairs was far from empty, but it was packed so tightly with a jumble of splintered wood, shattered crockery, and limp burlap sacks that it was clearly the graveyard for Yvo's failed spells.

He raced up the steps just as the door at the top of the stair-well began to swing shut. He caught it before it latched and stepped cautiously into the entryway.

Where, instead of stone gnomes, the entry was now full of chattering *live* gnomes in moleskin jerkins and green trousers, some with the traditional white beards and others more smooth-cheeked than Jordan's little brother. Gnomes, despite how humans chose to depict them, came in all shapes and appearances.

However, gnomes were creatures of earth, and while none came up higher than Nevan's mid-thigh, he braced himself in the doorway, preparing for their attack while cursing himself for a fool. Yvo had managed to drain him of enough water that he wasn't at full strength, and there were at least a dozen gnomes, all of whom had stopped their chatter and were staring up at him.

One of them, who had the face of an angel and an expression as fierce as a redcap, shouldered through their fellows and charged toward Nevan. Nevan planted his feet wide, ready for the blow, but instead the gnome stopped just out of arms-reach and looked up at him.

"Is it true? The mage is gone?"

"Yes."

The gnome narrowed their eyes. "Did you kill him, ceffyl dŵr?"

"No. My… partner doused him with water and rendered him into mud."

The other gnomes murmured to one another like the susurrus of wind through blackberry leaves, but their spokesperson kept their attention fixed on Nevan.

"So he will return."

Nevan curled his fingers into fists. "Not if I have a say. I intend to turn him over to the council for judgment. If you take issue with that, you will take it up with me, not my partner."

The spokesgnome widened eyes the color of new leaves

before bursting into laughter. "Issue? We had rather shower you with daisies and raise glass after glass of mead with you. The mage has kept us captive here for years. You have freed us."

Nevan relaxed a bit, but not completely.

Tick tick tick.

"My *partner* freed you, as he freed me. Will you all leave now?"

"It has been long since we've seen our burrows, our meadows, our hills. Long since we've gathered in Faerie beneath the One Tree. So yes, we will be departing as soon as may be."

"If I could ask a favor?"

"You may ask. We will judge whether we will comply once we've heard your terms."

"No terms. Only..." Nevan grabbed an umbrella stand shaped like an elephant's foot and used it to prop the door open again. "Yvo took my little sister, Luljeta. Lulu. She's an ora, but only a child. Would you help me find her? She must be here somewhere."

Regret darkened the gnome's eyes. "We will look, but I fear we will not find her. Although we were consigned to stone, we weren't insensible. We would have known if the mage brought another into his lair."

"Are you sure... I'm sorry, I didn't catch your name."

The gnome grinned, a display of very white, slightly pointed teeth. "Because I did not give it. Since you have freed us, however, I will gift it to you. I am Eike, of the Hirta clan."

"Are you certain, Eike? Certain that Yvo brought no one else here?"

Eike lifted a nut-brown eyebrow. "We knew he brought you, Nevan Quirke. We are certain. There is no one else beneath this roof or on these grounds. No one save us, your partner, and you."

Nevan's shoulders fell. "Shite." Where had Yvo stashed Lulu? Until he was reconstituted, Nevan couldn't force the truth out of him.

"Nevan?" Seb called from the stairwell, accompanied by the sound of his uneven footsteps on the risers. "I got most of him into the bucket, but I couldn't scrape it all off the floor. Do you suppose he'll be reanimated with parts missing? I think—" Seb froze next to Nevan in the doorway, eyes wide behind his spectacles as he took in the gnomes.

For their part, the gnomes took one look at Seb and all bowed deeply, humming low in their throats.

Seb sidled closer to Nevan, the bucket full of Yvo banging against his knees. "Um, Nevan? What's going on?"

Nevan smiled down at Seb. "I believe you're being thanked."

Eike straightened, although the rest of the gnomes remained bowed. "May I have your name?"

"Uh, Seb."

Eike's eyes narrowed. "That is not your true name. You needn't fear we will misuse it. We owe you lifelong allegiance for the service you have done us this day."

Seb blinked. "Oookay. My full name is Eusebio Ardelean."

"Hail to Eusebio," the gnomes intoned.

"Oh good heavens," Seb breathed, "it's like the Winkies after Dorothy melted the witch. How is this my life now?"

Nevan turned to Seb and took the bucket from his hand. "Eike says Lulu isn't here, that she's never been here."

"Oh, no." Seb's expression turned somber. "I'm so sorry. I know you want her back with you as soon as possible. But now that you're free, you can ask Jordan to find her for you. We can go back right now and—"

"We can't, cariad." Nevan heaved a sigh. "Mario is still in danger."

Seb's brows snapped together. "But Yvo's been neutralized. You're free." He nodded at the gnomes. "You're all free."

"That's true. However, simply because the contractee dies or is temporarily non-sentient, it doesn't cancel a guild contract."

"Won't Yvo's spell on the dagger be neutralized, though, the same as your geas was?"

"Not if the assassin already took possession, which we know has happened."

"But the Quest team is already working on that angle. Can't we leave it to them?"

Nevan cocked his head and gazed down into Seb's earnest face. "If it were one of your charges, would you be willing to leave their safety to someone else if you had the power to help?"

"Of course not!"

"We have an advantage that Quest does not—we've seen the dagger, touched it. We've scouted the assassination site." He gripped Seb's shoulder with one hand. "You have Quest's number. If we see anything, we can notify them at once."

The bucket in Nevan's hand juddered. He glanced down to see the mud inside heaving until a sullen bubble rose to the top and burst in a belch of sulfur. *Mud farts. Goddess preserve me.*

Nevan brandished the bucket, causing the gnomes to all jump back. "Yvo's already fighting to restore himself, but we don't have time to take him to the council." He glanced at the grandfather clock. It was past twelve-thirty. "Not if we're to make the Galliers' performance. Come on."

He headed for the front door, but slowed when he remembered the locks. Just when he was ready to find an axe and cut their way out, the locks all disengaged. He glanced down at the bucket. *Heh.* Apparently, the household recognized Yvo, even in his current incarnation. Good to know.

He flung open the door and strode to the well, Seb and the entire gnome entourage at his heels. After he set bucket-of-Yvo down on the dry grass, he hauled up another brimming pail of water. He glanced around, searching for a— *aha.* A metal cup hung from a nail on one of the well's pillars. Nevan grabbed it, filled it, and dumped the water on top of Yvo.

The mud immediately subsided, but for good measure, Nevan added another cupful.

Seb peered down at it. "Hmmm. Ex-earth mage. Just add water."

Nevan turned to Eike. "Will you and your clan guard him and keep him inert until we return?"

Eike took the cup from Nevan and tossed more water on top of Yvo. "With pleasure."

"Thank you." Nevan turned to Seb. "If we expect to save Mario, we must—"

"I know. Go back to the carnival." Seb sighed. "Maybe we'll be lucky for once and the clowns will all be on their lunch break."

CHAPTER 31

The drive from Yvo's lair in the West Hills to the fairgrounds in Hillsboro was complicated by an accident on Highway 26. By the time Seb parked the van in the grassy lot next to the carnival, his hands on the wheel were slick with sweat because his dashboard clock read 1:12.

Were they too late?

He tumbled out of his door as Nevan exited on the other side. He'd made Nevan drink two bottles of water from his pack as well as eat all the grapes, an orange, and a handful of almonds. Seb suspected it would take more than that for a true recovery from Yvo's horrible water diversion spell, and hesitated for a moment, his hand on the door handle as he looked at his pack. Right now, they needed speed and stealth more than healthy snacks and hand sanitizer, and the pack weighed him down, so he opted to leave it in the van.

He grabbed the third water bottle, though. Just in case.

They raced for the entrance and were able to walk right up to the ticket booth, since for once there wasn't a line. "Two, please," Seb panted as he tucked the water bottle under his arm and pulled out his wallet. He slid his credit card under the window.

"Welcome, Travelers, to Errante Ame's Carnival of Mysteries," the woman behind the window said. "All the rides and games are open right now, as well as the food stalls, but if you're interested in any of the tent acts, I'm afraid you'll have to wait a bit. They're all in the big top for the Grand Parade."

Seb cut a glance at Nevan, who wasn't paying attention, his gaze laser focused on the midway. "Grand Parade?"

"The acts circle the ring while Rafe, our ringmaster, introduces each of them to the crowd. Usually it only happens at the evening shows, but the boss decided to add another one for the first performance of the day."

"Are the clowns part of the parade?" Seb asked as she returned his card along with the tickets.

"Of course." She folded hands bedecked with at least two rings on each finger on the counter and smiled. "Our Grand Parade wouldn't be complete without Cleo's Clever Clowns."

Seb wasn't sure whether to be relieved or worried about that. They wouldn't encounter the clowns on the midway, but it would be harder to avoid them in an enclosed space like a tent, even a huge one like the big top. *Clowns are not the biggest problem now.*

"So the Galliers' performance hasn't started yet?"

She shook her head. "Not until after the Grand Parade."

"Thanks." Seb tucked his wallet back in his pocket and uncapped the water bottle. He nudged Nevan with his elbow. "We're not too late yet, but it's gonna be close. Here. Drink."

Nevan frowned at the bottle in Seb's hand. "I'm not thirsty."

"You're always thirsty. Drink."

"I'll drink after. At any moment, we could be too late."

He grabbed Seb's arm and hauled him forward, causing Seb to fumble the bottle cap and drop it in the sparse grass just inside the gates, right in front of the solemn guard in his velvet ensemble.

Seb pulled against Nevan's grip, conditioned by years of

convincing kids to pick up after themselves. "Wait. I dropped the—"

"No time."

"But I can't *litter*," Seb said, scandalized, gazing over his shoulder as Nevan towed him onward. "I *never* litter. The guard might throw us out, and then where would we be?"

However, instead of calling for them to halt, the guard bent gracefully and plucked the bottle cap off the ground.

"Sorry!" Seb called as they passed an enormous Wheel of Fortune, its teddy bear prizes bigger than Seb's torso.

With his litter nightmare behind him, Seb made an effort to match Nevan's pace as they raced toward the big top. Other than a couple of guys at the Buttons of Mystery game and a gaggle of truculent teenagers on the carousel, the midway was strangely devoid of fairgoers.

"Everyone must be inside the big top," Seb panted.

"Shite," Nevan growled, not sounding at all winded. "Can you imagine what will happen if this plays out in front of so many humans?"

Seb's steps faltered, the bottom dropping out of his heart. *Human. Like me.*

The sound of a calliope playing a jaunty tune drifted from inside the tent, along with the boom of the ringmaster's voice announcing, "I give to you Abdullah, whose fire-eating feats and sword-swallowing skills are sure to awe and amaze!" followed by the *oohs* of the audience.

Nevan looked down at him, brow furrowed. "What's wrong?"

"Nothing." He forced a smile, but he eased away from Nevan's hand, fussing with the water bottle. "Are you sure I can't convince you to drink?"

Nevan's expression softened slightly. "I'm fine, cariad. I will drink later, after we've saved Mario."

Seb nodded and ducked through the tent flap, nearly colliding with a carnie selling cotton candy and churros from a tray. The burnt sugar and cinnamon scents twined with the smell of sawdust and Seb's own rising panic.

The lights at the top of the tent turned the center ring brighter than the midway and cast the audience risers into shadow. Several follow spots swept the tent as though dancing in time with the calliope's music. One of them swept around the audience and caught Seb square in the eyes. He was still blinking away the afterimage when Nevan joined him.

"Shite," he said again. "The place is packed."

"Madam Persephone," the ringmaster—Rafe—in his crimson and gold uniform boomed. He held the hand of a willowy woman draped in yards of purple and lavender chiffon, who dropped a graceful curtsy. "She knows all. Sees all. Cross her palm with silver and she might be persuaded to share those secrets with you."

Madame Persephone glided to the edge of the ring to stand between a short, pale man in a black tails and top hat, and a dark-skinned, incredibly buff bald man in white linen harem pants, enough gold ornaments draping his bare chest to open his own jewelry store, and—*holy crap*—a giant sword.

"Nevan." Seb grabbed Nevan's duster lapel and drew him down far enough to speak into his ear in a near shout, because between the calliope, the audience applause, and the ringmaster's patter, there was no other way for him to be heard. "How are we going to find an assassin when we have no idea what they look like?"

"Cleo's Clever Clowns!" Rafe bellowed, and the clowns erupted into the ring and scattered, walking on their hands, feet, and, in a couple of cases, each other.

Seb tried to count them, but he couldn't. "It could be one of the clowns. I think there are more of them than before."

Nevan lifted a brow. "Since you refused to look at them, how can you be sure?"

"Well. I can't. But you have to admit, clown makeup would be the perfect disguise. Their face would be totally hidden."

"Perhaps, but I understand all clown makeups are unique. These would be familiar to the ringmaster and the other acts. I doubt a stranger could slip in unnoticed."

"I suppose," Seb grumbled. "But where do we even start looking? *How* do we start looking?"

"Gentleman Jim, Master of Knives, and his lovely assistant," Rafe announced.

Seb shuddered as the knife thrower escorted his assistant into the center of the ring, waving his Stetson at the crowd. *Knives. Ugh.* But at least Gentleman Jim's hands were empty of weapons for a change.

"They won't be high up in the risers," Nevan said, peering around through narrowed eyes. "The crowd would block their escape."

"Darius the Wonder Dog!" Rafe called, and the terrier who'd run off with Doop scampered into the center of the ring and executed a series of backflips.

"You mean—"

"They'll have to be in the first couple of rows, probably near one of the aisles. Better lines of sight that way, too."

Lines of sight. For throwing the knife. Seb pressed the hand holding the water bottle to his jittery middle. "That makes sense, I suppose."

"Samson. The strongest. Man. In the world!"

Seb spared a glance at Rafe and the latest act—a truly enormous man who, in his loin cloth, his bare chest glistening with oil in the lights, looked kind of like Fabio-and-a-half, but with a better proportioned neck. "So, how do we identify them?"

"Look for someone who doesn't belong," Nevan said. "Who's not paying attention to the show. Let's split up. You go left and I'll go right. Do a quick reconnaissance while the introductions are still going on." He pointed across the tent. "We'll meet up there, in front of the performers' entrance."

At that moment, seven people in form-fitting red and white

costumes, complete with satin capes, bounded out of the opposite entrance.

"The Flying Galliers!" the ringmaster shouted gleefully. "Marcel, Tia"—as Rafe announced each Gallier, they stepped forward and bowed with a theatrical swish of their capes— "Irena, Jamie, Paul, Bette. And last, but certainly not least..." The calliope boomed out a dramatic chord. "*Mario.*"

The boy stepped forward, his bow just as extravagant and his cape swirl just as practiced as the rest of his family's.

Oh heavens, he was so *young.*

Seb set his jaw. There was absolutely *no way* was he letting anybody hurt this boy. "Right. Let's do this."

He strode away from the tent flap, ignoring the clown who waved an enormous paper bouquet under his nose, and began making his way around the arena between the first row of risers and the ring railing.

He immediately recognized his mistake.

"Hey!" a middle-aged man in a Trailblazers cap in the front row said. "You're in the way."

Seb winced. "Sorry, sorry."

He crouched and scuttled onward, smiling apologetically at each person while he checked them out for... what? Looking assassanish? How could you even tell?

Think, Seb. You know how to read people. Assessing moods was a professional necessity when it came to heading off looming tantrums or derailing potential playground altercations.

Very few people would come to a fair all by themselves, right? So he really *looked*, but this time he looked for *units*. People who were *together*, here to share an experience.

"Today, my friends," Rafe said almost breathlessly, yet still in his booming outdoor voice, "you are in for a treat. Because today, in this *very tent*, in this *very hour*, Mario Gallier will perform his *very first* triple somersault—with *two twists*—and secure his place in his family's legacy."

Terror knotted Seb's belly. If Mario were about to perform—

"But first, direct your gaze above, where Paul and Irena Gallier will amaze you by their skill and daring on the high wire!"

Seb let out a shaky breath. A reprieve, but probably not a very long one. *Come on, assassin. Where are you?* When he looked at the risers now, he saw a field of... necks and chins, because everyone had followed the ringmaster's instructions and was looking up at the high wire.

Then his gaze caught on a face, a person who *wasn't* looking up. A person who was staring directly at *him*. His heart leapt to his throat, and he rose from his crouch.

But then he realized who it was—the guard from the gate, who was sitting in the top row, right next to the railing over the performers' entrance. He inclined his head at Seb, but he still didn't look at the high wire. Instead, he turned his attention to Rafe.

"Down in front," someone hollered.

"Sorry." Seb hunched over again and hurried forward, his eyes on his shoes so he could avoid stepping on the feet of every person in the front row. He rounded the corner and...

"*Ooof.*"

His head collided with something soft, and as he fumbled his grip on the bottle, it tipped and water shot out its neck.

He stood up quickly to discover he'd run head first into Gentleman Jim's assistant. Not only that, but he'd spilled half a bottle of water all over her bedazzled skirt, dimming the sequins' sparkle.

"Oh my word. I'm *so* sorry." Seb cursed himself for leaving his pack behind, because he had nothing to blot the water off her bling.

"Think nothing of it," she said. "It was an accident, after all."

Seb froze. *Something about those words...*

She turned away, and the set of her shoulders, her blonde updo, the line of her spine pinged Seb's memory.

"You said that before," he croaked. "In Starbucks. When I knocked that coffee on your skirt. It's you. *You're* the assassin."

She hardly paused for a moment before, in a flare and rustle of taffeta, she sprinted for the performers' entrance. And she was *fast*, faster than anyone wearing those pointy-toed, stiletto-heeled, vintage ankle boots should be.

For a moment, Seb couldn't move, rooted to the ground by shock and by the recollection of *why* he'd ordered that awful drink: He'd offered to buy her beverage for her as an apology, and she'd told him what she wanted, but then had told him not to bother.

He hadn't listened, of course, since he *had* stained her skirt, and ordered the drink for her anyway, although he hadn't been able to give it to her before Nevan had approached him, mistaking Seb for an assassin.

Finally, he shook off his shock and took off after her, only to be blocked by Fabio-and-a-half. Samson—the strongest. Man. In the world—planted his feet wide, arms crossed over a chest as broad as Seb's minivan.

"Performers only," he said.

"But—"

"Performers. Only."

"And now, my friends, the time has come," the ringmaster said. "I present to you... Mario Gallier!"

CHAPTER 32

*N*evan was beginning to share Seb's aversion to clowns. Or at least this cadre, since they kept popping up in front of him and blocking his progress. He was only halfway around his side of the tent when the ringmaster announced Mario.

Nevan froze as the spotlight landed on the boy, who stood at the foot of one pillar, his arm raised in the air to acknowledge the crowd's applause.

The calliope played its equivalent of a drum roll as Mario began climbing toward the platform where Tia Gallier waited for him. Marcel Gallier was on the opposite platform, a second trapeze in his hand.

Nevan scanned the crowd desperately. How could he spot the person who was focused on Mario when *everyone* was focused on Mario? This was impossible.

Mario reached the platform and when the calliope began playing another, vaguely familiar song, the ringmaster called, "Everybody join me in singing 'The Daring Young Man on the Flying Trapeze' to welcome Mario now. But be warned: Once he begins, we must all be very, very still, so as not to distract him.

Because, as you can see…" He swept out one crimson-clothed arm. "There is *no net*."

"Nevan." Seb nearly collapsed against him, his hair mussed and his eyes wild behind the glint of light off his lenses. "It's the assistant. The assassin."

Nevan shook his head, trying to make sense of Seb's words as the audience joined with the ringmaster's powerful baritone and belted enthusiastically if not tunefully, "Oh, he flies through the air with the greatest of ease."

"What?"

"The assassin," Seb said, gripping Nevan's arm. "Assistant. Assassin assistant." Seb slapped his forehead. "How clueless could we be? What better place for a knife-throwing assassin to hide than with the freaking *knife-throwing* act?"

"Wait. Are you saying—"

"Get *down*, you jerks!" a woman in the front row shouted.

Nevan grabbed Seb's elbow and towed him behind the risers near where he'd spoken to Yvo that first day. "Are you saying that Gentleman Jim's assistant is the assassin?"

"Yes. The second one, not the first one." Seb's eyes widened. "Oh my heavens, do you think she *assassinated* the first assistant so she could take her place?"

"I doubt it. Guild assassins only kill by contract. She probably just bribed her. But are you sure?"

Seb bobbed his head jerkily. "Absolutely. She was in Starbucks the day we met. I spilled coffee on her, and then I—"

"I remember. And I trust you. Explanations can wait. At least we know who we're looking for. Now we need to stop her from killing Mario."

"She was in her costume when I saw her just now, but she might have changed since I kind of, um, accused her of being the assassin."

"I doubt she'll change and risk her cover, but it doesn't matter." Nevan gripped Seb's shoulders. "We need to be smart about this, Seb. Smart and safe. I'll go find her. But you. You *must not* approach her."

Seb's expression turned mulish. "I'm not helpless."

"I know. However, you have a different task." He glanced over his shoulder. "I'd say you should speak to the ringmaster, but I doubt you'd be able to interrupt him in the middle of the show."

Especially as the man was waving his arms like a conductor, leading the crowd in another chorus of "The Daring Young Man on the Flying Trapeze."

"Not a chance. And we can forget about checking out the performers' area over there. There's a guy who makes you look like one of those gnomes blocking the way."

Nevan shook his head. "That doesn't matter. She can't execute her contract—"

"Please don't say execute," Seb said faintly.

"—if she doesn't have Mario in her line of sight. So she'll have to be inside the tent. Since the ringmaster isn't an option, I need you to go back to the gate and talk to that guard. He's bound to know something about carnival security."

"Probably." Seb scowled. "In fact, he'll probably think *I'm* a huge security risk. He already knows I'm a litterer. How will I get him to believe me in time?"

"If you have to, tell him that *I'm* the one who's the danger."

"But—"

"Seb. We'll straighten it out afterward." The calliope ended the song on a triumphant chord. "But we're officially out of time. Can you do it?"

Seb searched his face, but then took a deep breath, clearly capitulating. "Okay."

"Good." Nevan pressed a quick kiss to Seb's forehead. "Now go. I'll see you soon."

Nevan turned Seb and gave him a gentle push toward the tent flap. Then he straightened his shoulders and marched out to stop an assassin.

SEB INTENDED to follow Nevan's instructions, he really did. But he knew something Nevan didn't—that the guard wasn't at the gate at all. He was sitting in the top row, right next to the performer's entrance.

He eyed the narrow gap between the tent canvas and the bleacher struts. A little cramped, but better than risking the ire of the audience again.

Seb edged his way behind the risers, trying not to be distracted by the random bits of popcorn and peanut shells that pattered to the ground, dropped by fairgoers who clearly didn't share Seb's concern about litter.

As he reached the wooden railing next to the performers' entrance, the calliope swung into a highly embellished version of "The Daring Young Man on the Flying Trapeze," this time without the choral accompaniment.

"He's more daring than he realizes," Seb muttered.

The gap between the railing and the bleachers was even narrower than the space next to the tent, and the wooden railing wasn't as forgiving as the canvas. His polo snagged on a badly set screw when he was halfway along, and it took him a few precious seconds to free himself.

When he finally stumbled out next to the ring, the ringmaster intoned, "And now, my friends and fellow travelers, it's time. Time for Mario Gallier to take his place in the annals of Carnival of Mysteries lore."

Oh crap. Seb peered upward to see Mario, looking so tiny from this angle, although the trapeze platform was probably only about thirty feet in the air. Could the assassin actually throw a knife that far with any kind of accuracy?

Well, it's a freaking magical dagger, so who knows? Besides, if she missed Mario, she could still hurt somebody else, an innocent audience member, perhaps another child.

Seb peered up into the bleachers. Yes, the guard was still

there. He grasped the rail and began to mount the bleachers. There wasn't really an aisle here, but it was the most direct path to the guard, so he smiled apologetically at the people he displaced as he climbed.

"Sorry. I'm sorry. I just have to get up there. If you don't mind? Thank you. I'm sorry. I'm sorry. Excuse me."

The audience gasped, and Seb teetered, belly clenching. He jerked his head around in time to see Mario leap off the platform, swinging his legs to gain momentum as Marcel, on the second trapeze, timed his own swings to be in position for Mario's trick.

Any time. He's in the air, so it could happen any time.

When Seb turned back, the guard was gone.

He glanced around wildly, but the guard was nowhere to be seen. How could a guy *that* tall and noticeable just disappear? He spotted Nevan bulldozing his way around the ring but couldn't catch his eye to give him the *Now what?* shrug.

Fine. Okay. It was up to Seb then. He chewed on his lip. Who else could he— *Oh.* Fabio-and-a-half, who'd prevented Seb from following the assistant before.

Samson was part of the show. Surely that meant he could *stop* the show, or at least reach the ringmaster and raise an alarm. But when Seb peered over the railing, Samson wasn't blocking the curtain over the performers' entrance. Instead, he was standing at the end of the short aisle, next to the first row of risers, with Madame Persephone at his side and Darius the Wonder Dog at his feet. All of them were gazing up at the trapezes. At Mario, caught in the crisscrossed spotlights like a spider in a web of light.

Seb had no hope of reaching them before Mario launched into his trick—it had taken him forever to fight his way halfway up the risers and would no doubt take just as long to push his way down, especially since the people he'd dislodged were already cranky with him and wouldn't thank him for making them miss the signature event of the day.

Maybe he could... well, not shout. He didn't want to startle Mario, because if he missed his grip, falling from that height—and really, what was his family thinking, letting him do a dangerous trick without a net?—could kill him just as effectively as a magical dagger.

Seb leaned over the railing, the two-by-four cutting into his stomach. But as he was about to call Samson's name, the curtain fluttered and the assassin assistant slipped out. Her gaze, like everyone else's, was locked on Mario.

A very familiar dagger glinted in her hand, nearly hidden in the folds of her skirt.

Seb's heart flew up his throat and his hands spasmed on the railing, its edges biting into his palms. Even if Samson could hear him over the calliope's crashing chords, Seb couldn't force anything out of his mouth.

Was Nevan... No, he was still halfway around the tent, too far to reach the assassin in time, even if he could force his way past Samson, Madame Persephone, and Darius the Wonder Dog.

Dang it, where was a clown when you needed one?

The assassin hadn't spotted him. Her ice-blue eyes narrowed, and she lifted her hand, changing her grip on the knife's hilt. Nobody—literally *nobody*—was watching her, including her supposed boss, Gentleman Jim, who was clear across the tent, standing next to... Jeez, *there* was the guard, and how did he get all the way over there?

Below him, the assassin raised her arm.

Seb was out of time. He only had one option that he could see, and it was a stupid option—he was a nanny, for goodness' sake, not an action hero—but it was all he had.

Somehow, he had to spoil her aim.

One chance. I only have one chance to get this right. There'd be no do-overs, not like when Seb shepherded preschoolers through learning to skip or kicking a soccer ball for the first time.

With a muttered plea to any fates who might be listening,

Seb scrambled to the top of the railing and crouched there, wobbling, as the assassin drew her arm back, elbow tucked close to her ear and the hand holding the knife behind her head as though she were about to give herself a spontaneous haircut.

Then three things happened once.

Nevan, who'd obviously spotted Seb on his precarious perch, shouted, "Seb! No!"

The assassin's throwing hand whipped forward.

And Seb launched himself off the risers, arms outstretched.

Time seemed to slow then and Seb realized he'd miscalculated. He'd intended to bat the knife out of the air, but instead, he'd somehow rotated a quarter turn and his chest was directly in line with its trajectory.

This is going to hurt. Seb clenched his eyes shut and braced for impact.

Then another three things happened at once.

The audience burst into cheers and wild applause.

Warmth erupted in Seb's chest, directly below his heart, and he had an instant to be thankful for the shock that delayed the pain.

And he was snatched out of midair and held against a wide, naked chest.

He cracked one eye open to find that he was cradled in Samson's arms like a newborn. The assassin, her hands fisted on her hips, was glaring at Seb with Nevan looming next to her, neatly blocking her exit, while he, in turn, gave Samson the stink-eye.

Taking a shaky breath, Seb peered down at his chest and saw only his crumpled polo, bunched halfway to his armpits.

Wait. What?

Where was the blood? Where was the pain? For that matter, where was the freaking *knife*?

Oh, no. He covered his eyes with both hands, burying a moan. What had he been *thinking*? Of course he'd been doomed to failure. He wasn't capable of knocking a freaking *dagger* out of the *air*. He was a *nanny*, for goodness' sake. How many times had he tutored his charges on impulse control? Clearly he needed to listen to his own lectures, because—

"Let's hear another round of applause for Mario Gallier." Rafe's plummy tones penetrated Seb's fog of regret. "Mario, take another bow."

"Mario?" Seb croaked, peeking through his fingers at Nevan. "He's okay?"

Nevan smiled, his expression both proud and affectionate. "He is, cariad. But are you?"

"I, um..." Seb uncovered his face and did another quick assessment. His polo sported a few wet-looking blotches—probably from Samson's chest oil—but he seemed otherwise unscathed. "Yes. I'm fine. I think." Then he caught the glint of metal in the sawdust at Samson's sandaled feet.

The knife.

He looked up into Samson's square-jawed face. "Did you block the dagger?"

"No." Samson set Seb on his feet. "You did."

"Me? But I didn't even touch it."

Madame Persephone floated over in a cloud of violet and amethyst chiffon. "You have that backwards, zână. *It* did not touch *you*."

"Isn't that the same thing?"

"No, zână," she said. "It is very different."

He smiled at her, a little shakily. "My name's Seb, actually."

"It is not," she replied, her silver eyes glinting with specks of green and blue, like opals. "Your name is Eusebio Ardelean, and you are zână."

"Zână? Does that mean nanny in your language? Because that's what I am."

"No," she said. "You are zână, a being born to nurture children, protect them, cherish them."

"Like I said, I'm a nanny."

Nevan's face practically glowed with joy, which did funny

things to Seb's middle. "No, cariad. A simple nanny couldn't have stopped that blade in midair and sent it clattering to earth. But that is what you did."

"Wait." Something pinged in the dim recesses of Seb's childhood memories. "My bună told me tales of a Romanian spirit who watched over children. After my bunic, my grandfather, passed away, she told me another story about them every night to distract me and keep me from being sad. But when my imaginary friend showed up, she stopped."

Madame Persephone smiled enigmatically. "Your friend was not imaginary. He was your bunic, a zână, staying close to keep you safe until you no longer had need of him." She tucked her hand into Samson's arm. "Now, if you would be so good, Samson, escort me back to my tent before the crowd exits. You know how I loathe the crush."

They strolled past Nevan and the assassin, who hadn't bothered to try to escape, Darius bouncing at their heels. Seb stared after them, his mouth agape. His imaginary friend wasn't imaginary? His imaginary friend was his *grandfather*?

And I'm not really human. He was still a nanny, but more like... Supernanny?

He could live with that, especially since it meant Nevan wasn't technically in violation of the secrecy thingie with his council. *Maybe we have a real chance to be together.*

But before Seb could broach the subject, Nevan's expression turned somber. Threatening. Almost murderous. He glowered down at the assassin. "I would have your name."

She smirked at him. "You may call me Renata, but we both know that's not my true name."

Nevan grunted. "So, *Renata*, what must I do to prevent you from murdering that child?"

Renata flinched. "Child?" She peered upward, where the Galliers were continuing their act. "I didn't realize he was a *child*. The contract didn't specify that. I thought he was just short." She gestured to herself. "Like me."

E.J. RUSSELL

"For goodness' sake," Seb said, disgusted. "You work here at the carnival. How could you not know the other acts?"

She glared at Seb. "I've been part of the carnival for less than twenty-four hours, and I spent most of that time in Gentleman Jim's tent, dodging knives, smiling like a brainless twit, and wishing these shoes didn't pinch my toes. I'd never have taken the contract if I'd known." She sniffed. "Not that it matters now."

Despite himself, despite the revelation that he might be a creature out of folklore, Seb was curious. "Why doesn't it matter? Because once you take the contract, you're bound to complete it?"

"No. Because I was *made*." She flicked her fingers at Seb. "By you. I'll owe the guild a penalty for being that careless." This time, her smile was sharper than the blade at their feet. "Although that will be offset by the penalty they'll impose on the contractee for not disclosing the target was a minor."

"Exacting that penalty might be difficult," Nevan said. "He's presently a bucket of mud."

Renata shrugged, clearly unconcerned. "I'll let the guild handle the details." She brushed irritably at her still damp skirt. "For now, though, I'm losing this fucking male-gaze outfit and getting out of these shoes." She turned, but Nevan still blocked her way. "If you don't mind?"

"You're really done?"

"I really am. Like I said, I failed. Twice, actually. Once for being ID'd, and once for missing my mark." She winced. "That's a mandatory twenty hours of remedial practice in my future, but it can't be helped." She sidestepped Nevan and disappeared behind the curtain.

CHAPTER 33

The instant Renata vanished, Nevan took two strides forward and captured Seb in an embrace. "I thought my heart would stop when you jumped in front of that knife."

Seb's arms came around Nevan's waist. "So did I, when it comes down to it." He looked up at Nevan. "So. Zânǎ? Does that mean I'm, you know, a supe? Like you?"

Nevan smoothed Seb's tumbled hair off his forehead. "Not precisely like me. More like Lulu. A creature of spirit."

Seb glanced at the knife lying in the sawdust. "A creature of idiocy, more like. What was I thinking?"

"You were answering your nature, cariad. Saving a child. Keeping him safe."

"Does that mean we won't get into trouble with that council of yours?"

"I am… not certain. True, I didn't reveal our existence to a human, but I didn't know you were supernatural at that time."

"Spirit of the law versus letter, huh? Well, we can cross that stream when we come to it. But for now"—he glanced at the crowd, which was still focused on the Galliers' act, the calliope wheezing another merry tune now that Mario had accomplished his feat—"since Mario's safe for good, let's get out of here. We've got another child to rescue."

Nevan squeezed Seb once more before reluctantly releasing him. "We do. And Lulu has already waited far too long for me to come for her."

"We should probably collect Yvo from the gnomes, although they might protest." Seb grinned up at him. "They were having way too much fun dumping water on top of him."

"Yvo can wait." Nevan took Seb's hand. "We should go back to Quest. Formally ask them to locate Lulu. Once she's safe, we can decide what we do next. But Seb?" Nevan glanced down at their laced fingers. "Whatever that is, could we make that decision"—he peered up at Seb from under his brows—"together? I think we make a very good team."

Seb's smile bloomed, brighter than the spotlights. "I was hoping you'd feel that way, because I totally agree."

They made their way out of the big top, garnering a few more disgruntled comments from people in the front rows, although Nevan had no idea what they had to complain about. The show was thirty feet overhead. Even he couldn't block *that* view, not unless he shifted into his winged horse form and soared around the tent. Which, with Seb's hand in his and the promise of a future together, he was sorely tempted to do.

By the time Seb parked in front of the Quest offices, however, ice had twined around Nevan's spine and spread to his fingers. He sat, eyes straight ahead, as Seb turned off the engine.

"Nevan?" Seb placed a warm hand on Nevan's thigh, momentarily chasing away the cold that spangled Nevan's nerves like frost on a windowpane. "What is it?"

"What if they can't find her? What if only Yvo knows the secret? What if it will be too late by the time he's reconstituted?"

Seb tightened his fingers, spreading warmth a little farther. "Don't think like that. Just focus on how you'll feel once Lulu's back in your arms. One thing I've learned as a nanny—"

"A magical nanny," Nevan said with a wry smile.

"A *nanny*, is that while it's prudent to be prepared for any eventuality, you have to focus on the best outcome, not the worst. Because kids"—he kissed Nevan's cheek—"and apparently overprotective ceffyl dŵr can pick up on your mood, and *guarantee* that the worst will happen."

Nevan studied Seb's dear face. "Tell me, cariad. Have you ever encountered an eventuality for which you *weren't* prepared?"

Seb quirked an eyebrow. "Like being mistaken for an assassin, accosted by far too many clowns, getting stuck by a river out of time, and meeting a man who can transform into a flying horse? That kind of eventuality?"

Nevan grinned. "Yet you handled each of those with perfect aplomb." His grin widened. "Except for the clowns, perhaps."

Seb rolled his eyes. "Don't remind me."

"But in your work, your calling. As a nanny, have you ever been caught unprepared?"

A divot appeared between Seb's brows. "Now that you mention it? No."

"You see?" He leaned in and kissed that divot away. "A magical nanny. Now, let's go see whether a magical PI firm can bring my sister home."

They climbed out of the van and headed for Quest's door. As soon as they stepped into the vestibule, though, Nevan froze. Was that... Had he heard...

"Nevan?" Seb placed a hand on the small of Nevan's back. "Are you okay?"

"I thought I heard—"

And then there it was again. Unmistakable.

Lulu's laughter.

Nevan charged up the stairs and burst into the Quest lobby. Lulu, in her birthday outfit, complete with sword, was sitting in the middle of the floor, her legs straight out in front of her, with

Doop draped over her lap. Noah Tate sat next to her, tailor fashion, a book open across his knees.

"Lulu," Nevan breathed.

She looked up at him, dimples popping with her wide smile. "Nevvie!" She hugged Doop around the neck, earning a resigned eyebrow quirk from the giant hound. "Can we get a Ci Annwn for our very own?"

Nevan hunkered down next to her and smoothed her dark curls with a shaking hand. "I fear Herne might object, Lulu *fach*."

Her smile faded. "Oh."

Noah patted her shoulder. "That's okay. You can share Doop with me." He grinned up at Seb. "This book is *awesome*, Seb. Do you have more like it?"

Seb knelt next to Nevan. "I do. Lots of them, and I'm happy to share."

Noah turned to Lulu. "Seb says that with stories, you can share as many times as you want and they'll *never* run out, not like cookies."

"Where were you, *enaid*?" Nevan asked. "How did you come here?"

She tilted her chin up to meet his gaze. "That awful smelly man put me in a really boring room." Her eyes, the color of bluebells and as clear and bright as ever, widened comically. "It didn't even have a *single toy*, Nevvie. Can you *imagine*?"

"Truly a horror."

"I know! Luckily, I still had my golden sword." She patted the object in question, which was half covered by her skirt. "So I scared him off." She beamed at Noah. "But then Doop and Noah's brother came and got me and took me to their house and I got to play with Noah and Doop and *they* have lots of toys." She wrinkled her nose. "But you have to dig some of them up before you can play with them."

"Were you frightened, *enaid*?" Nevan asked, dreading the answer. "Are you upset with me for not protecting you?"

She patted his cheek with her soft hand, her fingers splayed like a tiny starfish. "Silly Nevvie. *I* protect *you*."

Nevan blinked. "What do you mean, you protect—"

"You gave Noah this book," she said to Seb.

Seb nodded. "I did. I'm Seb, and I'm very pleased to meet you, Lulu. Your brother has told me a lot about you. He loves you very much."

"I know," she said, matter-of-factly as she studied Seb, her head tilted to one side. "You're like me, aren't you?"

Seb glanced sidelong at Nevan, and Nevan gave him a small nod of reassurance. "I believe I am, in a way."

She smiled sunnily at him. "*You'll* take care of Nevvie."

Seb's eyebrows rose. "I'll certainly do my best."

"Good." Lulu leaned forward and dropped her voice to a very audible whisper. "'Cause I think Noah needs me more now, but I didn't want to say anything until I knew Nevvie would be looked after."

Seb laid his palm over his heart. "You can count on me."

"I know." She turned a melting gaze on Nevan. "Nevvie, Noah goes to a *school*. He says there's other kids there and I can learn to read just like him. Can I go? Please?"

"We'll see, *eniad*."

She turned to Noah. "That means yes." She pointed imperiously to the book. "What happens next?"

Noah began to read out loud in a surprisingly confident voice, Lulu hanging on every word as she stroked Doop's fur and ignored the adults completely.

Seb nudged Nevan's shoulder with his own. "I guess we're dismissed." He stood and held out his hand. When Nevan took it and rose to stand next to him, Seb looked down, toying with Nevan's fingers. "I guess Lulu doesn't object to me being part of your life."

"Yes, but—"

"Oh, hey, Nevan. Seb." Jordan trotted out of the hallway. "Good. You're back."

Nevan pulled Seb farther away from the children and gestured for Jordan to join them. "*You* found Lulu? How? How did you even know to look?"

"Well, see, it was like this." Jordan rocked back and forth from his toes to his heels. "When Doop and I followed the trail to the riverside again..." He turned to Seb, widening his eyes. "And seriously, *what is with* all the clowns? The Fun House was almost a relief."

Nevan attempted to herd Jordan back to the main point. "So you were able to follow the trail?"

He brightened. "Oh yeah. It was no trouble. I told you." He gazed at the enormous hound fondly. "Doop can find anything when he knows he ought to look. And if he's been somewhere once, he can *always* find his way back." Jordan shoved his hand into his pocket and drew out—

"Lulu's ribbon." Nevan all but snatched it out of his hand. "I thought I'd lost it."

"You sort of did. I found it on the riverbank. Or rather, Doop did. It was the only thing there except for your clothes, Seb. I brought those back too. Zeke has 'em in the staff room."

"Jordan," Nevan said, trying and failing to keep his tone nonthreatening.

"Right. Anyway, as soon as Doop found it, he got agitated, the way he does when he has to go outside and... Well, never mind that. But it was a breakthrough for him, you know? Usually, he waits for me to give him the find-it-out command. I could tell that this was a search *he* wanted to initiate. So I let him."

"And he led you to Lulu?"

Jordan glanced down at the children. "Yeah. She was in one of those pocket dimensions, like the C-suite demons are selling now that they're being decommissioned in Sheol. But it wasn't very well constructed. It was kind of..." He made a gesture with both hands, like compressing a ball. "...shrinking. No matter how she got there in the first place, obviously she couldn't stay.

264

So we took her back to the Doghouse with us. She hung out with Noah, Tahmina, Doop, and me last night."

Nevan managed to control his ire, because Lulu was safe now. Seb, however, wasn't as constrained.

"You could have *told* us," he said fiercely. "Nevan was so worried. Wait." He sucked in a breath and stared at Nevan. "*That's* why Yvo had you arrested. He really *didn't* know where she was."

"I'm really sorry," Jordan said. "But I didn't realize she was your sister. You never told me you were searching for her."

"No," Seb said crossly, "because he *couldn't*. Not with the geas. But I told you about her when I came here after the police took Nevan."

"I, um, wasn't here then. I saw you on the sidewalk, remember? But then I had to..." Jordan blushed. "And then I *tried* to tell you when I saw you next, but you ran out."

"Oh." Seb grimaced. "Right. Sorry."

Nevan lunged forward and hugged Jordan tightly, earning a surprised squeak from the young were. "Thank you. I am ever in your debt." He let go and stepped back to Seb's side.

"You're not upset that I didn't tell you sooner?"

Nevan shook his head. "You got her away from Yvo. Kept her safe and happy. That's all I could ask for."

"Just, you know"—Jordan jerked his thumb at Doop—"doing our job."

Nevan peered down the hallway. "Is Lord Kendrick about?"

"Right here," Mal called and strode in from the landing. "Just back from reporting to the King."

Nevan inclined his head. "I am pleased to report that the guild contract is neutralized."

"Neutralized how? We'd only just lodged the cease and desist order with the guild."

"Seb recognized the real assassin. Not only that, but he blocked a bespelled dagger midair."

E.J. RUSSELL

Mal whistled, long and low. "Midair? That takes skill."

"Not skill," Nevan said, gazing down at Seb fondly. "Magic. He's zână."

"Zână?" Mal narrowed his eyes. "How did I not know that?"

The typewriter clattered. Mal peered down at the paper and then shook his head. "Apparently, Miss Pennybaker is of the opinion that only unobservant fools could remain unaware of his blatantly obvious nature. But putting that aside, what of the mage?"

"He is presently out of commission."

"Out of commission?"

Nevan nodded. "Presently."

Mal quirked an eyebrow. "Care to explain?"

"He's, well, mud," Seb said, his cheeks rather pink. "In a bucket. Being guarded by gnomes."

At that, both Mal's eyebrows nearly reached his hairline. "Mud, you say?" He chuckled. "That'll make transporting him to the council a sight easier. My husband's never had the opportunity to reconstitute someone before. He might like to have a go at prepping the wanker for interrogation." Mal winked. "I'll make sure to tell him to make the process *really* unpleasant." He disappeared down the hallway.

"Does that mean..." Seb took a deep breath. "Is it over? Lulu's back, Mario's out of danger, and Yvo has been apprehended. Does everything go back to the way it was before now?"

Nevan took Seb's hands, gazing down at their twined fingers. "Not entirely. Because before now, I didn't know you. Before now, I had never... Is it too much to ask..." Mingled hope and apprehension nearly deprived Nevan of breath, but he managed to croak, "I would like nothing better than for us to stay together, whether here in the Outer World, in Faerie—"

"I could live in *Faerie*?" Seb whispered, his eyes round behind his glasses.

Nevan stroked Seb's cheek. "It's a possibility, although those not bred for it might find it lacking in certain conveniences." He kissed Seb's forehead. "Such as indoor plumbing."

"Oh. Ugh. Never mind then. We'll just visit."

"But Seb." Nevan took a deep breath and let it out slowly, willing his nerves to settle. "I'm not a good bet. I have no occupation, no treasure, no reputation. All I have is my lake and Lulu. And myself."

"Nevan, you do realize that's an absolute embarrassment of riches?" Seb said quietly. He smiled wryly. "Besides, *I'm* not exactly a great bet at the moment. It's not as though I have a job either. But I do have a house that's big enough for three. And we have friends. We'll figure it out as long as we're together."

From across the room, Lulu's laugh rang out, joyous, free, and easy, warming Nevan's heart. "What do you suppose she meant? That she protected me?"

"I was thinking about that." Seb wrapped his arms around Nevan's waist. "She's an ora, you said, a protective spirit who usually bonds with a child and remains with them throughout their lives?"

"Yes, that's right."

"I think she probably bonded with you."

"But I'm not a child," Nevan protested.

"I suspect need is more important than age. And when you met her, you were lonely, weren't you?"

Nevan's throat constricted, remembering just exactly how lonely he'd been then. "Yes," he croaked.

"You told me she was the first one who'd never seen you as a monster." Seb gazed up at Nevan, his dark eyes impossibly kind. "She did protect you, Nevan. By showing you that you're worthy of being loved." Seb's arms tightened, his palms flat against Nevan's spine. "And you are, sweetheart. *So* worthy."

Nevan cradled Seb's face. "As long as I'm worthy of you."

Seb pressed a kiss to one of Nevan's palms, then the other. "Well, *that* goes without saying."

"Then I am content." Nevan lowered his head and fitted his

mouth to Seb's, the kiss soft, tender, warm. A token of what Seb had gifted him. A promise of what Nevan offered in return.

He didn't linger overlong—they weren't alone here, and some tokens and promises were best exchanged in private. He slid his fingers from Seb's face to card them through his hair, mesmerized by the slip of the silky strands along his skin.

"Um, Nevan?"

"Hmmm?"

"I'm not sure you caught it," Seb said, smiling crookedly as he toyed with the buttons of Nevan's waistcoat, "but I think Lulu just handed you off to me."

Nevan stilled. "What?"

"I'm pretty sure she thinks her job here is done."

Ice filled Nevan's middle. "She's done with me? She's leaving me?"

"No, silly. I mean her job here"—Seb patted Nevan's chest, directly over his heart—"is done. She's found someone else who needs her, an actual child to bond with." He cut a glance to where Lulu sat with Noah. "She's ready to leave your care and feeding to me, and just be your little sister."

Seb kissed him then, dissipating the cold and filling Nevan with warmth and light and love. Nevan was happy to let it go on forever, except...

"Uh, guys?"

Jordan.

Nevan raised his head, but didn't release Seb from his embrace. "Yes?"

"Sorry to interrupt," Jordan said. "Like *really* sorry. But the thing is, Doop and I have a case and we have to leave right away. Tahmina's in Dewton, getting ready for her store opening, and the other guys at the Doghouse are about ready to leave for the summer."

"You'd like us to watch Noah for you this afternoon?" Seb asked.

Jordan grimaced, rubbing the back of his head. "Not... exactly? You're a nanny, right?"

"I am."

"A magical nanny," Nevan added, tightening his arms around Seb.

"Then..." Jordan hit them with full-on puppy dog eyes. "Can I hire you? Please?"

EPILOGUE

*S*eb nuzzled Nevan's nape, inhaling deeply to draw in that lovely forest pool scent that was now as familiar as it was intoxicating. "Good morning," he murmured into Nevan's ear.

"Mmmphmm." Nevan's hand flailed until it landed on Seb's hip, then he sighed contentedly.

Seb chuckled. After so many years of avoiding others who might take advantage of his nature, Nevan was happiest now when he was in contact with someone in the small circle of those he trusted. A couple of millennia of touch starvation could do that to a guy.

As ludicrous as it was to be the big spoon, given their size difference, Seb snaked an arm around Nevan's middle and cuddled close. "It's time to get up."

Nevan captured Seb's hand and moved it south. "I'm already up. Fancy a ride?"

"We don't have time."

"What?" Nevan rolled to his back and caged Seb's hand on his chest. "Lulu's at that sleepover with her jackrabbit shifter friend until this afternoon. It's barely dawn. We have plenty of time."

"In the first place, it's closer to nine. I'd never have guessed that ceffylau dŵr were such slugabeds."

Nevan kissed Seb's palm. "You wore me out last night." He grinned. "But that doesn't mean I'm not ready for another go."

"Trust me, I'd like nothing better, but you seem to have forgotten we've got a meeting to attend."

Nevan winced. "Shite. I had forgotten."

"More like you're in denial." Seb sighed and sat up. "I know the feeling." A summons from the freaking *King of Faerie* definitely had that effect. "Do you know what the meeting's about?"

Nevan shook his head. "Only that the King requires our presence."

"Yeah, like *that's* not ominous," Seb muttered. "Where *is* this meeting, anyway?"

"At the Quest offices."

Then Seb wouldn't have to wrangle breakfast. Zeke *always* had tea and pastries on hand, regardless of the hour. "You don't think they're going to punish you for revealing stuff to me before you knew I wasn't human?"

The set of Nevan's lips was grim. "I hope not, but I wouldn't discount the possibility. However, since I wasn't summoned to an audience in the throne room, we might yet be safe."

"Not exactly reassuring, Nevan." Seb quickly kissed Nevan and scrambled out of bed. "I'll shower up here. You can have the tub. Meet you back here in half an hour?"

Nevan nodded and Seb hurried into the bathroom, accompanied by a whole flight of stomach butterflies.

After nearly a month with Nevan and Lulu living in his house, nearly a month as nanny to an almost-nine-year-old werewolf and a six-year-old ora, Seb still didn't feel like a part of the Portland supernatural community. True, everyone had been kind to him, especially Jordan and Noah's housemates at the Doghouse, and Nevan had taken Seb and Lulu on several trips to Faerie to spend time at his lake.

Seb had even gotten up the nerve to ride on Nevan's back as

he winged over the waterfall, with Lulu tucked in front of Seb and laughing delightedly as the spray spangled her curls.

But he still felt like Dorothy, standing in the black-and-white house, with the technicolor world just out of reach beyond the door. And nobody had so much as *mentioned* the Secrecy Pact to him, either for good or ill.

Although that might change today. He sighed. He *really* wished the King was the kind of guy who sent out meeting agendas in advance.

After they both bathed and dressed, Seb grabbed his keys from the lopsided bowl Lulu had made on a school outing to Tahmina's new craft store. "Let's get it over with, then."

Nevan followed Seb down the stairs. "We could take the FTA through Faerie, if you prefer. As I understand it, there's a portal on one of Quest's upper floors."

A now-familiar frisson shimmered through Seb. He'd somehow become a guy who could take shortcuts through freaking *Faerie*, as long as he paid for the ride.

"While supernatural ride-sharing is cool and all, until we know what this meeting is about, I'd rather control our means of transportation, thanks."

The drive from their house in Hillsboro to the Quest offices wasn't bad when they weren't fighting rush hour, plus—bonus! —they were able to score a parking spot right in front of the door.

When they reached the lobby, it looked empty, but by now, Seb knew that didn't mean it was unoccupied. "Good morning, Miss Pennybaker."

"Good... morning... gentlemen." The rather mechanical voice emanated from the direction of the typewriter. "Please... proceed... to... the... conference... room... on... the... third... floor."

Seb shared a startled glance with Nevan. Guess Hector must have fixed her voice simulator. "Thanks. Have a nice day."

When they reached the third floor, Seb stopped, gazing first right and then left. "You know, I've been meaning to ask. This is a rectilinear building. Why is this corridor curved? For that matter, why does it extend in both directions when there ought to be a wall there?"

Nevan shrugged. "Magic."

Seb sighed. "I guess that's gonna be the explanation for a lot of things from now on, isn't it?"

Nevan looked at him worriedly. "Does that bother you?"

"Are you kidding?" Seb grinned up at him. "It's like a dream come true. And Nevan?" Seb kissed him softly. "No matter what happens, no matter what they lay on us, I'm with you. You know that, right?"

Nevan cupped Seb's face, running his thumbs along Seb's cheekbones. "I do. And you know I feel the same about you?"

"I do."

"Then we can face anything."

They walked toward an open door just visible before the hall curved out of sight. When they stepped into the room, Seb sucked in a breath.

For one thing, there were *a lot* more people in here than he'd been expecting. For another, even though most of them looked as human as Seb did, they were all incredibly beautiful, like a congregation of models or movie stars, except...

"Um, Nevan?" Seb murmured. "Does that guy over there have *antlers?*"

"Don't stare," Nevan muttered in response. "It's best not to draw his attention."

The man sitting at the head of the long conference table rose. He had to be at least as tall as Nevan and as classically beautiful as Mal Kendrick, but he was wearing a UO hoodie and worn jeans. "Welcome."

Beside him, Nevan bowed nearly double. "Your Majesty." Then angled slightly toward the red-haired woman at his right, gowned in the green of new leaves, her lovely face as serene and distant as the moon. "Your Majesty."

Hokey smokes, this was the King and Queen? Of Faerie. Seb wasn't sure whether to kneel, bow, or run.

"We do not stand on ceremony. Today I am simply one of our company," the Queen said. "Please join us at the table."

"Allow me to introduce everyone." The King turned to the extremely pale man at the Queen's right. "Kristof Czardos, vampire clan chief."

Seb's knees wobbled. Okay, Nevan had mentioned vampires, but if this Kristof guy was the clan *chief*, that meant there were enough other vampires to make a clan. *Not relevant now.*

Because the King was continuing his introductions, moving on to the dark-haired man with skin a slightly lighter brown than Seb's, who looked barely older than Jordan. "Tanner Araya, werewolf alpha."

The blond man at Tanner's left leaned forward and said, "*Supreme* werewolf alpha."

Tanner colored. "Chase, please. Not here."

Seb wasn't certain how he made it through the rest of the intros. Eleri Deilen, dryad. *Dryad.* AJ and Wash Hernandez, demon and witch respectively. The antlered man was Herne the freaking Hunter, and he loomed very protectively over Wyn Ellis, who was a corlun dŵr, another Welsh water being, but not a shifter like Nevan. Rafi Abbas was Tahmina's son, so apparently another djinn, and he was holding hands with Hector, Quest's hacker werewolf. Lachlan Brodie, a selkie, for goodness' sake—although at first glance, Seb assumed that Jason Momoa had joined them in his Aquaman costume—sat with his arm draped across the shoulders of the only human in the room, although Seb didn't believe for a single instant that the man's name was really Hugh Mann.

The King looked around at them, meeting each of their gazes somberly. "I imagine you're all wondering why I've requested your presence here today."

The human, Hugh, chuckled. "In most mysteries, doesn't that usually precede the unmasking of the murderer?"

The King quirked a smile. "That's not so far off the mark, Hugh. You're all here, including my lady wife"—he reached for the Queen's hand and laced their fingers together—"because each of you has had a potentially fatal interaction with a mage."

Rafi raised a hand tentatively, like a student who wasn't sure he could ask a question. "Excuse me, Your Majesty?"

"Please. While we're here, call me Eamon."

Rafi's brown eyes widened. "I couldn't."

The King sighed. "Very well. Please carry on."

"I don't think Hector and I qualify. We didn't encounter a mage."

"No. But you were targeted by a bounty hunter who was *hired* by a mage."

"Bounty hunters?" Seb squeaked. "There are—" He lifted a hand, palm out. "Never mind. Not relevant. I'm sorry for interrupting."

"Actually, Seb," the King said, "it's quite relevant. A very disturbing pattern is emerging." He turned to Nevan. "Your case was a wake-up call for us. It exposed several severe security risks to our community, as well as unacceptable collateral damage to human citizenry. Yvo Offerman, in his quest for power, didn't care that the assassination he contracted would not only be horrifying, but horrifyingly *public*, taking place in full view of hundreds of humans. The Guild should have rejected the contract for that alone."

"I still can't believe there's an assassin's guild," Seb muttered.

"Tell me about it," Hugh said.

"But what if Yvo lied about the contract details?" Seb asked. "I mean, he either lied or concealed critical information from Nevan when he made him take that lousy vow."

The King shook his head. "The Guild has magical safeguards in place to ensure that no assassin can ever target a human."

"And yet," Seb said dryly, "Yvo contracted for Mario Gallier's heart. To be carved out of his chest. In front of a packed house."

"There are some... extraordinary individuals who possess

extra-human abilities yet are not within our purview. While the Guild prohibits contracts on humans, if its spells detect that the target is such an extraordinary individual, the contracted assignment is allowed to proceed. Therefore, we can deduce that Mario Gallier is such an individual. However, since the spells didn't flag that the assassination would occur *literally* in the spotlight, their magic is clearly flawed."

"You think?" Seb said, and then winced. "Sorry, your majesty, but there are *so many* things wrong with that statement."

"I cannot disagree. Therefore, I'm establishing a task force to investigate mage activities, gather evidence, and hopefully prevent them from endangering others the way Yvo endangered Luljeta Zanash and Mario Gallier. I've invited you here because I hope that you'll all take part, share your experiences, and help us solve the problem."

Hugh raised his hand. "Count me in."

"Matthew," Lachlan said, warning in his tone.

"What?" Hugh said. "Like you were going to refuse? Do I need to remind you about what a certain necromancer wannabe intended to do to you?"

Lachlan sighed. "Nay. But I'd prefer that you stay out of harm's way."

"Because he's so good at that," Eleri said with a scoff.

"I know I'm kinda late to the party here," Seb said, his gaze traveling around the table, "but it seems to me that as long as there's, you know, an *assassin's* guild, not to mention bounty hunters and megalomaniacal assholes who can work *actual* magic, *everybody* is in harm's way. Like, all the time."

"Again, you are correct," the King said. "And should the mages discover our work, the danger could very well increase, especially for task force members." He paused, his expression somber. "Not to mention their loved ones. That is why, although you are my first choices for this work, participation is strictly voluntary."

"Seb is right," Nevan said. "Whether we participate or not,

our families, our friends, the entire supe community, are at risk. I, for one, will do whatever I can to eliminate that risk."

The King's expression lightened, although he didn't go so far as to smile. "I was hoping you would say that. Because I would like you, Nevan Quirke, to take the lead and coordinate our efforts."

Under Seb's hand, the muscles in Nevan's arm tensed. "Me?"

"Yes. As the team leader, you'll be an adjunct member of the Quest Investigations staff, with access to their resources. However, the case can't be officially on the Quest books."

"Why not?" Hugh asked.

"To retain the secrecy of the investigation. As long as the mages are unaware of our scrutiny, they'll be less likely to be on their guard, and therefore less likely to target the team and their loved ones."

Hugh frowned. "But Quest cases are confidential, anyway." He glanced at Nevan apologetically. "Not that I object to you joining us, because we've got plenty on our plate already, but why the extra layer of stealth?"

"Because," the Queen said, "we cannot be certain that Quest's records have not been... compromised."

Hugh shared a horrified look with Eleri. "You think we've got a leak?"

The King held up his hands and patted the air, which sent a warm, herbal-scented breeze whispering over Seb's skin, settling his heartbeat. Judging by the way Hugh and Eleri relaxed into their chairs, they'd felt it too.

Huh. Magical Xanax. Who knew?

"We have no reason to believe that Quest is more vulnerable than any other supe business, but in this instance, we must be extra vigilant." The King looked at Nevan. "Will you do it?"

"Of cou—"

Seb squeezed Nevan's arm to stop his response. Really, the man was terrible at leaping into situations without checking all the details. "I assume he'll be compensated appropriately?"

The King's eyebrows rose. "Naturally."

"All right then." Seb gazed up at Nevan. "See, sweetheart?" he murmured. "An embarrassment of riches."

Nevan stroked Seb's cheek with the back of his fingers. "My greatest treasure, cariad, is you."

The King cleared his throat, his eyes glinting in what Seb could almost call triumph. "And as for you, Mr. Ardelean, to mitigate the potential threats against our most vulnerable, our children, we would ask that in addition to your duties as nanny to Noah Tate and Luljeta Zanash, you accept a position as an aide at the supe school. Because beyond any other in our community, you are best suited to protect our most precious asset: our next generation." His lips curled in a half smile. "You, of course, will also be appropriately compensated."

Seb's throat tightened. A job. A home. He glanced up at Nevan, who met his gaze with eyes full of love. *A family.*

Not to mention, you know, *magic.* Life couldn't get any better than this.

"I accept."

A MESSAGE FROM E.J.

Dear Reader,

Thank you so much for reading *Assassin by Accident*. I had such great time merging my Mythmatched world with Carnival of Mysteries, and I hope you had just as much fun accompanying Seb and Nevan on their adventures!

Wondering what to read next? If you're a fan of contemporary romance, you might like *Camera Shy*, where a cocky LGBTQ activist/talk show host gets his comeuppance after his ill-advised on-air fake engagement announcement to his PA gets turned into a reality competition for wedding planners.

Assassin by Accident is my eighteenth (sheesh... really?) Mythmatched story, so if you're in the mood for more paranormal romantic comedy, you might want to travel back to where it all began: *Cutie and the Beast*, where a cursed fae warrior turned psychologist clashes with his determined temporary office manager. As you might imagine, hijinks ensue!

You can catch the deets on all my books and audio on my website, https://ejrussell.com. (The QR code at the bottom of the page will get you there with your smartphone camera or other code reader.)

Would you like exclusive content and ARC giveaways, not to

mention gratuitous dance videos? Then I'd love for you to join me in Reality Optional, my Facebook fan group (https://facebook.com/groups/reality.optional). My newsletter is the place to get the latest dish on new releases, sales, and more. I promise I only send one out when I've got...well...news. You can subscribe here: https://ejrussell.com/newsletter.

All my best,
 —E

CARNIVAL OF MYSTERIES

Welcome, Traveler! Join us for a series of M/M fantasies by a talented group of both new and established authors. Whether you enjoy mystery, action, danger, or just sweet romance, there is something for everyone at the Carnival of Mysteries!

Kim Fielding * L. A. Witt * Kaje Harper

Megan Derr * Ander C. Lark * E. J. Russell

Morgan Brice * Sarah Ellis * Kayleigh Sky

Nicole Dennis * Elizabeth Silver * Ro Merrill

T. A. Moore * Z. A. Maxfield * Ki Brightly

Rachel Langella

ALSO BY E.J. RUSSELL

Paranormal Romance

Mythmatched Universe

Fae Out of Water Trilogy

Cutie and the Beast

The Druid Next Door

Bad Boy's Bard

Supernatural Selection Trilogy

Single White Incubus

Vampire With Benefits

Demon on the Down-Low

Other Mythmatched Romances

Howling on Hold

Possession in Session

Witch Under Wraps

Cursed is the Worst

The Skinny on Djinni

Assassin by Accident (*part of Carnival of Mysteries*)

Mythmatched Companion Stories

Rusty's Really Bad Day (free to newsletter subscribers)

Second First Date (free to newsletter subscribers)

Quest Investigations Mysteries

Five Dead Herrings

The Hound of the Burgervilles

The Lady Under the Lake

Death on Denial

Art Medium Series

The Artist's Touch

Tested in Fire

Art Medium: The Complete Collection (omnibus edition)

Legend Tripping Series

Stumptown Spirits

Wolf's Clothing

Enchanted Occasions Series

Best Beast

Nudging Fate

Devouring Flame

Royal Powers Series (shared world)

Duking It Out

Duke the Hall

King's Ex

Magic Emporium Series (shared world)

Purgatory Playhouse

Monster Till Midnight

Historical Romance

Silent Sin

Contemporary Romance

Camera Shy

The Thomas Flair

Mystic Man

For a Good Time, Call... (A Bluewater Bay novel, with Anne Tenino)

Holiday Shorts (separately)

The Probability of Mistletoe

An Everyday Hero

A Swants Soiree

or all three together in

Christmas Kisses

Geeklandia Series

The Boyfriend Algorithm (M/F)

Clickbait

Writing as Nelle Heran

(traditional cozy mystery)

Crafty Sleuth Series (with C.K. Eastland)

Die Cut

Mixed Media

Found Objects (*coming soon*)

ABOUT THE AUTHOR

E.J. Russell (she/her), author of the award-winning Mythmatched paranormal romance series, writes LGBTQ+ romance and mystery in a rainbow of flavors. Count on high snark, low angst, and happy endings.

Reality? Eh, not so much.

She's married to Curmudgeonly Husband, a man who cares even less about sports than she does. Luckily, C.H. also loves to cook, or all three of their children (Lovely Daughter and Darling Sons A and B) would have survived on nothing but Cheerios, beef jerky, and Satsuma mandarins (the extent of E.J.'s culinary skill set).

E.J. also writes traditional cozy mystery as Nelle Heran. She lives in rural Oregon, enjoys visits from her wonderful adult children, and indulges in good books, red wine, and the occasional hyperbole.

News & Social Media:
Website: https://ejrussell.com
Newsletter: https://ejrussell.com/newsletter

ACKNOWLEDGMENTS

First off, I want to thank Ari McKay and Rachel Langella for concocting the Carnival of Mysteries world and for inviting me to come play in it! I had a terrific time and am incredibly fortunate to be in the company of so many amazing authors.

Thanks also to Dianne Thies of LyricalLines.net for the gorgeous series covers; to lyric apted for beta reading and reality checking; to the Crit Posse, L.C. Chase and Lee Blair, for pointing out problems but still saying, "More, please!"; to my long-suffering editor, Meg DesCamp (who's making a dartboard —or perhaps a drinking game—featuring all the words I use far too frequently); to my fabulous PA, NOLAKim, for boundless encouragement, humor, and patience.

To my family—Jim, Hana, Nick, Ross, and Billy—love and thanks for being there for me even when I'm clearly off wandering in another universe.

And, of course, to you, my readers. Your enthusiasm for my stories makes it possible for me to continue doing what I love.